# BELL HATH NO FURY

## A Samantha Bell Mystery Thriller

### JEREMY WALDRON

jeremy@jeremywaldron.com

# ALSO BY JEREMY WALDRON

Dead and Gone to Bell

Bell Hath No Fury

# CHAPTER ONE

ADRENALINE PULSING THROUGH HIS VEINS KEPT HIM ALERT. Months of preparation were finally coming to fruition. His heart knocked inside his chest as he dropped to one knee and clicked open his hard-shell guitar case.

Inside, the black metallic pieces of his rifle reflected a dull shine that left him feeling breathless.

Suddenly, the penetrating rays of sun broke through the massive battleship clouds overhead. The warmth draped over his shoulder like a wool blanket. Tipping his head back, he briefly watched the gray air glide beneath the crisp blue sky.

He had planned meticulously to get to this point. Hundreds of hours and sleepless nights dreaming about what would happen next. He'd waited patiently for this moment and could feel the blessings of the day shining down upon him as if it was written long ago. Here, now, was what he was born to do—his contribution to the world.

Inhaling the dry cold air, he felt his nerves calm. His muscles flexed and prepared for battle. Today, everyone would learn of what he did while keeping his anonymity. The war that started decades ago brought to the forefront. Their lives—as well as his—would be forever changed.

On his exhale, the Sniper swiftly lowered his gaze back to his .338 Lapua Magnum bolt-action rifle. He assembled it in record time, finishing the task by inserting the magazine of ammunition into the firearm.

A playful grin pulled at his lips just as he flicked his wrist and checked the time. The digital watch said it was five minutes after 9AM. "Showtime."

Laying his rifle down on the cold rooftop next to him, he retrieved the high-powered Nikon binoculars from the case and gripped both sides between his fingers, scoping his target to the southeast.

Light snow fell lazily from the sky.

He gauged wind speed and direction before turning toward the breeze's source. To his west was Mt. Evans towering over the Continental Divide at an impressive 14,264 feet above sea level. Socked in by what was sure to be a blizzard, the Sniper brought the binoculars back to his eyes and looked once again toward North High School.

A handful of students carelessly roamed school grounds. He swept his gaze to the left where the gym class was outside on the track, boys and girls screaming as they ran and chased each other around. Sweeping his attention back to the north entrance, bicycles were parked outside. There was no movement to his plan; a perfect day to die.

"You're late," he muttered to himself. His partner wasn't anywhere to be found.

The Sniper patted his pants pocket when reaching for his cellphone. Remembering he'd purposely come without it— fearing it could be used to trace him to the rooftop from where he was perched—he couldn't call to check in.

His head snapped up when the first shot rang out.

His heartrate spiked as he dropped his binoculars and

rushed to exchange them for his rifle. Locked and loaded, he extended his trigger finger and lowered his eye to the scope.

Eyeing the school entrance through his long-range scope, he felt his veins open up. Despite the cold, he began to sweat. Sweeping the area, it didn't take him long to find the first victim. A young male lay on his stomach in a hot pool of blood near the north entrance to the school.

"Well done, son," he whispered to himself.

His index finger pressed firmly into the trigger guard. Itching to join the fight, he clenched his stomach and resisted the urge knowing patience was his friend. The wind changed direction and the chaos unfolding only a short distance away could now be heard.

Inside, he smiled; outside, he kept focused on his mission.

The school's seams burst in a roar of screams as students poured from the building from all sides. Sprinting for their lives, he watched the young terrified faces fill his crosshairs. Tapping the trigger guard with his index finger, he pretended to shoot them all.

Sirens wailed in the distance like a call to prayer.

The Sniper closed his eyes and calmed his breathing. *This is your moment. Your time to shine. A moment to live in infamy. To country, God, and glory.* By the time he opened his eyes, the paramedics were already on scene. Then came the cops.

Lowering his eye to his scope, he gripped his rifle harder, pushing his stock deeper into his shoulder.

Several police cruisers arrived in succession. *Just as he suspected they would.* The moment the first uniformed officer stepped out, the Sniper chose his target. Then, when he had the officer's face locked between his crosshairs, he brought his index finger off the guard and onto the trigger.

Holding his breath, he took the shot.

A single red dot exploded on the officer's neck just above his protective vest.

The Sniper watched the other officers scramble to figure out where the shot had come from. More students came running out from the school. Chaos ripped through like a tornado. Another half-dozen police cruisers arrived on scene and the Sniper's chest expanded.

The shot cop lay on the ground gripping his neck between his hands. Risking his own life, his partner rushed to his side, pulling him safely behind their car and surely calling it in.

A grin pulled the Sniper's lips. His plan was unfolding better than he had imagined.

He zeroed in, calmed his breathing, and prepared to fire off his second shot. Through his scope, he watched the police officer looking toward the school thinking the shot that killed his partner had come from there. A grin pulled at the Sniper's lips when he squeezed the trigger and watched the second officer hit the ground next to the first.

# CHAPTER TWO

I STRUGGLED TO BREATHE AS I DROVE AS FAST AS POSSIBLE from the newsroom to North High School. Two of the men I cared most about were inside the building when news broke about the shooting. The thought that my son, Mason, or the man I was dating, Alex King, might be dead made me sick.

I pounded on my horn, cursed slow drivers, and weaved through morning traffic praying that both were alive and well and that I would be able to see them again.

Their voices echoed between my ears and I didn't know what to make of it.

When I hit a red light, my chest swelled with sudden panic. I shoved my fingers through my hair and felt my neck muscles tense. I was paralyzed by disbelief. It didn't feel real. The moment I closed my eyes, the first of the tears squeezed out of the corners.

My throat closed as I began sobbing uncontrollably.

The floodgate to my emotions poured from my lungs in thick bursts. It was all too much—too sudden of a surprise. I wiped my tear-filled eyes with my hand and saw that the light was still red.

"C'mon, dammit!" I slapped the steering wheel.

I needed to get to the high school—wanted desperately to hold my baby and feel his heart beat against the palm of my hand. He had to be alive. He just had to be.

The light refused to change. Seeming to be forever stuck on red, I felt my hand ball into a fist as my cries turned to anger. Hitting the center of my steering wheel over and over again, I was losing control. The sudden sting cracked my knuckles red just as the light flicked over to green.

I gasped and hit the gas with my foot, hearing my tires speed off the line. It made little sense to rush but logic had nothing to do with my motherly instinct to protect my cub from harm. I knew there was nothing I could do to stop the situation currently unfolding, but something about being there—waiting anxiously, holding onto hope—kept me believing that Mason would be okay and that I could take him home and away from the danger.

The radio news broke, covering the situation. Quick to turn it off, I'd had enough bad news for one day. Reaching for my cellphone, I tried calling Mason again.

"C'mon, baby, pick up. Mason, please pick up," I pleaded as the line rang and rang.

Mason wasn't answering, and neither was Alex.

The tightness in my throat closed even further.

I glanced to the rearview mirror when I head the sirens approach from behind. Jerking the wheel, I pulled off to the side and held my breath as I let the ambulance pass. Quick to point my hood back onto the road, I drafted off their lane as I followed closed behind, ignoring the illegality of what I was doing. I didn't have to guess to where they were heading because we were all making our way to the same destination.

Feeling my hands go numb on the wheel, I couldn't stop thinking back to what I'd seen on Dawson's TV.

*Breaking News. North High School is currently on lockdown as*

*an active shooter is on scene. One student has already been confirmed
dead but authorities and emergency services are expecting the number
to rise.*

I stared at the emergency lights flashing in front of me,
unable to erase the image of Trisha Christopher's face from
my memory. How my colleague's hand trembled over her
mouth as she stared in terror and disbelief by what we were
witnessing. My heart shattered in that same moment and I
blamed myself for putting my son in harm's way.

A sharp stab in my side twisted with regret as I wished I
would have driven Mason to school myself or have sponta-
neously made the decision to insist we all take the day off. We
were all together—Mason, me, and Alex. Happy and laughing,
everything was perfect. *Why did I let them leave?*

The prayer wheels inside my head never stopped spinning.
I muttered thousands of them past dry lips like a mantra that
grew and spread out like branches the more I said them. I
needed to put good energy out into the world, afraid that if I
didn't, good news wouldn't come my way.

I broke off the tail of the ambulance as soon as the high
school was within sight.

Applying more pressure to my brakes, I scanned over the
dash, feeling my face pale with disbelief at what I was
witnessing. I pulled into an empty space, not needing to get
any closer. Kicking the door open, I stood and gaped at the
unbelievable sight.

Police cruisers circled the school like an army. SWAT vans
were parked next to tactical teams. Ambulances lined up,
waiting to be called to duty. Fortunate students who'd
managed to escape alive huddled in each other's arms, staring
through wet eyes and crying at the horror they'd witnessed.

Unease flipped my stomach.

Digging my sneakers into the pavement, I slammed my
car door behind me and hurried to an open vantage point

where I hoped to find Mason and King. The world spun around me and I moved fast but my vision came in spotty waves as everything seemed to come to a complete stop.

Past the bubble of hearing my own heart thrashing, there were voices and cries mixed between the screams of terror. I wanted to hold each and every one of them as I popped my head in and out, above and below, searching for my son.

"Have you seen Mason Bell?" I asked.

No one had and I couldn't find him anywhere. Before I knew it, I'd come to the police barricade somewhere in the middle of the school parking lot. They had secured the area, not letting anyone out without first being checked as a possible suspect.

Students clasped their hands behind their heads as police patted them down. Backpacks and school books were thrown to the ground and I watched a tactical team, heavily armed, enter the building.

Twirling around, I shoved my hands through my hair and tugged at the roots. I felt helpless in my pursuit, convincing myself I was too late.

My heart stopped the moment I saw it.

Then I couldn't take my eyes away.

A thick red stain spread over the sheet covering the first casualty. While being protected by an army of officers, two paramedics wheeled the gurney into the back of an ambulance, quickly shutting the doors and rushing back toward the entrance to help with the next.

A woman wailed over my shoulder.

I shuddered and felt my breaths quicken. When my cellphone rang, my heart was shocked back into rhythm. Hoping it was Mason or King, I was let down to see it was Erin. I couldn't answer. Not with Mason still missing. I tried his phone again, but he still didn't answer. *King is with him,* I reassured myself. *He'll protect Mason as if he was his own. They have to be alive. I can't let them die today.*

My breath hitched with the surprise of hearing Mason's phone click over to voicemail.

"Mason, oh my god, call me back," I rambled off quickly, not wanting to miss the opportunity. "I'm here. At the school. Please, call me back ASAP. I love you and I need to know you're okay."

# CHAPTER THREE

HE FELT HIS RIBS SQUEEZE AS THE ELEVATOR SLOWED TO AN unexpected stop. The Sniper drew his brows together and glanced at the floor number. His pulse throbbed in his neck as he wondered who could be waiting on the other side of the doors.

Maintaining his composure, he pulled his baseball cap over his eyes with his free hand as the doors slid open. A woman lifted her head and greeted him as she stepped through the doors. The Sniper said nothing. Only nodded and smiled. The woman turned to face the front and he relaxed, appreciating her lack of interest in prolonged eye contact and awkward conversation. The last thing he needed was to be seen—remembered and later linked to the rooftop.

By the time the elevator started up again, the Sniper smiled and cast his gaze to the floor, keeping one firm hand on his guitar case.

Not a minute later, the doors chimed open once again and he followed the woman in professional attire onto the lobby floor, quick to blend in with the others. He focused on his stride, being sure to keep it much slower than his racing heart.

The soft murmurs came from all directions. He could hear others discussing the details about the shooting in progress happening in real time two blocks away, guessing to who was behind the attack and how many were dead.

*Three dead outside—two police officers and one student*, the Sniper thought to himself. *But you'd never guess why we did it.* He grinned as he kept walking, keeping a lookout for police activity.

"One can only imagine the carnage inside with nowhere to run," the Sniper overhead someone say as they stared at the television screen.

Pulling his sunglasses from his jacket pocket, he slid them over his eyes with pride blooming across his broad chest. No one paid him any attention. All the authorities were responding to the school. He was invisible. His secret safe— at least for the time being.

Stiff-arming the glass double door entrance, he exited the building and scampered down the front steps, coming to a stop near the street curb.

Swiveling his head on his shoulders, he watched with bewilderment as the sidewalks filled with curious civilians all heading in one direction. It seemed that everyone's initial intuition was to run *toward* the danger rather than flee it. Tilting his head to the side, the Sniper took note of the behavior, promising to remember for a later time.

Stepping into traffic, he trudged across the street and worked himself into the crowd of people. What began as a trot quickly widened into something closer to a run. Zig-zagging their way closer to the school, he picked up his own pace once the familiar building was within sight.

Breaking off from the crowd of people, the Sniper took

refuge near a group of parents congregating beneath a lamp post. He joined them in staring at the front entrance on the north side of the school. He mimicked their expressions, looking on with the same wide, unblinking eyes as if he couldn't believe it himself.

He prided himself on being a master of disguise. Related it to the soldier's camouflage that kept him hidden in battle. It was an easy way to move undetected, take pride in his work, and hear firsthand what kind of reaction his work elicited.

It was almost boring, he thought as he looked around at everyone pressing their cellphones to their ears. He was quick to remind himself that this was only the beginning of what was to come—and that gave him purpose.

Picking up his feet, he wanted to get closer.

Terrified faces were everywhere. It was impossible to decipher the good from the bad. As police officers treated innocent subjects as suspects, no one knew how many shooters there were or if there was more carnage to come. It was all going as planned and he could only assume the soldier inside was still fighting a good fight.

Weaving between parked cars, he struggled to keep himself from smiling.

They thought it couldn't happen here, wouldn't happen to them. They were wrong. For those who had forgotten what happened so long ago, they would soon be reminded that the seed that had been planted long ago had finally grown into something big and dangerous.

The Sniper shortened his stride when coming within sight of the police cruiser first to arrive on scene. His gaze flicked to the dark stains on the pavement where he'd taken out his intended targets. Though the bodies were now gone, he knew with absolute certainty they were dead.

Turning around, he faced the road.

A line of media vans and reporters trampled the grass, spouting off live updates as they unfolded. Gripping his guitar case tighter, he lowered his brow and headed straight toward them.

# CHAPTER FOUR

ALLISON DOYLE WAS BUSY TAPPING AWAY ON HER keyboard when her Chief of Operations, Patty O'Neil, interrupted. "Allison, do you have a minute?"

Sweeping her gaze away from her monitor, Allison was quick to notice the concern lining Patty's face. "Everything all right?"

Patty bit her cheek and swallowed. "I think it's best if you see it for yourself."

Allison cleared her throat and pushed back from her desk. Standing firmly on two feet, she followed Patty across the hall and into her office. Patty's two large computer monitors lit up the dim back corner of the room and Allison drew her brows together with intense curiosity.

Patty lowered herself into her chair and said, "I was monitoring Philip Price's account when I came across this."

Allison stared into Patty's round eyes for a split second before bending at the waist. Leaning in to take a closer look at what Patty was bringing to her attention, her eyes began scanning the comments below their advertisement.

Allison's shoulders tightened and she didn't know what to say.

It appeared their message had gotten lost. What had started on sound policy quickly deteriorated into a heated debate on immigration and the need for racial division.

Allison rubbed her brow as she thought through her options.

Philip Price was one of their best clients and currently making a run for the governor's office. He certainly wouldn't like the way people were responding to his ad with the election just around the corner.

Allison flicked her gaze to Patty. "We have to put out these fires by deleting these comments."

"I'm afraid I can't keep up," Patty said.

Allison continued scrolling down. She felt her stomach flutter when someone turned the conversation to blaming the media for spreading lies. Instantly, Allison's mind turned to her friend, Samantha Bell.

"Then we temporarily suspend Price's online campaigns until this stops." Allison kept reading as she spoke. Both women knew that stopping any advertisements with the election so close wouldn't go over well with their client, but they saw no other choice.

The hairs on Allison's neck lifted further with each word. A dozen more comments poured in and there seemed to be no end in sight. "What is this everyone is talking about?" She turned to look at Patty. "A school shooting?"

Patty shook her head and shrugged.

"Turn on the TV."

Patty reached for the remote, pointed it at the screen hanging on the opposite wall, and clicked it on. The screen flashed as she clicked through the channels before landing on a local news station.

They both felt their throats close as they couldn't believe the breaking news.

Allison cast her gaze back to the computer monitor. "Look at this." She pointed. "Apparently, someone is airing live from within the school."

Allison hovered her finger over her mouse, debating whether or not to click the link. *Did she really need to see the terror live?* Her imagination could surely fill in the gaps. She would have let it pass if it weren't for the fact that the link to the live newsfeed was on *her* company's advertisement. She finally clicked, knowing she wouldn't be able to un-see whatever came next.

A new webpage opened and a live Facebook video streamed.

Allison felt her lungs stop working as the office suddenly went completely silent.

The video was dark, a bit grainy, but both women knew what it was they were seeing. Not long into the video, the women shared a look. Neither of them could believe their eyes. The gunman inside the school was *recording* his own massacre.

"I can't watch." Patty turned away and dropped her head into her hand.

Knowing Sam's son, Mason, attended North High, Allison didn't want to look away but knew she had to call her friend. Running across the hall, Allison retrieved her cellphone and was about to call Sam when Patty began screaming.

"He showed his face. The sick bastard is showing his face."

Allison sprinted back into Patty's office and dug her heels in when seeing the shooter's face for the first time. When she covered her mouth with her hand, she felt her chin trembling.

"You thought you could push me around. Well, today, I'm

here to tell you that you can't," the shooter said into the camera. "You people thought this school was yours. You treated the halls like they were yours to be taxed. Remember my face because I'm not inferior like you made me out to be." Screams filled the speakers. The shooter looked up before turning the camera back on himself. "Well, I'm here to tell you that we *are* superior, the chosen race, and your day of reckoning is upon you." He pointed his handgun to the ceiling and fired off two shots, aiming the third inside a classroom full of students.

# CHAPTER FIVE

Every drop of hot blood left my knuckles as I clutched my smartphone tightly inside the palm of my shaking hand. I was only speaking to Mason's voicemail but, even then, I didn't want to hang up.

The air filled with shouts and orders being barked. Heavy boots pounded against the concrete as tactical units were put in place.

I spun on a heel and felt my breath hitch.

A man wearing a baseball cap caught my eye. His look of shock mirrored my own and we shared a silent message of reassurance. I wanted to tell him not to worry, that everything would be okay when I couldn't even honestly convince myself it would be.

A large SWAT van rumbled into position.

The stranger broke our stare and looked toward the school.

It was as if the same images of classrooms filled with students were running through both our minds. The thought of children running and screaming flashed behind my eyelids as a shot unexpectedly rang out.

I ducked for cover and continued to stare at the school's entrance.

A mobile command unit buzzed with activity. Radios filled with chatter. And I kept praying for it to end. Suddenly, school fire alarms bellowed, echoing off the thick concrete walls.

My heart panicked.

If it weren't chaotic enough already, now the police had to deal with that.

A stream of students funneled out of the school faster than the authorities could handle. More screams and shouts, young faces crying and not knowing how to handle the intense flood of emotions that came with what they'd had to witness inside.

With their hands held high in the air, they were being led out of the building by a line of cops in helmets, guns raised. Mild relief swept over me. I searched for Mason but, again, didn't see him. My worry that something happened to him only grew.

Whipping my head around, I glanced back to the man I'd shared a look with only a moment ago. He was gone. Looking everywhere, I couldn't find him and couldn't explain why I cared.

A hand landed on my shoulder and my feet left the ground.

I turned to see who it was and when I saw her glistening eyes looking down on me, I fell into her compassionate embrace like a tree toppling over.

"Mason and King are still inside," I told Erin, hearing my voice crack. "They were doing a school project together."

Erin palmed the back of my skull and squeezed me harder. She had an uncanny sense of always seeming to know where to find me and I couldn't have been more grateful for it.

"We'll find them, Sam," Erin said into my ear.

I nodded into her shoulder, feeling the tears stream from my eyes.

"King is trained for situations like this. If he is able, he'll be the first to confront the shooter."

I pulled back and looked my friend in her eyes. "I don't know if he has his gun with him."

Erin's brow wrinkled before she pulled me against her chest. At a loss for words, we held each other as if believing somehow it would bring Mason and King out safely.

When I heard a second round of students exit the building, I released Erin and turned to scan the horizon, hoping to find Mason. Bouncing my gaze from face to face, I held my breath, crossing my fingers for a little bit of luck. Then my heart sprang into my throat when I saw my son running with his hands held high in the air.

Erin nudged me forward and I sprinted toward him, needing to feel his heart beat against my own just to convince myself he was in fact alive and this wasn't a dream.

# CHAPTER SIX

My vision tunneled with a single mission as I pushed my way through three bystanders before swinging my arms wildly around a tight turn. Then I ducked beneath the barrier that kept me from getting to my son, adrenaline guiding my way.

"Mason!" I yelled, waving my arms wildly above my head.

I kept screaming until stealing his attention away from everything that was happening around him. The moment his eyes lifted and met with mine, he broke free from the pack.

We ran toward each other as fast as we could, jumping into each other's arms somewhere in the middle.

Throwing my arms around him, I patted my hands over his back and down his arms, beyond grateful to know he'd survived something so horrific. Suddenly, I pulled back when my fingers brushed over a damp spot on his clothes. Lowering my gaze to his stomach I asked, "Is that blood?"

Mason's eyes puffed up and froze before beginning to cry.

Pulling him in for another hug, I held on to him like I had when he was much younger. Rocking him back and forth, I glanced over his shoulder and kept searching for King. My stomach dropped with worry, afraid he was still inside.

Mason shuddered in my arms.

"Are you okay?" I asked, taking a step back to lead him away from the building.

Mason tugged on my arm and stopped me mid-pursuit.

"Mason, c'mon, we can't stay here." His look was enough to tell me something wasn't right. "What is it?"

"It's Nolan." His cheeks were wet with tears. "He's still inside."

Closing the gap between us, I reached up to brush his tears away. "Is he okay?" Mason's eyes drowned. "Were you with him?" When he didn't respond, I said, "Mason, you have to tell me. I wasn't inside. I don't know what's going on."

Mason lowered his gaze to the ground and I watched as his lips curled and frowned. "Mom, he shot him."

Instantly, my heart shattered into a million pieces. My stomach fell to the floor and, for a moment, I was speechless. All I could see was a young man dead, sprawled out across a hallway floor.

"Where is Alex, honey?" I asked, holding my breath and hoping that I would receive the answer I needed. "Were you with him?"

Mason's head hit my shoulder like a dead weight. I gripped the back of his skull as he murmured, "He's with Nolan. Please tell me that Alex will be able to keep him alive."

Mixed emotions spiraled out of control. Parts of me were tense with agony, other parts loose with relief knowing that King was still alive and attending to Mason's friend. Tipping my head back to the heavens, I closed my eyes and exhaled a deep breath of Colorado air and began praying.

I dropped my chin when a male voice told us we had to step back.

I acknowledged the officer and guided Mason to safety. All I wanted was to go home, take my son far away from here. I didn't want to be anywhere near the school or the terror that had exploded here today. But King was still inside, and I, too, needed to feel his touch inside the palm of my hand.

Afraid to let go of Mason's hand, together we threaded our way through the parking lot until seeing Erin who was already busy working. I wasn't surprised to see her interviewing students, parents, anybody she could get to go on record. As soon as she saw Mason and me coming, she broke away and came directly to us.

"Mason, thank God, you're okay." Erin hugged my son. Then she turned to me and gave me a look that asked, *Is he okay?*

I insisted Mason sit down on the curb's edge before stepping out of his earshot. "What did you learn?" I asked Erin.

"There seems to be a consensus that the shooter was a student. One person I interviewed thought maybe he graduated last year but, either way, everyone can agree that there was only one shooter involved."

I glanced back to Mason. "Why would anybody do this?"

"Sam, there is something else I learned."

I rolled my neck back to Erin, arching a brow along the way.

"Apparently, he recorded the entire episode on Facebook Live."

I folded one arm over my stomach and lifted the opposite hand to my face. The thought of having the world watch this sicko act out his violent actions was enough to make me want to vomit. But, before I could do that, I heard my name being called.

"Samantha Bell," a TV news reporter called.

As I watched the man approach, I felt a shell harden over me. Since Erin and I had solved The Lady Killer serial murder case only a week ago, I was starting to find my newfound celebrity more cumbersome than helpful.

"Is that your son?" The reporter pointed to Mason as his cameramen struggled to keep up with his pursuit.

I stepped in front of Mason, blocking his face from the cameras, and held up my palms in an attempt to get the reporter to hit the brakes and stop. I watched him shorten his stride and was again surprised by his bold request.

"Let me interview him. Talk to you both," he said.

"Not today." I grinded my teeth as I fought to remain polite.

"Another day perhaps?"

Erin turned to me. "You take Mason home and I'll take care of this."

"Thank you, but with Alex still inside—" I wouldn't finish my thought.

Erin's brows knitted as she locked her eyes with mine.

"Mason's friend was shot. I think Alex is with him."

Erin shoved a hand through her hair and cursed. "Okay then." She glanced back to the reporter. "But I still have something I need to say to this asshole."

I grinned and watched Erin march straight up to the reporter, berating him for his bad judgement and disgraceful professionalism. Turning to Mason, he was still staring up at me. A part of me told me to wait for King, but with reporters now trying to take advantage of both Mason's and my relationship to the school, I knew I needed to get him out of here as soon as possible.

As if reading my mind, Mason stood and stepped toward me with shoulders rolled back and head held high. I watched with increased curiosity as the crease between his brows deepened into something serious.

"Mom," Mason said in a deepened tone, "I'm not leaving here without Nolan."

# CHAPTER SEVEN

ALEX KING KEPT BOTH HANDS FIRMLY PRESSED INTO THE bullet wound of 16-year-old Nolan Dreiss. "You're going to make it," he told Nolan. "We'll get you out of here as soon as possible. Stay with me, buddy."

The warm blood pulsed between his fingers as he watched Nolan's breath shorten. King kept looking toward the school library entrance, hoping help would get to them soon. He wasn't sure how much longer Nolan could hold on without receiving proper medical assistance.

Nolan gasped as she struggled to swallow.

"Help is on its way," King said, maintaining eye contact with Nolan.

King's head pounded with worry as he wrestled with his own shortcomings. Regretting many things today, the first was one he wouldn't ever forgive himself for.

What was he thinking not keeping his department-issued handgun on him? At the time, the decision was easy to make. Seeing it more as a burden and potential risk, he decided it was safer to keep it out of the school rather than to bring it inside. But the biggest regret of all was not stopping the shooter before Nolan was shot.

King noticed Nolan go quiet. He felt Nolan's chest rise and fall. His pulse was weak, but he was still alive.

Growing impatient, King flicked his gaze once again to the entrance. *Where were they? What was taking them so long?* As difficult as it was to admit, King knew in his heart that Nolan wasn't the only one wounded in the attack. He was sure there were casualties as well.

Darting his gaze around the library, the fire alarm lights flashing, he felt his heart break.

Textbooks were left open on tabletops. Next to them, reports were being written and researched, homework getting done. An array of backpacks remained tucked beneath chairs or dropped on the floor. It looked like a stampede of cattle had ripped through here, leaving only himself and Nolan.

"Where is Mason?" Nolan asked, his voice barely audible.

King stared into Nolan's eyes. "He went to get help."

Nolan wet his lips with his tongue. "You should have gone with him."

"He's safe." King's throat collapsed with uncertainty in his statement. He hoped it was true but he couldn't be sure. "The police are here. Mason was escorted to safety."

"Am I going to die?" Nolan's eyes slowly shut.

The sound of a hundred shoes *pitter pattering* their way through the halls grew faint as the police worked to clear each classroom currently on lockdown.

Just as King was about to answer Nolan, he heard voices call out. Two paramedics arrived behind the protection of two officers. "Over here," King answered back. Then he turned back to Nolan. "You're going to make it."

King pulled back and let the paramedics work on Nolan. They loaded Nolan up on a gurney with King telling the young man that he was strong, a fighter. He planted his hands on his hips and quickly glanced down into his blood-soaked palms. Inside his head, he could still hear the gunshots popping off.

Once Nolan was secured to the gurney, he held his hand out for King's attention. "There is something else you need to know."

The paramedics pushed Nolan out of the library and down the hall. King kept pace, marching right alongside of them, knowing he wanted to stay with Nolan until the boy was safe.

"You can tell me anything," King said.

Nolan's hooded eyes locked on King's, life suddenly returning to them. "Mason needs to know what the shooter said just before he shot me."

King's brows wrinkled with interest. Nolan patted King's hand and the detective tilted his head to the side, continuing to march quickly to the exit. Supporting himself with one hand on the gurney, he lowered his ear close to Nolan's mouth, wondering if he had heard him correctly.

"Say that again," King requested.

Nolan repeated his words exactly as he had stated them the first time.

When King learned of the shooter's secret, his entire body froze with disbelief.

# CHAPTER EIGHT

"ALL I'M SAYING IS THAT HE WAS A BETTER QUARTERBACK than he is a general manager."

Dr. Benjamin Firestone grinned and leaned closer to his date. "I'll admit the Denver Broncos are having an off year, but the problem is not with John Elway."

Susan Young loved the way her new boyfriend's eyes sparkled with passion when delving deep into a heated debate. He was quick, intellectual, and a sports fanatic. All very good qualities to her.

Staring into his dark, coffee colored eyes, she said, "You would think that with his experience as a quarterback he would actually be able to draft a decent one."

"We had Peyton Manning, didn't we?" Benjamin turned his palms up to the ceiling and fell back into his chair with his smile crinkling the corners of his eyes.

"Anyone in the league would be able to win with Manning." Susan took the corner of her lip between her teeth and locked eyes with the man she desired.

"I hate to say this, Susan, but you sound like a fair-weather fan."

Susan pinched her straw between her fingers and stirred the ice in her glass of tea. The early and unexpected lunch date Benjamin had surprised her with today was thrilling, even if she would have preferred a romantic night out on the town. His insane working hours, she was learning, meant she had to be flexible with her own if she wanted to make this relationship work.

"You're wrong," she said.

Benjamin's eyebrows lifted high on his head.

Susan held her gaze inside of his and murmured, "I'm a concerned fan, is all. I like to see my team win."

Benjamin cast his gaze to the table. Their vegetarian meal had been both artistic and delicious but Benjamin wasn't ready to leave just yet. He picked up the menu and looked for dessert options. "Then I suppose I should find someone else to come to the game with me this Sunday?"

Susan caught his eye as he peeked over the menu's rim and arched a brow. "Who are they playing?"

Benjamin dropped his head and laughed. "Only a fair-weather fan would care."

Susan tipped forward, perching an elbow on top of the table, and rested her chin inside her hand. "And a true fan, what would they do?"

Benjamin looked her directly in the eye and said, "They would drop everything in order to attend the game."

Susan laughed.

Then Benjamin said, "The New England Patriots."

Her eyes lit up. "Then I'm in."

"Tom Brady?"

Susan wiggled her eyebrows, eliciting another gasp of disbelief from Benjamin. Without warning, Benjamin's work pager went off. Susan watched him glance to his waist and her stomach dropped, knowing that their date had officially come to an end.

"Is it important?" she asked, feeling her muscles slightly tense.

Benjamin lifted his gaze and smiled. Hoping his answer was no, Susan held her breath as he said, "If you'll excuse me, I need to make a quick call."

Susan leaned into his lips as he brushed them against her cheek when he stood. Hanging onto his hand, she didn't want to let go, didn't want their lunch to end yet. Benjamin's fingertips slipped from her grasp and, the moment she was alone, she turned her gaze out the window and blew out a heavy sigh. Dating a doctor wasn't easy, but she couldn't deny how much she liked him.

A minute passed and Susan glanced over her shoulder.

Benjamin was still on his cellphone, his gaze pointed to the floor as he talked. She could tell by the look on his face that something was seriously wrong. The second he ended his call, she straightened her spine and brushed off her feelings of loss.

"Is everything all right?" she asked when Benjamin returned to the table.

"I'm afraid not." He reached for Susan's hand. "There's been emergency and I'm needed at the hospital."

Susan tilted her head and gave him a questioning look. "I thought you just left."

He nodded. If he was being called back in after his overnight shift, this emergency was serious. "I promise to pick up where we left off as soon as I'm finished."

Susan nodded and squeezed his hand as he leaned down to kiss her cheek.

"Don't worry about the tab, I'll take care of that on my way out."

"No. You go. It sounds urgent. I'll take care of the bill," Susan insisted. When Benjamin pressed his thick lips against hers, Susan closed her eyes and felt her stomach flutter. Then Benjamin was off, hurrying to the exit at a quick clip.

Susan twirled her hair between her fingers, trying not to let Benjamin's sudden departure get to her. Besides, it wasn't like she didn't have a pile of work waiting for her back at the office. All things happened for a reason.

Diving into her purse, Susan checked her cellphone out of habit. Having silenced it before sitting down for lunch, her heartrate spiked when she noticed a dozen missed calls from Allison, all since she'd arrived at the restaurant. Fearing something had happened, she called her friend back without taking the time to listen to her voicemail.

"Susan, where are you?" Allison asked in a hurry. "I've been trying to get hold of you."

Susan's pulse pounded. "Having an early lunch with Benjamin. Why? What's going on?"

"You haven't heard?"

"Heard what?"

"There was a shooting at North High School and Sam is there with Mason now."

A sudden coldness hit Susan's core. Words to express her feelings escaped her. Then she realized Benjamin's emergency had to be related. "Where are you? I'll come to you."

"Meet me at my office," Allison said. "We'll travel to Sam's together."

# CHAPTER NINE

As I stared into my son's eyes, I had only respect for him. This was what I had taught him to do. Be kind. Show respect. And remain loyal to those we loved.

With watering eyes, I lifted my arms and hooked my hands on his shoulders. "Okay. We'll stay and wait for Nolan."

"Thank you, Mom."

Sliding my arm through the crook of his elbow, I led him to my car. Here, we were close enough to see what was happening at the school, yet far enough from the chaos to not get caught up in the tornado of activity.

As the minutes passed, we didn't say much but I kept a firm hold on his hand.

It seemed like forever as we waited for something to happen. The snowflakes came and went, like the students who had made it out. And as I stood there staring at the school with my son, I prayed for Nolan, King, and the other students who might still be inside.

Soon, a uniformed officer approached, encouraging all of us to go home.

I gripped Mason's hand tighter. Together, we watched the crowd disperse.

The entire mood changed. The air grew colder and the sense of urgency from earlier had withered. When I asked what the officer knew, he only responded, "It's best if we can have the area cleared."

Mason gave me a concerned look.

I released his hand and approached the officer. After a quick introduction, I said, "Can you at least tell me if you have heard from Detective Alex King?"

"The investigation is still ongoing. I'm afraid that's all I can say at this time."

"Officer, last I heard, Detective King was assisting a wounded student, Nolan Dreiss. Can you please ask your superior officer if they have any information concerning those two men?" I glanced back to Mason. "I can't leave here until I know that they are both okay."

The officer flicked his gaze to Mason before saying, "Mrs. Bell, off the record, I wish that I could tell you something, but we just don't know at this time."

A stone lodged in my throat that I couldn't work down. I wanted to keep my promise to Mason but we were losing control and daylight.

"Now, please, go home," the officer said. "If I happen to see Detective King, I'll tell him you were looking for him."

"Thank you," I whispered. Spinning around to face Mason, I said, "We have to leave."

"Mom, but you promised."

"There is nothing I can do. The police need to do their job. It's best we stay out of their way." I marched to my car with a heavy heart. When I opened the door, Mason was still standing in the exact spot I'd left him. He looked defeated and broken and I felt like I had let him down. "C'mon. Let's go home."

Mason slouched in the passenger seat after buckling in. I cranked the engine and turned on the heat. "Why couldn't he tell you anything?"

"Protocol."

"Don't they know who you are?"

"It doesn't matter."

"But they know if the shooter is dead or not. Why can't they just tell you that much?"

"They don't want any misinformation to get leaked before they compile a report of what happened."

Mason sprang up. "A report of what happened?! I know what happened."

I watched my son breathe heavily through his nose, anger swirling in his young eyes. When I reached for his hand, he pulled away. I clenched my stomach, wishing I knew what to do. Inside, I was still crying but I fought to appear strong for my son.

"One second I was in the library with Nolan, then next thing I knew I was coming out of the bathroom to the sound of gunfire."

I rolled my gaze over the hood and watched my vision blur. My bones quaked and it destroyed me to know that Mason would live with this memory for the rest of his life. It was the nightmare none of us wanted to experience.

"We'll find Nolan," I murmured.

"It should have been me. I should have been there with him." Mason crumbled like an accordion into his seat.

Fighting back the threat of tears, I put the car in gear and started to drive.

I understood Mason wanting to blame himself—allowed him to begin his grieving process. Like me, he felt helpless to change the outcome of what happened. It was a noble idea to want to take a bullet for his friend, but I was so thankful that he hadn't.

By the time we arrived home, the snow had really started to come down. Mason kicked the car door open and scampered up the front steps, entering the house to an ecstatic yellow lab.

When I stepped into the house myself, I checked Cooper's water bowl before sticking my head into Mason's room. He was already lying on his bed, hugging a pillow while curled up in the fetal position. Cooper was pressed up against his leg, staring at me, knowing that something wasn't right.

"Can I get you anything? Are you hungry?" I asked Mason.

Mason only shook his head.

The home phone started ringing and I left to answer the call. It was my editor, Ryan Dawson. "Sam, how is he?"

I turned toward Mason's room and sighed. "Alive but not well."

"It's horrific."

"His friend was one of the victims."

"Sweet Mary, Joseph." Dawson sighed.

"Last we heard, King was with him and he was alive, but that was hours ago."

"Anything I can do for you?"

"Thanks, but there's nothing you can do that I can't do myself."

"Sam, I'm calling from your desk. We have to be out of this newsroom no later than tomorrow."

"Shit." I closed my eyes and pushed my fingers through my hair, completely forgetting about *The Colorado Times* having to move offices because of the paper downsizing.

"I can hear you have your hands full," Dawson said. "Let me help by taking your stuff to the new office."

"Thank you but don't bother. I'll be in first thing tomorrow morning."

"Sam—"

"Dawson, I'll be there," I said firmly. "I should be the one to tell today's story."

"That's not what I'm asking."

"Maybe not, but you know that's what both of us need."

Dawson didn't argue and said his goodbyes. Once we ended our conversation, I began making calls to hospitals across the Denver area with hopes of finding both Nolan and Alex.

# CHAPTER TEN

PASTOR DWAYNE MICHAELS KNEELED ON BOTH KNEES WITH his head bowed in prayer.

His soft whispers swirled around his lean body as he sought guidance and strength during this time of tribulation. The news that had broken earlier today had been both unexpected and heartbreaking but with the son of God hanging over him, the pastor knew he wasn't alone.

Deep in meditation, the pastor looked for answers to the most difficult of life's questions. They came to him in waves but one truth remained; this week of all weeks would be one to test his community's resolve.

With his eyes closed, bright lights flashed behind his lids. A variety of colors swirled inside his head like a kaleidoscope pointed into the light. Ignoring the sharp pain digging into his kneecaps from the hardwood floor, it felt like he was floating in air. His old knees had been through a lot over the years but he welcomed the agony and considered it a simple reminder that he, too, had chosen a life of sacrifice.

His lips moved faster, his whispers growing louder.

The pastor imagined himself inside the school. He could

see students he knew and suppressed the growing resentment toward the evil person who'd set out to destroy so many lives.

Then the entire church went silent.

Pulled back to earth, the aging pastor tipped his head back and slowly opened his eyes. As difficult as it was to know that such evil existed in his city of birth, unfortunately this wasn't the first hate crime the pastor had seen destroy his community.

He found himself smiling at his savior hanging from the cross, enjoying a moment of peace.

Pinching his expression, the pastor stood when noticing something peculiar. Needing a closer look, he extended his index finger and reached for Jesus's cheek. He gasped and pulled away. Feeling the dampness on the tip of his finger, he couldn't believe what he felt.

Jesus was here, inside his church, weeping alongside him.

Feeling his heart begin to race with sudden excitement, the doors opened behind him.

When he turned his head, his body followed. The pastor expected more members of his congregation to follow just as they had streamed through his opened doors steadily since mid-morning but, this time, the man was alone.

"Welcome, my brother." The pastor clasped his hands in front of him and smiled. The stranger hid beneath a worn baseball cap and took a moment to look around. "Please, come inside. This is a safe place for all."

Without responding, the man swept his gaze across the walls before locking on the pastor's eyes. The pastor felt his ribs squeeze when the stranger's dark, piercing gaze narrowed on his own. The man's look was not one of grief or sorrow like the other faces he had seen pouring through his doors today. Instead, his was one of confusion.

"Speak with me, my brother." The pastor took tiny steps

toward his visitor. "What is it that brings you into God's house tonight?"

The stranger lifted his foot and walked confidently toward the pastor at a relaxed pace. He carried a guitar case and didn't appear bothered by the pastor continuing to speak without receiving a response.

"If you are here to speak about what happened today at the school," the Pastor said, "you have found your place of refuge." Today, the pastor had prayed alongside many grieving visitors, answered questions to the best of his ability, and done his best to bring peace to their troubled lives.

The stranger stopped within arms-reach of the pastor and continued to stare. "Forgive me, Pastor, for I have sinned."

The pastor tucked his chin into his neck and grinned. "Lucky for you, you have come to the right place. For I, too, am a sinner." Bringing his hands to the stranger's strained shoulders, the pastor said, "Let us pray."

They both bowed their heads, the pastor's prayers echoing between the many rows of pews behind them. The stranger stood without moving, hanging onto his guitar case as if it were part of himself. When they finished, the stranger muttered a quick thank you.

"Are you new to the neighborhood?" the pastor asked.

Keeping his gaze pointed to the floor, the stranger shook his head. "I must be going."

"Please stay, I could use some company." The pastor extended his arm to an empty pew.

The stranger declined and stepped away from the pastor's warm hands. "Really, I must be going."

"Very well then." The pastor didn't argue.

The stranger spun on a heel and quickly trotted toward the exit. But, before leaving, he stopped, turned, and said, "Forgive me, Pastor, I didn't catch your name."

The pastor tipped his head back and said confidently, "Dwayne Michaels."

A knowing smirk pulled on the stranger's lips.

A wave of chills rolled beneath the pastor's collar and the initial odd feeling he'd had when the stranger arrived was back, stronger than before. He turned his head to the side, hoping the stranger would offer his name freely in a kind gesture.

"Yes, that is right. Now I remember," the stranger said, bobbing his head.

The pastor stared with a quizzical look on his face, thinking the stranger's response was rather odd. "And yours, brother? What is your name?"

The stranger pulled his hat further over his eyes, flashed a broad knowing smile, and then pushed his way through the doors, exiting the building without another word.

# CHAPTER ELEVEN

THE CORDS IN MY NECK FLEXED AS I FOUGHT BACK THE urge to groan. I released the phone onto the table and dropped my head into my hands. My fingers curled deep into my scalp as I struggled to understand why no one could give me a straight answer.

Nolan and King were still missing. I didn't even know if they were alive.

The sound of my teeth grinding filled my head. I wished I could go back in time, relive the laughter that filled this house twelve hours earlier. No matter how hard I squeezed my eyes shut, those memories were drowned out by everything that had happened today.

I fell back into my chair and cradled my unsettled stomach.

Even worse than getting the run-around at hospitals was that King wasn't picking up his phone or responding to any of my dozens of messages. Worry tangled my stomach into uncomfortable knots and, when I began shaking uncontrollably, I knew the trauma of today was finally catching up with me.

I told myself that I was stronger than what I felt but it was only a lie.

Flipping my head around to the corkboard on the back wall, I stood and plucked Mrs. Dreiss's phone number away from its tack. Staring at it, I knew I should have done this hours ago, but I struggled to find the words I wanted to ask. I had to do it—make the call and hope that I would receive the news I wanted to hear.

I watched my thumb tremble as I dialed Nolan's house.

Sucking back a quick breath of air, I put the phone to my ear and listened to it ring. I held that little breath inside until my lungs burned. My nerves were getting the best of me. I was afraid and uncertain and hoped that I wouldn't be the one to break the news to her. Mason's words about Nolan's shooting was something I would never forget—something that would make me count my blessings daily.

The line clicked over and I got the family voicemail.

With parted lips, I paused. After taking a moment to collect my thoughts, I said, "Natalie, it's Mason's mom, Samantha Bell. I was calling to tell you that we are thinking of you and your family. Call us if you need anything. Anything at all."

Then I hung up, feeling regret pinch my gut as I thought how lucky I was to have my son safe and at home with me now. The front door clicked open. When I turned to see who it was, Susan and Allison stepped inside.

"Sam, I hope you don't mind that we brought Chinese for dinner." Susan held up two huge plastic bags of food.

I leaned against the threshold leading into the kitchen. Crossing my arms, I couldn't even force a smile. Even without eating since breakfast, I wasn't hungry. "Thanks, but I don't have much of an appetite."

"Me either," Allison said, leaning in to give me a tight bear hug. Then she pulled back, bounced her gaze around, and, without saying it, I knew what she was thinking.

"It's happening again," I said, thinking how tonight was beginning to remind me of when everyone came over after solving The Lady Killer murders.

Allison rolled her misty eyes over me and flashed a weak smile. "It feels that way, doesn't it?"

"And here I'm starting to believe that maybe I'm bad luck."

"Just stop with that right now," Susan interrupted after setting the bags of Chinese on the kitchen table. "You know that's not true," she said, wrapping her arms around me.

"It's how it feels, though," I muttered into her shoulder.

"We're not going anywhere," Susan said with Allison's approval. "And you're *not* bad luck."

I called both of them in and the three of us dropped our heads together and hugged each other as tight as possible. Tears started to fall. When I stared into their doting eyes, it only made me cry harder.

Allison rubbed my back and asked, "How is Mason?"

I swiped my hand over my eyes and said, "He's alive."

"And we're thankful for that." Susan nodded.

"His friend was shot," I said, hearing a collective gasp suck all the air out of the room. I looked my friends in the eye and added, "We don't know anything yet. I called everyone and no one can confirm his whereabouts."

"Not even Alex?"

I choked on my next words. "I haven't heard from him, either."

"Jesus." Susan reached for me again.

Feeling weak and exhausted, we moved to the kitchen table. The three of us sat there staring at our hands, not knowing what to say. The phone rang and my eyes flew open, hope blooming across my chest.

Susan gave me a look that said, *what are you waiting for, answer it already.* I jumped to my feet and answered. "Sam, oh, thank God, you answered. How is Mason? Is he home?"

I turned back to the girls and shook my head. Covering the mic with my hand, I whispered, "It's my sister."

"Sam, are you there?"

"I'm here, Heather." I sighed. "Mason is here, too."

"I've been so worried. It's all over national news. Have you spoken with Mom?"

I stared through the kitchen window, catching my own reflection in the darkness of night. I thought of my mom living in Arizona and how I had forgotten to call her with all the other phone calls I had been making. "No," I said to Heather.

"Sam, you have to call her." Heather was always telling me what to do, even with her living on the East Coast. "If she sees this on the news, she's going to freak. Hell, I freaked. I mean, you just broke that big serial killer case, and now this?"

"It's been an incredibly difficult day, as I'm sure you can imagine." I turned around to see Erin had arrived. I gave her a small wave and watched the girls greet her with another round of hugs.

"It sounds like you have company."

"The girls are here."

"I'll let you go," Heather said. "I just wanted to call and tell you that I was thinking of you."

"Thank you."

"I'm glad that Mason is okay. Please hug him for me, will you? I miss you guys."

I promised Heather I would, saying, "I'll call you once things die down."

"Sam, don't worry about Mom. I'll call her for you."

Heather closed out our call and I pulled my phone away from my ear. Erin's sullen look was even worse than my own.

I padded to the table, squeezed her shoulder, and dropped into the empty chair. Then told her I still couldn't find Nolan or Alex.

Erin cast her gaze to the table and didn't act surprised.

"How many?" I asked, staring at Erin from beneath my brow.

Talking to the table, Erin muttered, "When I left there were 11 confirmed causalities."

"Was Nolan one of them?"

Erin lifted her gaze and I felt my heart pause when wanting to ask if any of the dead were King. "Names of the deceased haven't been released, but there were nine students and two officers."

"How many critically injured?" Susan asked.

Erin turned to Susan. "Fourteen in critical condition."

"Two police officers?" Allison's brow furrowed and glanced to me.

Holding my breath, I was hanging on to the word *officer*, never once hearing *detective*. King was alive. He had to be.

"The first two officers to arrive on scene." Erin frowned.

The kitchen fell quiet. No one was eating and we sat silently as the food went cold—still tucked away in their neat little boxes. Tears hit our eyes and we all wished we could have done something to have prevented this. The immense suffering I was feeling was intense. Just as I was once again struggling to maintain my grasp on what little information we had to work with, I heard a small knock on the front door. A second later, King stepped inside.

# CHAPTER TWELVE

I PUSHED AWAY FROM THE TABLE AND RAN THROUGH THE house, jumping into Alex's arms. The moment King wrapped his arms around me, I melted into his hard chest and hung off his thick neck. Then I began to shake.

"I thought I lost you," I admitted.

"You didn't." He squeezed harder.

I tipped my head back and pounded my fist against his breast. "Then why didn't you call?"

His eyes said what he couldn't; they spoke of immense grief and devastation. "Did you find Mason? Did he make it out safely?"

Tears pooled in the corners of my eyes as I nodded. "He's here. In his room."

King's large hand cupped the back of my skull and pulled my head against his body. I listened to his heart pound like the bass in an orchestra. "I saw everything, Sam."

"I know. Mason told me you were there."

The tips of his fingers dug deeper into my flesh as I felt him struggle to contain his grief.

"I have been trying to track down Nolan." My words

were muffled by his jacket. "No one is telling me anything. What happened to him? Where is he? Mason said you were with him. We waited for as long as we could but you never came."

King lowered his gaze and took my face between his hands. Stroking my cheek with his thumbs, he murmured, "Sam, Nolan was shot and is hurt really bad."

I felt my expression fall from my face. I swayed my eyes inside of King's blues, and was afraid to ask the dozen follow-up questions that were swirling between my ears.

"Nolan got out." A small smile curled King's lips. "He was alive the last I saw."

I moaned and rubbed my forehead. "Thank you, Lord."

"I don't know where they took him, Sam." King's fingers massaged my tense neck loose. He closed his eyes and said, "But we'll find him."

"Did they catch the shooter?" Erin asked from the kitchen.

King lifted his head. With hooded eyes he said, "The shooter shot himself. He's dead."

"Coward," I heard someone mutter.

"Come inside." I tugged on King's hand and moved to the living room window. Staring outside, it still didn't make any sense to me why someone would shoot up a school.

King worked the room, giving each of my friends a hug. Words were quiet, sentences short. And as we each let our heads drop into our hands, King made his way back to me.

Snaking my hands around his tight waist, I touched his face, looked him in his eyes and asked, "How are you?" He cast his gaze to the floor. "Are you okay?"

A subtle shake of his head had me worried. His eyes lifted. "Can we talk in private?"

My breath caught in my chest as I nodded. We excused ourselves and went to the kitchen. "Are you hungry?" I asked, pointing to the meal no one had touched. "Susan brought Chinese but none of us are hungry."

King declined and rubbed the back of his neck.

Something was on his mind, his actions worrying me further. I shuffled my feet over the floor and said, "What is it?"

King stared. "Something Nolan told me as he was being wheeled out by the paramedics."

I crossed my arms and tucked my hands deep into my armpits.

King scrubbed a hand over his strong jaw and glanced to Mason's closed bedroom door. "The shooter said something to Nolan just before shooting him."

My brows pinched. "What?"

Licking his lips, King lowered his voice to a whisper and said, "That he was looking specifically for Mason."

I did a double take with my eyes. Suddenly, my entire flesh burned with tiny needle pricks. "Why would he be looking for Mason?" I asked.

"Let's just put it this way: Nearly all of today's victims were black."

I flicked my gaze to an old photograph of my dead husband, Gavin, and found myself staring into his chocolate eyes. It didn't take me long to recall Mason's recent bullying episode at school and receiving a call from Principal Craig to come speak to him about fighting.

"But Nolan is white," I said.

King raised his eyebrows. "A white kid who is friends with Mason."

Struggling to accept what King was telling me, I argued, "I'm white—"

"And Gavin was black." King's words were clipped and if it weren't for the fact that he knew Gavin as well as anybody, I might not have accepted his tone when speaking of my late husband.

My chest rose and fell as I paced from sink to counter and back, helping to lower my rising blood pressure. "What are you saying, that this was a hate crime?"

"The early assessment makes me think so."

"What you're saying is Nolan got shot because he's friends with a 16-year-old biracial kid from the Highlands?" When I heard my voice rise, I immediately regretted it, hoping Mason didn't hear.

"Sam, I'm only sharing what Nolan told me. There is a lot still unknown, but I thought it worth mentioning to you so that maybe we know what to protect Mason from."

"The world?" I shook my head and King sighed. I turned my back to him and said softly, "Then maybe the shooter got what he deserved."

"Sorry to interrupt," Allison announced as she stepped into the kitchen.

"We're in the middle of something." I spun around with my hair swishing across my shoulders. One glance and I could see that Allison had something she wanted to say. "I'm sorry. I'm not feeling myself."

"None of us are, Sam." Allison was quick to forgive. "But I saw what the shooter said. I watched his live feed at the office."

"You did?"

Allison nodded. "I'll never be able to erase his voice from my head." Allison shook her head. "But King is right. This was a deliberate attack on the black community, *my* community." Allison pointed at her chest. "The shooter said it himself. And if Nolan was shot for being friends with Mason, we can't ignore it."

"Did you see the video?" I asked King.

He shook his head.

"It was taken down," Allison confirmed.

"The shooter is already dead." My bones ached. "What else can we do?"

"Pastor Michaels has his doors open late." Allison stepped forward. "People are gathering, coming together to show their solidarity. Maybe it would be good for Mason to be with his peers?"

I gave King a look.

"This isn't a time to hide," Allison added.

I was still staring at King when he finally nodded. "No, you're right." I glanced to Allison. "We need to stick together. I'll see if Mason's awake."

# CHAPTER THIRTEEN

Mason opened the door before I even knocked. Surprised, I blinked and stared into his coffee bean eyes and said, "Pastor Michaels—"

"I'm coming Mom."

My eyes opened further. Then my gaze drifted to his right shoulder as my head titled on its side. "Okay, well..."

"I heard what Allison said." Mason raised his chin, still looking me directly in the eye. "She's right. We can't hide here. It's not going to do us any good."

Nodding, I wondered what else he might have heard. Cooper jumped off Mason's bed and nudged his head against my thigh. Rubbing his ears, I said, "King is here. I think he would like to see you."

Mason's gaze lifted a second before I heard King's deep voice travel from over my left shoulder. "Hey buddy."

I glanced over my shoulder and smiled at King, appreciating all he had done up to this point and over the years. He was like a father-figure to Mason and nothing was more comforting to me than knowing King was here now. Gavin would be proud, I thought.

"Where is Nolan?" Mason asked him. "Is he all right? Did you get him out?"

"He's hurt pretty bad but the paramedics were able to get to him."

"What hospital is he at?" Mason whipped his head around and stared wide-eyed at me. "We need to go see him."

"We don't know those details yet," I said.

Mason looked to King. "But you do, right?"

"We're still working on it," King said somberly. "In the meantime, how about we go see what Pastor Michaels has going at the church?"

Mason dropped his head, stared at the floor for a brief pause, then nodded.

King gripped my shoulder as he side-stepped around me to hook his hand around Mason's neck. Then he pulled my son under his arm and guided him into the kitchen.

Following their lead, I offered Mason food but he wasn't hungry. Telling the girls our plan, I tucked the two massive bags of Chinese in my half-empty fridge and prepared to leave. With Mason already stepping out the door, I grabbed King's hand and said, "Thank you."

"Stop, Sam." His friendly gaze put butterflies in my stomach. "You don't have to thank me for loving your son."

"But I do." I smiled.

We all shuffled out of the house, locking the front door on our way out. I knew that if it weren't for King, I didn't know where I would be today. Mason took to him better than anybody and, together, they remained strong—even in the face of adversity.

"We'll follow you," Erin said, standing behind her opened driver's side door.

I nodded and dropped into the front seat of King's car. Mason was tucked into the backseat and the girls were with Erin. It was a short drive to the community church and, as

King drove, I stared out the window thinking about the Facebook Live video Allison had seen.

Questions rolled around my head like dice and I wondered how I could get my hands on it. I needed to hear what the shooter said, see what he looked like, and know if he was a lone wolf or if there were more. The dangers that would follow my son through this world were everywhere. Even with the shooter dead, it didn't feel complete. There were still too many questions left unanswered, not to mention the gaping hole today's event left in my heart.

When we pulled up to the entrance, the parking lot was as full as Sunday worship. I flicked my gaze to the cross, shining bright on the outside wall, and smiled. King parked in an empty spot in a dark corner and I stepped out to little sound. Misty clouds of breath billowed in front of me as I breathed in the wintery air.

The girls parked three spaces down and quickly met up with us. King met me near the trunk, pressing his large hand in the small of my back. We shared a quick glance before I latched onto his arm. With Mason off to my side, our small group made our way to the entrance. The snow-covered ground crunched beneath our feet as we walked. Not one of us said a word.

A member of the church greeted us at the door and Mason was quick to recognize other families from the school, many of whom regularly attended Pastor Michaels's sermons.

The choir sang and the organ played. With each step further inside, my emotions began spilling out of me. Tears prickled the backs of my eyes and everything was so beautiful that it had me choking up all over again.

I spotted Pastor Michaels off to the side, edging the wall, holding the hands of a teenage girl. We locked eyes and I nodded and waved. King took an empty pew in the back and we all followed him. We sung and held hands, searching for peace and understanding in a familiar place each of us knew well. In our home of spiritual refuge, we hoped to find answers to why, but mostly we wanted to show that love would overcome evil.

When I closed my eyes, memories came to me in waves. The day Gavin first brought me to his place of worship. The day Pastor Michaels officiated our marriage. The countless Sundays I attended sermon after Gavin had passed.

A gentle touch to my shoulder and Pastor Michaels was there, greeting us all. Then he requested to speak to me alone. "I promise not to take you away from your family for very long."

I squeezed Mason's hand and worked myself to the end of the bench, my brain trying to guess what could be so important that Pastor Michaels had to speak with me now.

He took me to somewhere quiet and, when he turned to face me, he held his opened palms out for me to take. I dropped my hands inside of his and felt his warmth radiate and transfer to my core.

"It's good to see you, Samantha." He smiled.

"Good to see you too, Pastor."

"I know it is a bit late but I wanted to personally congratulate you on breaking the serial killer case open." His genuine smile spread.

"Thank you." I dropped my gaze to our entwined hands. "But none of that matters now."

The pastor lowered his gaze. "You were there today?"

I nodded. "I was." Flicking my gaze up to meet with his, I added, "The shooter took his own life."

"The Devil comes in many forms." He paused, then asked about Mason.

I turned my head and let my gaze travel to my son. Blowing out a shaky breath, I said, "Detective King discovered the shooter was specifically targeting African American students."

"And Mason was one of them?"

I nodded, unable to look the pastor in his eyes. "He shouldn't have made it out alive today."

"But he did." The pastor smiled. "The Lord chose him to live. There is a reason for it, Samantha."

My head was still nodding when I said, "He doesn't even know." The pastor's head pulled to the ceiling and I watched him glance to my son. "I haven't been able to tell him, or figure out if I even should."

"The answer will come to you when you're ready."

I stared into his eyes and we both shared a knowing look. "I should warn you that today's event, though assumed to be isolated, might not be."

The pastor released my hands, turned to his church, and smiled. "Hatred and bigotry walk through my doors every day. We can't make decisions for others, but we can certainly show them that there is an alternate path. One of kindness and compassion and forgiveness."

Pastor Michaels glanced over his shoulder, then back to me. "Have you recently received threats?" I asked.

The pastor looked away, shaking his head. "I've seen a steady stream of visitors today but nothing compared to this." The pastor grinned then dropped his gaze back to mine. "Sam, there is talk of a vigil being held tomorrow evening. Would you be able to help spread the word?"

I told the pastor about the *Times* being under new ownership and its uncertain future. "I'll see what I can do."

He thanked me and said, "Bring Mason. Keep him involved. It's important he doesn't lose hope."

"I will."

"It will be good for him." His slender hand landed on my shoulder. "We'll get through this together."

# CHAPTER FOURTEEN

I COULDN'T SLEEP. THERE WAS TOO MUCH ON MY MIND. Slipping out of bed, I went straight to work. First, I checked my email to see if Dawson responded to my request for a slot in today's paper to mention the vigil. There was nothing and I feared it might have been too late. Then I went searching for the Facebook Live video.

My finger tapped the mouse and I scrolled and flicked through a couple dozen sites, always coming up empty. The video was gone and a part of me was thankful for it. I didn't need to see it. No one needed to relive yesterday. Our minds would do that for us—often when we least expected it to.

Threading my fingers together, I leaned back in my chair.

Ignoring my own emails piling up, I couldn't stop thinking how Mason's name was on a kill list. I thought about hate crimes, racism, and bigotry in today's complex world and it left me speechless. The shudder down my spine seemed never-ending.

So many questions spiraled between my ears. I kept asking myself if I was the reason for Mason being targeted.

I didn't need to read what people were saying about me.

There was plenty of it, and I could already guess. Threats were nothing new to me. I received them weekly in some form of another, but lately there did seem to be more of them since solving the serial killer case. But none of them were because of my race, and none—that I knew about—were directed at Mason.

In exposing The Lady Killer, I had ruffled a lot of feathers in an extremely powerful community. It seemed like everybody was taking sides and you either hated me or loved me. But was it revenge directed at my son? Or was it simply jealousy of my newfound fame and I was an easy target to express their hatred for great journalism?

My stomach flexed involuntarily.

Normally, these were the kinds of things I would choose to ignore. It wasn't worth the wasted energy. But this was different. This was personal. People were killed because of someone's hate and that bothered me a great deal.

Tipping forward in my chair, I opened up a blank word document and started writing my column, reporting on the horrific events of yesterday from a mother's perspective. It was my way of coping, explaining the unexplainable. The words poured out of me like water. An hour passed in the blink of an eye and I snapped out of my head when King greeted me from behind.

"Did you get any sleep?" he asked.

Pulling away from my keyboard, I spun around and said, "Not much. You?"

"About what you'd expect."

He was a sight for sore eyes. Refusing to leave me home alone, I did what I thought I wouldn't do; I asked him to sleep over. Even with me insisting he sleep on the couch—still wanting to keep things slow for Mason—he agreed and I appreciated the gesture. It felt good to be kissed goodnight—to have a man in the house again. All night I considered myself lucky to have my son home and unharmed, yet still worried about how this would all play out.

I extended my arms and reached for King's hands.

Pulling him closer, he asked what I was working on. "I can't help but feel that maybe I was the reason Mason's name was on the shooter's kill list."

"Sam, don't beat yourself up about this."

"It makes sense," I pleaded. "My face is plastered everywhere and not everyone likes what I have to say." Beneath that, and what I couldn't admit to King, was how old memories resurfaced and reminded me of the bigotry I'd experienced during my marriage to Gavin.

King tucked a loose strand of hair behind my ear. "Mason is home. He's safe."

"But will he remain safe? Like you said last night, there is still a lot unknown."

"You need someone to blame?" He raised his brows. "Blame me."

"What? Why? No."

King lowered his tailbone and sat on the edge of the desk. Turning his gaze out the window, he said, "I can't stop thinking how I let Mason get out of my sight minutes before the shooting began." He rolled his neck and looked me directly in the eye. "If something happened to him," he cleared his throat, "I would have had to live with that the rest of my life."

I stared into his ocean colored eyes, realizing that I wasn't the only one wanting to take the blame. After a moment of silence, King's phone rang from his pocket. He gave me a pained look, but we both knew he had to take it. He stood and pressed his lips against my forehead, then walked out of the room. I closed my eyes and sighed.

My article wasn't finished, but I closed the document and leaned back in my chair. There was no way I could blame

King for anything that happened yesterday except keeping Nolan alive. At least, I hoped he was still alive.

Alex walked back into the room and put a hand on my shoulder. "That was my lieutenant calling."

His tone made me tense. He'd learned something, I could tell. But I didn't know if I wanted to hear it.

"Sam, they're releasing the name of the shooter. I thought you might want to hear it before it's all over the news."

I nodded and stood. "I want to know who did this to our community."

King paused before saying, "Timothy Morris."

The name meant nothing to me. I'd never heard it before. Now I'd live with that name for the rest of my life.

King took my hand and I met his eyes. They held an understanding that told me I didn't have to say anything. He would live with the name forever, too. It would color one of the darkest days of our lives but we would endure.

"I'm going to shower and head to the school," he said. "If I come across any answers to your questions, I'll call."

"Thank you," I whispered and watched him disappear into the bathroom. As soon as he closed the door, the house phone rang.

Lunging for it, I answered.

"Samantha, it's Natalie."

"Natalie, thank you for calling me back. How are things?" I held my breath.

"Nolan had a long night in surgery but is expected to make a full recovery."

"That's wonderful news." My legs wobbled. "Mason will be thrilled."

"He's already asking to see Mason." Natalie sounded exhausted.

"Mason would like that." We arranged a time and promised to see each other then. As soon as I set the phone down, Mason strode into the kitchen running a hand through his messy hair. "Hey, baby, how did you sleep?"

He shrugged. "Who were you just talking to?"

"Nolan's Mom." The corners of my eyes crinkled.

"How is he?" Mason perked up.

"He had a long night in surgery but is doing well. He would love to see you." I smiled.

"Can we go now?"

Lowering myself into the kitchen table chair, I said, "No, honey. He needs to rest first."

"When?"

"Soon." Cooper came in from the living room to greet Mason. "Can I ask you something?"

"What about, Mom?"

My heart skipped a beat. "The shooter."

# CHAPTER FIFTEEN

ERIN TATE SAT BEHIND HER COMPUTER IN HER HOME office pouring over past school shootings. Digging through what seemed to be endless headlines from around the country—many of which she was familiar with already—she was looking for patterns.

With pen to pad, she scribbled off notes. Her lips fluttered soft whispers as she scanned the text, reading aloud to her quiet, empty house.

Keeping her personal emotions at bay—as hard as it was —Erin didn't have to argue the fact that the country was experiencing a sickening epidemic. After yesterday, she still couldn't believe how close it had hit to home. There seemed no end in sight.

Without looking, she reached for her coffee mug and curled her lips over the rim. Realizing she had already finished her second cup for the day, she told herself she didn't need any more. Already buzzing with energy, she kept working.

Nearly every shooting was performed by a male—just like yesterday's shooting spree. Some of them were blamed for lacking maturity while other outbursts were blamed on unful-filled masculinity and an over-exposure to violent video games. But, to Erin, these excuses only skimmed the surface of what was actually going on.

Biting the pen cap between her teeth, Erin still didn't have the name of the shooter. She only knew the gender. It was a start, but to learn who this person really was she would need to know his name.

Flicking her gaze to her wooden trimmed wall, her mind quickly took her back to last night. Remembering what King said about the investigations' early assessment being a hate crime, Erin curled her fingers over the keyboard and began typing.

Turning her attention to the high school's social media page, it didn't take her long to get sucked down a rabbit hole. Here, she found herself navigating through a half-dozen student social circles, getting a feel for the lives of these kids. Her lips parted as she read and scanned everything these teenagers publicly posted. There was little filter and she couldn't believe half of what she read and saw.

Backing away from her monitor, her mind painted a picture of what it was like to be a student at North High. There was racism and hate, bullying and harassment. It was all happening online, out in the open for all to see, and Erin could only imagine what it was like to experience the same kind of language in person. *Was the school administration doing anything about this?*

Erin had never read such awful things. She had read how children killed themselves over things like this but, until now, she never realized the magnitude of what was actually happening. It was so different than her own high school experience that she remembered with fondness.

She kept scouring the web.

Inside, she wanted to believe that these were only sick

jokes, a cruel game between peers, but she would be a fool to think otherwise.

Sitting in the church last night, she couldn't help but notice how as soon as the doors closed and everyone began filing out to go home, everyone divided themselves up by race. She thought about it for a long time, thinking how we was the cause of our own crimes.

Erin went back to the internet browser and one funnel led her to the next before finding herself coming to an abrupt halt. Her lips parted. She stared with dry, unblinking eyes, unable to believe how quickly she'd found herself staring into the hazel colored eyes of her friend, Samantha Bell.

Only a second ago she was in the circle of teenagers and now, suddenly, she had managed to jump portals and find herself snooping the online profiles of her peers. Shaking her head, Erin wasn't at all surprised to see adults acting in the same disgraceful manner. An online mob had formed and together they called journalist hacks, phonies, and even wished some in the profession would die.

Erin scrolled back up to Sam's face.

She was an easy target, Erin thought. Not only was Sam a great investigative reporter, but she was also female.

"You should feel intimidated by us," Erin muttered under her breath.

She and Sam had already proven what they were capable of doing when locking in on a story. But knowing Mason had been singled out by the shooter only intensified things. She knew that this story would be different than any others she had worked on before.

This one was personal.

Reaching for her phone—worried for Sam—she quickly reminded herself that Sam was with King. The small television in the corner of her office stole her attention. Erin turned to the screen and listened.

"This just in," the news anchor started. "We have just learned the name of yesterday's school shooter. His name is Timothy Morris. He was a senior, set to graduate in the spring—"

Erin spun back to her computer and typed a quick inquiry into the search bar. Keeping one ear on the television, she watched her screen populate with hundreds of hits. Clicking the first option, Erin quickly learned the basics of who this young man was.

Timothy Morris was called smart, loved books, and looked happy.

Erin didn't need to see yesterday's video to ask who purchased the weapons used or whether Timothy acted alone.

She turned back to the television.

The news anchor kept showing clips of Timothy. The people interviewed had plenty to say about him. Each interviewee wanted to be an expert on the life we all wanted to know more about. To Erin, the images she saw online of a happy kid didn't line up with the images being painted of Timothy as a monster.

Erin's brows knitted as she tapped the end of her pen on her legal notepad.

A minute later, she flipped the channel to CNN. Rolling her eyes, the talking heads were already guessing to why the shooter did what he did. Of course, little of it was actually based on fact, nearly all of them speculating and assuming Timothy was like past school shooters. Erin knew better than to make such grandiose assumptions until the official police report was released and clicked the television off.

Her phone dinged with a message.

She glanced to the display screen and saw that it was an email from her source.

After a quick message back, she opened the email. There,

waiting for her inside, were the names of yesterday's victims along with a link to a digital yearbook.

Feeling eager to solve the mystery, Erin quickly matched the names of each victim to a face.

"King was right," she said to herself.

All the victims were of color except for Nolan. Even the two cops were African American.

A minute later, she had the two police officer's faces pulled up on her screen. "How did Timothy manage to kill you two and not Nolan?" The discrepancy in marksmanship didn't make sense.

Erin fell back into her chair, her mind churning with possibility.

Did Timothy intentionally keep Nolan alive because they shared the same skin color? Or did the shooter get knocked off his shot when firing on Nolan? Because there was no way a person could kill two officers wearing protective vests and miss their shot on a student who wasn't.

Erin flipped her browser back to Timothy Morris and said, "Someone taught you how to shoot, but who?"

# CHAPTER SIXTEEN

Mason sat across from me at the kitchen table with his head hanging to his chest.

Gripping a cold apple between my fingers, I stared at him counting his vulnerabilities. He appeared so fragile. And it wasn't even his innocence that I was thinking. Mason knew how to navigate his world—this city—better than most kids his age. But now I had to decide if maybe I should reign in his freedom until I was sure this danger had passed.

"Did you know him?" I asked of the Timothy Morris, deciding how best to ask my son what might actually be going on inside the high school's walls where he spent so much of his time.

"I didn't see him." Mason reminded me he was in the bathroom at the time of the shooting inside the library.

"No, but I know you know who he was."

Mason's body seemed to freeze. He appeared frozen stiff. There were no signs of life, like the walking dead, he was so quiet.

"Mason," I set the apple down and splayed my hand flat on the table, "it's important we talk about this together." I paused, hoping to get some kind of response. When there wasn't any, I continued, "I don't expect you to manage this on your own. We're in this together even if it doesn't feel that way." Tipping forward, I slid my hand closer to him. "Tell me what you're feeling."

The cords in Mason's neck tensed and I watched him make a fist with one hand.

"It's okay to be scared," I said.

He sniffed and blinked his eyes. "I can't stop hearing the pops of gunfire." He wiped his nose with the backside of his hand before adding, "Each time I close my eyes, my head fills with screams and all I can hear are the people crying."

My ribs squeezed the air out of my lungs. I drowned in my own sorrow, my pulse faint. Not wanting to lie, I knew the noises Mason was hearing might live with him forever. It broke my heart to know that Mason would have to battle the demons of PTSD just like his father had. I couldn't tell him that. At least not now.

Mason lifted his head and stared beneath a heavy brow. "I was scared I was going to die."

I was sure of the answer, but I still had to ask him, "How did you get blood on your shirt?"

"I ran into the library looking for Nolan. That's when I found him with King."

"And King told you to leave?"

Mason nodded.

Standing, I skirted around the table and let my arms fall around my son. "You did the right thing. You survived. Even Pastor Michaels said there is a reason for it."

"It's not fair, Mom." Mason snapped, getting my eyes to bulge.

I stepped back. "I know, sweetie, and as cliché as it is to hear, it's the way this world works. We can only decide for ourselves how we want to move forward."

He rolled his eyes and turned away. "There must be something I can do to make this right."

"You'll know it when the time comes." I stepped back around the table and lowered myself down into the chair. "I'll be honest with you, Mason. Things won't ever be the same. You have an incredible support system surrounding you. You can talk to any one of us."

Mason's brows pinched as he kept staring out the window.

King entered the kitchen a minute later. I smiled, letting my eyes drift down his sport coat. "Would you like to eat before you leave?"

"I'll get something on the way."

Mason spun around in his chair. "Nolan made it out of surgery," he told King.

King lifted a fist and Mason bumped it. "That's excellent news."

I nodded when King glanced to me. "We're going to see him later this morning."

"Are you okay with me leaving?"

My gaze softened, appreciating King's caring words. "We'll be fine. You have work to do."

"I'll call you later." King squeezed my shoulder, said goodbye to Mason, and I watched Cooper follow him to the front door. As soon as he was gone, I turned back to Mason.

"Did he sleep on the couch?" Mason asked.

"I thought it would be nice if he stayed with us."

"Because you're scared?"

I held Mason's eyes inside of mine and nodded once. I realized, then, that asking Mason to talk about his feelings from yesterday was too much too soon. Even I couldn't muster the strength to voice my fear. My anger. My complete loss of control. So I changed the subject. "Tell me what you know about the shooter."

Mason slumped in his seat and groaned.

"They said his name is Timothy Morris, did you know him?"

"Not really."

"But you *did* know him?"

"Everyone knows everybody." Mason looked me in the eye when he spoke. "There are no secrets in that school. There is nothing anyone can hide. Eventually, everything gets out." Mason paused and gave me a questioning look. "Why do you want to know, anyway? Are you going to write a story about it?"

"Would it bother you if I did?"

Mason shook his head.

"It's all very confusing, as you can imagine." I brought my elbows to the top of the table and threaded my fingers together. "I can't stop thinking about my meeting with Principal Craig a couple weeks ago when he said you were fighting." I arched a brow. "Do you remember that?"

"We don't have to go over this again." Mason's mouth turned down. "I already told you it was nothing."

My other brow raised. "But you never told me who was bullying you. And what did they say to make you want to fight them?" I replayed what Mason said that day inside my head. *You should have heard what they said about me.* I couldn't get it out of my mind and I deeply regretted not asking more about it at the time.

"I don't want to repeat it." Mason's eyelids drooped.

When I pulled my head back, my shoulders rolled forward. "Did they say something about you being of mixed race?"

"People say all sorts of things about race. It's just people joking around." Mason seemed confident in his assessment. "Tim never talked to me. He was a loner. A recluse who everyone picked on."

"Did you pick on him?"

When Mason hesitated, I feared the worst. The knots tangled in my stomach with paranoia that things might escalate if Timothy wasn't an isolated case and things were as bad as Mason was making me believe.

Erin entered the house, knocking the snow off her boots, just as I was about to ask Mason his thoughts on school. I peeked my head around the wall and greeted her.

"I hope you're ready to work," she said, hitting the brakes the moment she saw Mason. "Oh, hey, Mason."

After Mason said a quick hello, I told him, "Honey, why don't you go take a shower and get ready for our visit with Nolan."

Mason headed to the back of the house and Erin quickly gave me a questioning look. "Nolan? Did you find him?"

I caught Erin up to speed.

"That's great news," she said. "About Nolan, I mean. Awful about what these kids are saying to each other."

Picking up the apple again, I paced the kitchen floor and began expressing my grievances. "I feel like I need to blame someone, someone other than the shooter who is already dead."

"Careful, you might get what you ask for."

I stopped and looked to Erin. There was a glimmer in her eye that made me suspicious. "What are you talking about?"

"In my scouring of the web this morning, your son isn't the only one whose life is being threatened." Erin raised her wrinkled brow. "Yours is, too."

I shook my head and pursed my lips. "C'mon, really? No one really means harm against me. It's just their emotions responding to the articles I write. I've been receiving threats long before yesterday."

"Maybe so, but something tells me that these new threats against you might be designed to lure you in."

"Lure me in? What are you talking about?"

"I don't mean to frighten you, as this is only a theory, but look at what I found." Erin dug out a manila folder filled with printed papers from her shoulder bag and began spreading them out across the table. I stood over her, assessing the data. "There is a discrepancy in the shooter's skills as a marksman." Erin rolled her neck to meet my gaze. "How did the shooter kill two cops wearing protective vests but only injure Nolan?"

"Okay, I see your point." I pinched my chin. "But what does this have to do with me?"

"Either there was a second shooter, or Nolan got lucky. Because somebody clearly knew how to shoot."

I swept my gaze to Erin's. "So what? I still don't see the connection. You think they'll come after me next? That they only let Nolan live because they couldn't get to Mason, which was their way of getting to me?" Suddenly, she was making sense.

Erin shrugged. "It's worth exploring."

I stared at the data, thinking back to my concern earlier. Erin, too, thought I might be the reason Mason was targeted. As much as I wanted to discredit the idea, I knew we had to see if the theory checked out. "We need to ask Nolan."

Erin smiled. "My thoughts exactly."

# CHAPTER SEVENTEEN

SUSAN STOPPED MID-STRIDE TO READ THE TEXT MESSAGE from Benjamin.

Holding her breath, she opened her phone and scanned the screen.

*I'm sorry but I have to cancel lunch. Work is rather hectic at the moment.*

Susan pressed her lips tightly together and stared at Benjamin's words. Wanting to not be disappointed, even though she was, she knew that he was doing good work. After his abrupt departure yesterday, she had learned later last night that her boyfriend was called to emergency surgery in response to yesterday's event. When she reminded herself of that, feelings of pride bloomed across her chest.

*You're doing great work, Doctor. See you when I see you,* Susan messaged back.

Lifting her head, she continued making her way to her office. Suddenly, the air cracked with the sound of a gunshot.

Ducking, Susan whipped her head around to look in the direction of the noise.

Feeling her heart hammer against her ribs, she scanned

the street for danger only to realize the sound was actually a car backfiring and not a gunshot. Her nerves were jumpy. Though she might not admit it, she was plagued by nightmares with images of yesterday still filling her head.

Forcing herself to stand taller, Susan brushed her bangs straight and clutched her handbag tighter between her fingers. Calming her pulse to slow, her heart was still heavy with agony for the community and the open threats King had learned about Mason.

Susan's steps were small but she began walking once again.

In her head, she prayed that today would be better than yesterday. She couldn't see how anything would ever get any worse but she wasn't willing to put it to the test. Remembering what Pastor Michaels said last night about now being the time to express kindness, Susan relaxed, believing in the power of love.

With her chin held high, she stepped into a chaotic office.

Her brows pinched with sudden concern.

Darting her gaze around the room, none of her staff bothered to turn and greet her. Their attention was glued to the television. Stepping forward, her colleague, Carly McKenzie, turned to Susan and whispered, "The name of the shooter has just been released."

Susan stared, reading the name *Timothy Morris* as it flashed across the bottom of the screen. It meant nothing to her. Just another ugly reminder of the evil people were capable of committing.

"The Governor is standing by and is about to comment for the first time on yesterday's event," the TV news anchor told her audience.

Susan set her bag down near her feet and folded her arms, curious to hear what Governor John Scott had to say. She watched him step up to a podium and greet the members of the press. Then he began speaking of the tragedy, briefing the citizens of Colorado on the investigation, before mentioning a vigil being held tonight at Pastor Michaels's church.

Susan watched, thinking of Benjamin, but mostly of Sam and Mason.

When the Governor opened the podium for questions, a reporter asked, "Is there a victim's fund? And, if so, where can people send their donations?"

The Governor covered the microphone with one hand and tipped back to consult with his Chief of Staff. A second later, the Governor removed his hand and said, "Donations are being taken by the United Network of Colorado Charities organizer, *Extraordinary Events*."

Susan gasped, feeling her heart freeze. The Governor just mentioned her company. "Did anybody know about this?"

Her small staff of a half dozen shook their heads, equally as shocked as she was.

Carly stepped closer. "Did you not know about this?"

Sweat poured down Susan's back and her blood pressure went through the roof. "I wouldn't be asking if I did."

Bending down, Susan swiped her handbag off the floor and hurried into her office. Falling heavily into her chair, she opened up her computer and checked her emails. There was nothing from the Governor, no notice from anybody asking if this was something her company could handle. Shaking her head, she knew that she wasn't prepared for the sudden influx the Governor predicted was coming.

Holding her knotted stomach with one hand, Susan now regretted agreeing to take on the United Network of Colorado Charities as a new event to organize and manage. It was a lofty idea at the time, but now it seemed impossible.

When Carly stepped into her office, Susan lifted her eyes, and said, "Who authorized this?"

"I'm as surprised as you are."

"Did anyone contact you?"

Carly shook her head.

Susan's body felt heavy. "We're not ready for this," she whispered. "Nor are we set up to handle something this large with no notice."

"What if we contact the governor and say we can't meet his request?" Carly proposed.

Susan flicked her gaze over Carly's shoulder and glanced to the television. Her head spun in circles when she saw her website's address prominently displayed across the bottom of the screen. "Too late, it's already coming in."

# CHAPTER EIGHTEEN

An hour later, Mason was showered and dressed and the three of us were saying goodbye to Cooper as we stepped out of the house on our way to visit Nolan. The air was brisk and I tugged on my jacket collar to fight off the cold, but the sun was shining strong.

"Hey Mason." The voice of fourteen-year-old Lucy from across the street managed to get us all to hit our brakes and pause.

Lucy stood on her front porch, her tall frame wrapped warm in a hoodie sweatshirt. She smiled and lifted her arm to give a small wave of her hand.

Erin flicked her gaze to me, holding her hand over her heart as if it was the sweetest thing she had ever seen. I felt my own lips form small curls as I waited to hear what else Lucy had to say.

"It's good to see you made it out," Lucy said.

"You too," Mason responded.

In that moment, the wind was knocked completely out of me. My heart shattered. I was completely heartbroken to be hearing these kids congratulate each other on not winning the mass shooting lottery. I couldn't recall the last time I had seen Mason interact with Lucy but, because of yesterday, they now had more in common than ever before.

"Hey Lucy," I said. "How are your parents?"

"Hey Mrs. Bell." Lucy's eyes drifted over to me. "They're doing good."

"Tell them I said hi, will you?"

"I will."

"I heard about Nolan."

A stone lodged in my throat.

"Yeah," Mason's voice dropped, "we're going to see him now."

"Tell him I'm praying for him."

Lucy said her goodbyes and ran back inside. Meanwhile, I felt my eyes swell, but before I started to cry, I got behind the steering wheel of my Subaru Outback and started the engine. Mason and Erin followed suit. The right tires bounced on the wheel well when both of them sat at the same time.

After ensuring everyone was buckled in, I pulled away from the curb. My mind spiraled into a dizzying array of thoughts but I kept coming back to Erin's theory that Timothy Morris had been trained to shoot. If it was true, that would mean maybe he had an accomplice still somewhere on the loose.

I glanced to the clock, wondering when I would be receiving an update from King.

Anxiety spilled out of me and kept my nerves jumpy.

"Music anyone?" Erin asked, wanting to break the silence that consumed us all.

No one was interested and I was thankful. I didn't want to turn on the radio and risk hearing more talk and speculation about what happened. And I certainly didn't want Mason to have to relive it through the eyes and ears of people who hadn't experienced it themselves.

"Maybe we could get Nolan a burger and fries?" Mason suggested.

I flicked my gaze to the rearview mirror and grinned. "Great idea."

Erin shared a look with me and smiled. "There is a *Good Times* not far from here."

A half hour later, we arrived at St. Joseph Hospital munching on salty fries. Everyone's bellies were full by the time we parked and started making our way toward the building.

My jaw tensed when I saw them coming. Maybe it was the skills I'd honed, or just a journalist's natural instinct to recognize the approach. But there wasn't any question that we were their target.

"Samantha, hey," the local TV news reporter, Nancy Jordan, called after me. "Are you here to visit Nolan Dreiss?"

"I'm not here for business," I said, knowing it was only a half-truth.

Her eyes flicked to Mason. "Wait, has anyone interviewed both of you at the same time?"

"No." I kept walking. "And we don't plan to. If that story is ever told, I'll be telling it myself."

I picked up the pace, Erin and Mason one step behind, and we left Nancy in the dust as I stiff-armed my way through the hospital's entrance.

Everyone was stuck on Timothy Morris while I was certain that Erin was on to something bigger. This was our angle, our story, and even though I didn't want to capitalize off Mason's access to Nolan, I knew we had little choice considering what King said Nolan knew about Timothy targeting Mason.

Soon we found our way to Nolan's floor. Natalie had just stepped outside Nolan's room when she saw us coming. Heavy bags of sadness swung beneath her eyes and her face was lined with grief. With a constricted throat, I stepped up to her and immediately gave her a hug.

"How did this happen?" she asked softly.

"That's what I've been asking myself," I said. "I don't know."

"Samantha, promise me something." Natalie clung to me tighter. "If you tell this story, don't let the shooter win the spotlight."

I closed my eyes and whispered in her ear, "I'll do my best."

When Natalie released me, she reached for Mason. I smiled as I watched Natalie hug him as if he was her own. "Nolan is so excited to see you."

"We brought him a burger." Mason held up the paper bag.

Natalie smiled. "He'll love it. Why don't you go give it to him?"

We watched Mason disappear into Nolan's room, stepping to the wall to let a nurse pass by. "Natalie, I would also like to ask Nolan some questions. With your permission, of course."

Her brow furrowed. "About what?"

"Has Nolan talked about yesterday with you?"

Natalie dropped her chin into her chest and I watched her hand tremble. Staring at her feet, she murmured, "A little, but I haven't had the courage to ask too many questions." Her gaze swept up and landed on me. "I'm afraid it might trigger him."

"I understand."

Natalie flicked her gaze to Erin, then back to me. "You know something, don't you?"

Keeping tight-lipped, I nodded.

"What is it?"

I shared a look with Erin.

"Sam, if I'm going to allow you to interview my son, the

least you can do is show me the same respect by telling me what you're hoping to learn."

My tongue swiped over my bottom lip before I said through a cracking voice, "According to Nolan, the shooter was looking for Mason."

Natalie gasped.

"It's why we'd like to speak with your son," Erin said. "Figure out if maybe Nolan knows more about the shooter's motive and if he said anything else that might be useful to the investigation."

"Is this not finished?" Natalie's eyes darted between mine and Erin's. "I heard he killed himself. What does it matter now?"

"The police will want to ask the same questions," I said. "I assume they would also like to know if this case is closed or needs to remain open."

Natalie closed her eyes and compulsively nodded her head.

"It also matters to the families who would like to see some kind of closure when trying to understand why their child or father died in yesterday's events," Erin added bluntly.

Natalie blew out a heavy sigh before finally agreeing. "But, please, don't push him if he doesn't want to talk."

I reached for Natalie's shoulder. "I promise we won't."

Turning on a heel, I knocked on the opened door. Mason turned and smiled. Nolan managed a small smile as well. "Hey, Nolan. It's good to see you."

"You too, Mrs. Bell."

"Mom, look at the scar Nolan is going to have."

Nolan peeled back his hospital gown and I watched his face fill with pride.

"Mason, would you mind giving us a moment to speak with Nolan alone?"

Mason stole a fry off Nolan's tray and said, "If she starts harassing you, just holler."

The boys laughed and seeing them get back to being teenagers filled me with hope that maybe they would be able to move on from this with only minimal bruising.

I pulled up a stool and took a seat next to Nolan. Erin shut the door and I asked Nolan how he was doing.

"Sore, and a little tired, but otherwise I'll be fine."

"We're very thankful for that. I know your Mom is, too." I paused to collect my thoughts. "I was hoping to ask you some questions about yesterday. Do you think you'd be up for that?"

Nolan's smile flat-lined. He cast his gaze to his hands—his fingers fidgeting with the bed sheet. "I didn't tell Mason what I told Detective King."

"Neither did I. And we can keep that a secret for now if you would like."

Nolan shook his head. "Mason should know."

"Why do you think Timothy Morris wanted to find Mason?"

Without moving his head, Nolan rolled his eyes to me. "To shoot him."

Hearing that Mason was a target never got any easier, and hearing it from Nolan somehow made it even more real than before. "Do you remember how Timothy phrased his words to you?"

Nolan cast his gaze back to his hands. His eyebrows pulled together as he filed through his memory. "I was hiding under the library table when I saw him come straight toward me. I remember my heart feeling like it was about to explode inside my chest I was so scared. Then he asked where Mason was. I told him I didn't know. Maybe went back to class."

A tear rolled down Nolan's cheek and I reached for his

hand. "And what did he do after you told him that? Did he believe you?"

"Tim kept saying weird stuff," Nolan continued after a minute of silence.

"What kind of weird stuff?"

Nolan shook his head. "Something about how he was a patriot of God, put here on earth to cleanse it of its sins, or mistakes. Something like that."

Hovering over my shoulder, Erin asked, "Did you see Tim shoot his gun before he turned it on you?"

Nolan nodded. "He was spraying bullets across the walls. We heard him coming and someone screamed for us to hide."

"Did he appear to be comfortable with his weapon?"

Nolan flashed a quizzical look.

"What Erin is asking is, did Tim appear to take aim when firing his weapon?"

"I don't know."

"Do you think he shot you on purpose?"

Nolan nodded. "I know he did."

"You know?" Suddenly, I felt lightheaded.

"He told me so." His voice was so small, so quiet.

Natalie's words rang in my head but I couldn't stop. I had to know. If this was Mason in the hospital bed, I'd ask him the same questions. "What did he say?"

Nolan looked me directly in the eye and said, "Tim said that he was going to let me live so that someone could tell his story."

"But he still shot you?" Erin sounded surprised.

Nolan lifted his gaze to her. "Because, according to Tim, a hero is always remembered but a legend never dies."

# CHAPTER NINETEEN

THE SNIPER COULDN'T SETTLE DOWN. STILL RUNNING ON the adrenaline high after yesterday's attack, he paced back and forth, drumming his fingers on his thighs. The TV flashed, its light flickering across the walls.

He was hidden safely inside the darkened bedroom. Now that he had managed to gain national attention, he had the curtains drawn. The drapes were so thick he couldn't tell night from day.

He stopped to pause and listen.

No one knew of his secret but soon they would be looking for him.

The news anchor was speaking of Timothy Morris when they switched over to the police captain. Hot, thick breaths spilled from his nostrils. A grin tugged at his lips. He liked everything he heard. The captain couldn't reveal too much into their investigation, but the Sniper assumed they were still trying to fit the pieces of the puzzle together.

"Good luck." He smirked.

It was all going according to his original plan. Perhaps even better than he would have expected. Now all he needed was to hear the final list of confirmed dead to know if he was ready to move on to his next attack.

When the program flicked to a commercial, he threw his fists in the air and cursed the screen. He was dying to hear more, wanted to hear the victims speak for themselves. Their stories would glorify his genius and water the revolution he'd set out to finish.

Turning to face the bed, he glanced at his rifle.

His heart fluttered inside his chest. He felt his cheeks blush with sudden warmth.

The guitar case in which he carried his rifle lay open on the floor next to him. He was proud of that, too. The brilliance in disguising his weapon to be carried in the open for all to see.

It was easy to move undetected in a city that appreciated the arts. Musicians were a dime a dozen and no one suspected a thing. Not even Pastor Michaels.

When the news came back on air, it was a fresh cycle to start the top of the hour.

The Sniper lowered himself to the edge of the bed, feeling it sink beneath his weight. He leaned forward, propping himself up on his elbows that dug into his knees.

Shaking his head, he knew how they would speak of Timothy. Timothy was a boy who was lost. A troubled student; a recluse; an angry loner who was bullied. So many excuses, so little answered.

"You only know half the story." He chuckled.

Yes, the Sniper knew Tim Morris was all those things, but that wasn't the reason why he did what he did. Again, he thought himself a genius for the puzzle he had left behind for the investigators to piece together. All he needed was enough time to keep them at bay to allow him to complete his mission. Then, his name would live in infamy.

The news anchor touched his earpiece. "I'm just learning

that," he looked up into the camera lens, "we now have the names of the confirmed dead."

Reaching for the remote, the Sniper turned up the volume not wanting to miss a name about to be read off.

One by one, the faces of the dead were shown on the screen before the news anchor cut to a reporter in the field. "That's right, Kyle, fourteen are still in critical or stable condition, including sixteen-year-old, Nolan Dreiss, who we are being told came out of surgery early this morning."

As if reacting with his sixth sense, the Sniper reached for his rifle and stood. Gripping the cold metal with both hands, he said, "Tell them your story, Nolan. Let them know that the terror reigned down yesterday is only the beginning and that the legend will never die."

# CHAPTER TWENTY

"Here, take some money for food." I opened my purse and handed Mason a twenty-dollar bill. He crumbled it into the palm of his hand. "If you decide to leave early, call me. I'll come and get you."

Mason cast his gaze to his shoes.

"Did you hear me?" I gripped his shoulder and ironed my hand down his arm.

He lifted his gaze and nodded.

"If Nancy Jordan tries to talk, tell her to get lost." The corners of his lips curled. "In fact, tell any reporter who tries to talk to you to do the same thing. Got it?"

"Don't worry, Mom. I got this."

"I know you do, sweetie." I released Mason's arm and turned to Natalie. "Thank you for letting him stay."

She shook her head, *not a problem*. "Go get 'em, Sam. I want to know why as much as everyone else."

As difficult as it was to leave Mason, I knew he was in good hands. There was plenty of work that still had to be done, and Erin and I hurried out of the hospital on a renewed mission to find some answers to our growing list of questions.

Erin waited until we were outside before talking her way through a plan. Stopping one foot outside the door, I scanned the area for any sights of Nancy Jordan. I didn't want her approaching Mason without my consent, and I knew she was hungry for a story—hungry enough to skirt the line I had drawn in the sand earlier and go against my wishes.

When Erin caught up with what I was doing she said, "Maybe she went to the school."

I exhaled a breath of air and glanced to Erin. "What do you think the shooter meant when he said, *a hero is always remembered but a legend never dies?* It sounds familiar."

We began walking, Erin already on her phone searching for something.

"Maybe that he's the legend and Nolan is the hero?"

I felt my face tense as my thoughts churned.

"That makes sense, right? I mean, you heard what Nolan said. Tim wanted him to tell his story of what happened."

"But Nolan is no hero."

"What are you thinking?"

Picking up my pace, I lengthened my stride. "I'm thinking Tim wanted to be the hero that never died. Of course, now we know that isn't the reality. He had to know that he wasn't going to walk out of there alive. Whether he killed himself or the police did him the honor, he was a dead man after he committed his first murder."

"Okay, then what about the legend?"

When we were within sight of my car, I stopped and turned to face Erin. "The legend is the story."

"That Tim wanted Nolan to tell?"

"Or one that we haven't learned yet."

Erin's expression pinched.

I raised my brows and stepped around my car, unlocking the doors. "There is something else Nolan said that I can't stop thinking about."

Erin opened the passenger door.

Staring over the windshield, I said, "Tim said he was a patriot of God put here to cleanse the earth of its mistakes."

"What do you think he meant by that?"

"We know he was targeting Mason as well as other African American students. I assume Tim was referring to Mason's mixed race when speaking of cleansing the earth of its mistakes."

Erin paused and I watched the blood leave her face. "Have you ever heard that phrase before?"

I shook my head. We were both settled into our seats when Erin mentioned how Nolan made her believe that Tim was shooting from the hip. "He didn't have the skills required to kill those officers. Not with their training to defend themselves."

"Only an expert could make those shots."

Erin picked up her phone when I asked, "How many rounds did the officers shoot off?"

Staring over the dash, Erin swiped through her phone, digging through the notes she'd made earlier this morning. A minute later she turned to me and murmured, "None."

I gnawed on the inside of my cheek. "It's not adding up." My head was still shaking back and forth. "It was like these officers weren't prepared, or didn't even confront the shooter."

"Yet they were some of the first to die. Tim had to know that officers would come. Could he had actually been targeting them?"

I started to push the keys into the ignition but held off on starting the car. "Possible, yes. Maybe the shots that killed the officers came in from a different angle?"

Erin snapped her head around. We shared a look and she said, "That's it. Oh, shit. Someone else was helping Tim. It's the only thing that makes sense."

I exhaled a heavy breath. "Let's not get too excited here. You heard Nolan. He was scared for his life. I'm not sure he has a good grasp of what actually happened."

Erin knitted her brows. "Have you heard back from King yet?"

I shook my head. "We need to get ourselves inside that school. See for ourselves what the library looks like, put ourselves in Nolan's shoes."

"We'll never get past the police line."

"We have to try." My phone chimed with an incoming text message. Turning it screen-side up, I saw that it was Dawson.

*Love the article. I had it run in today's print. However, I missed the email about the vigil. Sorry. I posted it to our social media pages. Hope that is okay?*

"Damn. Dawson didn't get the word out about the vigil." I swiped my thumbs over my phone's screen, responding to Dawson.

*No prob. Thanks. I'm working a story. There might be more to yesterday's event. Stay tuned...*

"I saw it mentioned by the TV news crews. Word will get around." Erin seemed convinced.

I nodded, knowing she was right. Yet I still felt bad about not being able to help Pastor Michaels spread the word.

*I'm not surprised. Let me know if I can help.*

I put my phone down and Erin had picked hers up. "So, where should we go from here?"

Erin flipped her phone around and showed me the address. Based off the location, I had a good assumption to where she might want to take me. "And whose address is that?"

A glimmer caught her eye. "The residence of Mr. and Mrs. Rick Morris."

# CHAPTER TWENTY-ONE

NOT MORE THAN TEN MINUTES PASSED BEFORE WE WERE parked in front of the Morris' house. And we weren't the first ones to arrive.

"How the hell are we going to break through that line?" I asked.

Erin glanced to the front door, then rolled her neck to look me in the eye. "What line?"

I stared at Nancy Jordan and her crew unpacking their gear by their TV news van. Relieved she was here, I no longer had to worry so much about Mason. But Nancy wasn't the only other reporter hoping to interview Timothy's parents. Every single Colorado news station was here, along with a half-dozen national organizations and their affiliate stations.

Grinning at Erin's comment, I said, "I have an idea. Follow me."

Together, we stepped out of the car and pulled our sunglasses over our eyes. I stuffed my hands deep inside my jacket pockets. Erin and I paled in comparison to what the other reporters carried with them. Armed with their large cameras and fluffy microphone pieces, we traveled down the sidewalk with only our wits. I was hoping that would be enough to get us inside.

Nancy Jordan caught sight of me and scampered across the grass. "Where's Mason?"

Not bothering to look at her, I muttered, "You're really starting to wear on me, Jordan."

"Sam, we're both after the same thing. We're not enemies here."

I stopped and turned to face her. Looking her directly in the eye, I said, "Then stop asking about my teenage son."

Nancy pulled back, her lips parting below stunned eyes. "Then tell his story for us. He's a student at North High School. He was at school yesterday. We want to hear what happened from someone who knows."

Shaking my head, I felt Erin grip my arm. "C'mon, Sam. We have work to do."

Nancy kept her gaze locked with mine. Refusing to look away, I said, "It's not my story, and Mason doesn't need any additional weight on his shoulders. Keep away from him."

Erin tugged again on my arm and I finally broke eye contact with Nancy as I turned to the Morris household.

"Wanting to interview Mason is no different than you wanting to sit Timothy's parents down for your own interview." Nancy lobbed her words over my shoulder like exploding mortars that barely made me flinch.

When we got to the front door, Erin said, "You know she's right."

"It's different." I jabbed the doorbell with my finger. The chime rang loud enough for me to hear it through the covered windows.

Turning to face the army of news crews, I wondered how many had already tried their luck at getting the Morrises to speak. Probably all of them. If I couldn't get Tim's parents to talk, I would have to try my luck with

King and make use of his influence to get us inside the school.

Erin rang the doorbell again. Then she knocked. Refusing to walk away without getting what we'd come for, I couldn't fault her for being the same obnoxious reporter I thought Nancy was.

My breath hitched when I heard the deadbolt click over.

Suddenly, my blood vessels opened up. When the door cracked, I lifted my sunglasses to the top of my head and couldn't believe Mrs. Morris was actually standing just inside the threshold.

"Please, just go away," she said. "My decision hasn't changed."

"Mrs. Morris, my name is Samantha Bell. Our boys knew each other."

Mrs. Morris squinted her eyes as if deciding whether I was worth the risk. "Have we met?"

"I don't believe so."

"Our son isn't the monster you people are making him out to be. He's a good kid who made a mistake."

"I know."

"Then what do you want?"

"I was told that your son was looking for my son yesterday."

Mrs. Morris's cheeks hollowed. "Did he..."

"No." I exhaled. "He wasn't injured."

With heavy lids, she muttered, "I'm glad to hear that."

Inching forward, I said, "I was hoping maybe you could shed light on why Tim might have wanted to find my son, Mason."

"Please, can we come inside, Mrs. Morris?" Erin asked nicely, introducing herself without mentioning her crime podcast. "We don't need these reporters to make the wrong assumption."

Mrs. Morris flicked her gaze over my shoulder and I watched her spine slump when she saw the growing number of vans. Then she nodded.

Wedging our way inside, I allowed myself a quick assessment of the house. It was a comfortable size with a large living room and an updated kitchen. It was clear the Morrises were financially comfortable—money didn't seem to be a problem. And, as Erin and I followed Mrs. Morris onto the couch, I couldn't help but notice the strong military history glorified on their walls.

"Please, have a seat," Mrs. Morris said. "Can I offer you something to drink?"

There was a television on somewhere in the back. I declined the offer for a drink, unable to stop myself from staring at the old muzzle loader hanging above the fireplace mantle next to a wooden Christian cross.

"I'm fine, thank you," I heard Erin say.

Men in uniform were framed next to images of patriotism. Medals were encased in beautiful wooden boxes and laid atop American flags. Everywhere I looked highlighted the strong patriotism and support for our country's military. Any other day, I wouldn't have thought much into it but now I couldn't stop thinking about what Nolan said Tim muttered about being a *patriot of God.*

"Mrs. Morris, was your husband in the military?" I asked, hearing the house suddenly go quieter than only a moment before. The TV had turned off, alerting us to another's presence somewhere in the house.

"Ginny, who are these people?" a man's voice barked. "I told you, no interviews." Mr. Morris emerged from the back and planted his hands firmly into his hips.

Both Erin and I remained silent.

"Our son—" Ginny began saying before being interrupted.

"Our son was a great boy." Mr. Morris's hot breath spewed

out of his flaring nostrils. "I'm not going to let the media tarnish the memories we have of him."

"That's not the reason we're here," I said.

"I know who you are. Your face is all over the news." Mr. Morris flicked his gaze over to his wife, then back to me. Ginny seemed tense. "It's your fault, you know?"

I raised a curious brow—refusing to take the bait.

"If it weren't for the media's glorification of each mass shooting, turning these tragedies into spectacles, then maybe my son wouldn't have declared war on that school."

My own stomach clenched as I shielded myself from his anger. "Did you know your son was going to do what he did?"

"Jesus," Mr. Morris threw up a hand, "you're already twisting my words around."

"Mr. Morris, the reason—"

"We didn't know that our son was planning to do anything. You're just like the police. Acting as if we had something to do with this." Mr. Morris shook his head. "Our son is dead, too, you know?"

Ginny stood and set a supportive hand on her husband's shoulder. "Honey, Tim was looking for her son yesterday."

"What's your son's name?" Mr. Morris asked.

I swallowed the sandpaper lining my throat. "Mason Bell."

Mr. Morris narrowed his eyes. "And what did Mason do to make my son want to kill him?"

Erin jumped to her feet. "Stop it. There is enough pain inside this room to go around. We don't need to add to the flames."

I stared at the floor, feeling the sting build behind my eyes. My heart raced and I began to hyperventilate. Without looking, I heard Mr. Morris turn to his wife.

"Whatever they're going to publish about Tim is on you." Mr. Morris swiped his arm up and pointed his sharp finger at me while looking at his wife. "Don't think for one minute that they are our friends."

I lifted my eyes and stared at Mr. Morris from behind a thick curtain of lashes, listening to my short, fast breaths.

"I can promise you that they will cast us in the same dark spotlight they have already done to Tim."

"Please, Rick." Ginny pressed both her hands into her husband's big arms. "Maybe you should leave. There is hot water ready for tea."

Reluctantly, Rick followed his wife's advice and finally left the room. As soon as Mr. Morris disappeared into the kitchen, I released my flexed muscles and gasped three full breathes of air.

"You all right, Sam?" Erin's voice was small, caring.

I looked her in the eye and nodded. "I'll be fine."

"I'm sorry about my husband's behavior." Ginny turned her attention back to us. "I can assure you he didn't mean what he said." She sat once again on the sofa chair. "He's been edgy since the police came asking questions."

"When were they here?" Erin inquired.

"Nearly as soon as Timothy was identified as the...shooter." Ginny's chin quivered a second before she dropped her head into her hand, crying. "I'm sorry."

"It's perfectly all right." I leaned forward and took her hand inside of mine.

She received it extremely well. "Thank you."

"Could I see Tim's room?"

Ginny sucked back a deep breath, turned her head, and wiped her cheeks. "Certainly."

We followed her down the hallway and into Tim's room.

"What was Tim like?" I asked as his mother opened the door. I wondered briefly if anything would ever change inside or if it would become a shrine to their son.

"He was a smart boy. Though High School had been tough for him."

"How so?" The walls of Tim's bedroom were plastered with baseball memorabilia—trophies from childhood, posters of the greats. I caught Erin's eye and gave a subtle nod toward Babe Ruth on the wall. The words *heroes get remembered, but legends never die* rang in my mind. Tim had said nearly that exact thing to Nolan.

"Tim seemed to have trouble finding his crowd. You know how it is at that age." Her lips pursed. "He was depressed, didn't seem to fit in with most other kids." She smiled at a memory she wasn't willing to share. "His love of baseball fizzled a few years ago when he didn't make varsity as a freshman. He never found a passion to replace that with."

"Was he on any medications?"

Ginny nodded. "It helped some, but there is a lot of pressure put on these kids to be popular, peer-pressured into thinking they have to be a certain way." Ginny paused when her gaze landed on Tim's bed and she started crying again.

I put my hand on her shoulder.

"I thought he was starting to find himself when Rick and I encouraged him to enroll in a couple of classes at Community College of Denver."

"Did he?"

Ginny's eyes brightened as she nodded. "I really believed he would make it to graduation and he'd make a turn for the better."

"High School has been tough for Mason, too."

Ginny rolled her gaze to me. "Can I see him? Do you have a photo of your son?"

I reached for my back pocket and unlocked my smartphone. Pulling up a photo of Mason, I handed it over to Ginny. "Looks like a good kid," she said, handing the phone back.

"What class was Tim taking at the community college?"

"Political Science."

Erin stepped forward with her eyebrows knitted. "Does being a patriot of God mean anything to you, Mrs. Morris?"

"We are Christians, Ms. Tate. And my family is full of men who would consider themselves patriots." Her smile spread to her ears when she turned back to Tim's bed. "We love our country as much as we love God."

# CHAPTER TWENTY-TWO

ALEX KING WAS SWAMPED AT WORK. THERE WAS MORE evidence to comb through than he and his partner, Detective John Alvarez, could handle themselves.

After working through a couple of classrooms, they moved down the hall and entered the library. Without realizing it, King came to a dead stop and paused.

Suddenly, his head spun with memories of yesterday. He could still smell the burning gunpowder, hear the conversation he was having with the librarian when he nodded at Mason as he left for the bathroom. The pops of guns firing and the cries that traveled the walls with terror. In that moment, it hit him like a freight train and it hurt bad.

With parted lips, he stared at the blood stain on the floor in the exact location where he'd assisted Nolan.

Rubbing his fingertips together near his thigh, King could still feel the blood coagulating as Nolan fought to hang on. King had seen a lot over the years, but something told him that this crime scene was going to stay with him forever.

Alvarez turned to look at his partner. "Was this where you were when it happened?"

"Yeah," King exhaled.

"You never did tell me how Sam's son is doing."

Without looking, King muttered, "It's going to be a long road to making sense of this, but he's strong. He'll find a way to turn this into a positive."

Stealing his attention away from the nightmares still playing out inside his head, King blinked and came to when a handful of FBI officers followed a couple of investigators into the library.

"Hey, looks like Lieutenant arrived." Alvarez stood straight.

King scrubbed a hand over his face and shook off his emotions.

"What have we got, besides the FBI?" Lieutenant Kent Baker asked without greeting his detectives.

Seeing King struggle to form a response, Alvarez stepped in and gave Lieutenant a quick rundown of the work they had been shuffling through. King stood and listened, catching his breath. Lieutenant Baker didn't seem to notice King acting strange.

"What do we know about the shooter's movements?" the Lieutenant asked.

"Shooter entered the building through the north entrance at approximately 9:09AM. First shots were fired outside and he worked his way down the halls, firing dozens of shots along the way until entering the library where we are standing now."

King stood, listening to Alvarez explain to Lieutenant the shooter's course of action, but all he could feel was the pang of regret for not having his gun with him when he needed it most. It twisted like a knife and King wouldn't ever forgive himself for knowing he could have stopped the murder spree from spreading.

Lieutenant Baker rested his hands on his hips and looked

around. "Looks like a bomb went off in here."

"Either the perp was trigger happy or, most likely, he didn't know how to properly aim." Alvarez furrowed his brow.

The Lieutenant rolled his gaze to Alvarez. "Then tell me, how does that explain why two of my men were shot outside?"

Alvarez shared a quick glance with King.

"Well?" Lieutenant Baker grew impatient.

"The ME is working to recover the bullets from each of the victims," Alvarez informed his superior. "She'll have them sent over to the lab to run a ballistics test—"

"Okay." Lieutenant rolled his shoulders back and eyed Alvarez. "Tell me something I don't already know."

"Until the tests come back, we won't know for sure, but King and I have been over this a dozen different times and the scenario keeps coming out the same."

Lieutenant narrowed his eyes.

Alvarez sighed. "It's best if we tell you this where it will make sense."

The three men left the library and weaved their way through the halls until they were standing outside near the place where the two officers had been shot.

"Okay, now that you brought me into the sun," Lieutenant squinted, "what is it you have to show me?"

With the fresh Rocky Mountain air working its way into his bloodstream, King was feeling much better. He stepped forward and said, "Lieutenant, we don't believe that our officers were killed by the perpetrator."

Lieutenant raised his eyebrows.

"I'll bet my entire pension," King continued, "that when those lab reports come back on the bullets that killed our men, it will show that there was a second shooter."

The cool air was still for a long pause as the detectives gave the Lieutenant time to form his response. "Explain."

King went into great detail about the trajectory of each bullet that made it impossible to have come from the direction of the school entrance. King led them to the blood-stained pavement and discussed how the officers were thought to have fallen, the direction of their blood splatter, as well as how the officer's vehicle was positioned. "These officers were ambushed by a high velocity rifle the moment they arrived, which I believe came from there." King turned and pointed to a nearby hotel.

"They didn't have a chance," Alvarez added.

Lieutenant cocked his jaw and flicked his gaze between the hotel rooftop and the pavement where they were standing.

"I'm guessing this second shooter is either military trained, or perhaps a cop." King was confident with his delivery.

Lieutenant gave King a sideways glance.

"We know for a fact Timothy Morris was specifically targeting blacks, but it's worth asking ourselves if this second shooter was also targeting blacks or if he was going after cops."

Lieutenant stared ahead and King watched his posture go rigid. "Christ."

"What do you want us to do, LT?" Alvarez asked.

"If we are in fact dealing with a cop killer, then we better find whoever is behind this before another officer dies."

# CHAPTER TWENTY-THREE

As soon as we exited the Morris household, camera shutters began clicking at a dizzying speed before their operators realized it was only Erin and me.

I lengthened my stride, smirking at the disappointed faces we passed, and made a beeline for my parked car.

From the edge of the Morris property, I spotted Nancy Jordan glaring. When we locked eyes for a brief moment, I watched her face lift before she trotted along and quickly caught up with us.

"I'm not interested in speaking with you, Jordan." I kept walking. "My answer is still no."

"What did they say?" Nancy was now at my side. "You were in there for over a half-hour, you must have something you can share with me?"

I was still feeling a bit queasy from the way Rick Morris attacked me. The nerve he had to suggest that Mason was the reason Timothy wanted to kill him. "I have nothing for you, Jordan."

"Samantha." Nancy stretched her neck, taking up more of

my vision. "The Morrises have refused to be interviewed by all of us. What makes you so special?"

Erin spun around so fast her hair lifted off her shoulders. Blocking Nancy with her small frame, we all came to an abrupt halt. Erin narrowed her eyes and stuck her face near Nancy's. "Maybe we were invited inside because we weren't being pushy."

Nancy's jaw dangled on its hinges. Her eyelids blinked like shutters. "Well, did they agree to sit down for an interview or not?"

"Check our website for details, Jordan," I called over my shoulder after beginning to move down the sidewalk once again. "You know where to find us."

Shaking my head, I was looking forward to stepping away from my colleagues. Nancy was grinding on my nerves. Without giving it much thought, I swiped open my phone and texted Mason just to see how he was doing.

Dropping our bottoms into my car, Erin said, "I'd like to know what the police said to them and if they took anything from the house."

"Whatever it was, it clearly got on Rick's nerves." I slid the key into the ignition and paused with a striking thought.

"What is it, Sam?"

Rolling my gaze to Erin, I said, "Did you get the impression that Rick didn't have the best relationship with his son?"

"Yeah, I got that." Erin's brow wrinkled.

Pinching the loose skin on my throat, I pursed my lips and recalled everything Ginny Morris mentioned about her family and son. "It's just speculation on my part, but does it make sense that maybe Tim was trying to prove to his father he was a soldier, just like him?"

Erin stared ahead without blinking.

"I mean, what does it even mean to be a man in today's

world?" When I heard my question, I immediately thought about Mason.

"If that is what went on here, it's a strange way of going about it."

Bringing both hands to the steering wheel, I said, "The whole house smelled of testosterone."

"*We love our country as much as we love God.*" Erin repeated Ginny's words.

"Rick's anger bothered me," I admitted.

"But can you blame him?" Erin turned to me, tucking a loose strand of blonde hair behind her ear along the way. "Because of what their son did, they're victims of his crime. No one wants to sympathize with them. I know I wouldn't want to be in their shoes."

"There is something more going on with him." I stared at the Morris house. "I can't put a finger on it but I think it might be worth looking into."

When I started the car, Erin said, "We also need to check out the political science course Tim had enrolled in."

I nodded, once again feeling the wave of guilt that maybe I was the reason behind Mason being targeted. "I got the feeling that his parents encouraged him to take the class. Maybe Rick's political views will shed some light on Tim's motives. It's clear he has a thing against journalists, but does he express that same anger toward minorities, too?"

Erin was jotting down notes by the time I pulled away from the curb. I mentioned my need to collect my things from the newsroom and Erin was fine with a quick detour. Besides, it would be good to catch up with Dawson and inform him of what I was working on.

A quick fifteen-minute drive later and I was dipping the front hood of my Outback into the parking garage. Erin wanted to stay in the car to continue researching, and I promised to be quick.

The newsroom was quiet as a tomb. No one was around and only a handful of boxes remained. Including mine. Reaching for it, there was a sticky note from Dawson.

*In case you're looking for your orchid, I took it to make sure it received the care it needed. See you at the new office. - R.D.*

I smiled and scampered out as fast as I'd entered. There was no time for nostalgia.

"Rick Morris has his own Facebook profile page," Erin said as soon as I was back behind the wheel.

Gripping her phone with both hands, she kept scrolling. "Anything interesting?"

"You could guess most of the boring stuff from what we saw of him."

"Enlighten me."

"White-collar engineer job with a military weapons manufacturer, heavily involved in politics, and the real humdinger," Erin flashed me a quick sideways glance, "He loves his guns."

"Sounds accurate."

"Then, there is this." Erin turned her phone's screen toward me. "Read what he wrote yesterday at 8:38AM— approximately thirty minutes before the first shot was fired."

With a hesitant heart, I took the phone between my fingers and squinted my gaze at the post.

*But the Helper, the Holy Spirit, whom the Father will send in my name, he will teach you all things and bring to your remembrance all that I have said to you. - John 14:26*

After reading it for a second time, I lifted my gaze and we stared into each other's eyes.

"Rick's anger became Timothy's." I shrugged.

"He said it himself."

*"...then maybe my son wouldn't have declared war on that school."* A cold shiver moved up my spine.

Erin sucked back a deep breath. "Are you thinking what I'm thinking?"

"If he did train his son to kill—"

"Or instructed him to go inside—"

"We better find out."

# CHAPTER TWENTY-FOUR

"What an insult," Erin whispered as she followed me inside our new newsroom.

It didn't feel real. As I glanced around and took in the new office myself, it was a clear punch to the gut. A flood of old memories hit me as I thought back to the time when journalists had been respected. People in high office would agree to speak with us, give us statements. And, in turn, we would assist them with sharing stories and public service announcements with the community. But now, working from our print facility, how could we exert that same authority and expect to be respected?

"It even smells like death."

I flicked my gaze over my shoulder and smirked at Erin's comment.

"Does it not?"

"Let's find my desk."

"And how do you expect to do that?"

"Use your nose." I scrunched my nose and made sniffing noises, getting Erin to chuckle.

I had no idea where to even begin my search. It was clear

that half the staff was now gone, another consequence of the decisions made by our paper's new owners residing in New York City.

"Sam," I heard Dawson calling. He waved his hand as he approached. "Have you found your desk? No, of course not." He shook his head. "This place is a mess." He rolled his eyes. "Follow me. I'll show you your new home."

Only a week ago Dawson encouraged me to leave the paper. He recognized the platform Erin and I were building with my writing and her podcasting. He knew that was the future of journalism. Not here. Not getting demoted and being treated like second class citizens. As tempting as it was, and even with his blessing, I wasn't ready to leave my column just yet.

Dawson stopped at a small wooden desk. It had a strange resemblance to the tables I once sat at in high school. "It's not much—"

"It's perfect," I said, reaching for my orchid. "Though this guy might have to find a window."

Dawson gave me an apologetic look. Then he asked with obvious concern lining his brow, "Sam, how's Mason?"

"He's at the hospital, staying with his friend."

"You don't have to be here, you know. I'll have your leave approved the moment you ask for it."

"Are you trying to get rid of me again?"

Dawson laughed.

I shook my head. "I just took a week away from the office," I said, thinking back to last week and how Dawson refused to let me work from the office after cracking the serial killer case. "We were just visiting with the Morris family."

"Whoa." Dawson shoved a hand through his thick head of hair. "I heard they weren't allowing anybody to interview them."

"It's true. However," I shared a brief look with Erin, "we were invited inside."

"Anything worth reporting?"

Thinking of Natalie's request, I said, "I'm not going to glorify the shooter and make him out to be some anti-hero."

"People are curious to know why he did it."

"I understand."

Dawson cocked his head to the side and gave me an intense look.

Erin stepped forward and stretched her neck thin. "We believe Timothy Morris might have had an accomplice."

A gasp sucked the air out of the space between us. I watched Dawson raise his eyebrows as he flicked his gaze back to me.

"The Morrises didn't say that," I assured him. "But there are several inconsistencies in the stories coming out of yesterday that make us believe we might be on to something."

With his hands rooted into his hips, Dawson lowered his voice and said, "Then I suggest you keep all your preliminary theories to yourselves until you find the facts to back up your claim."

"Goes without saying."

"So now what?"

"We're pursuing a few leads from people who we believe might be able to confirm these theories."

"Good." Dawson nodded. "Until then, perhaps I could have you report on tonight's vigil."

My cell started ringing in my jacket pocket. "Consider it done," I told Dawson. Stepping away, I answered my phone to talk to King. "Hey."

"How's Nolan? Did you visit with him long?" King's gravelly voice rumbled through my earpiece.

"He was in good spirits."

"And Mason?"

"He stayed behind, wanting to keep Nolan company."

There was a long awkward pause that caused my stomach to flip. I could hear that something wasn't right in King's voice and I braced myself for the impact I felt coming.

"Are you still at the high school?"

King said he was, then told me, "I told you I would call if I found something."

Pinching the bridge of my nose between my fingers, I closed my eyes and muttered to myself a soft plea. *Please tell me it's not about Mason.*

"Can you meet me here?"

I checked the time. "What's this about?"

"It's important you hear this in person."

# CHAPTER TWENTY-FIVE

As soon as I ended my call with King, I turned to Erin. Feelings of anxiety roiled my gut. My silence made her ask what my mind was swimming in.

"King found something," I said in a whispery tone.

"What?"

"I don't know. But it sounded urgent." I reached for my orchid and told Dawson to put it near a window.

"Where are you off to?" he asked.

"North High."

"Promise me you'll be careful."

I answered him with a single look and followed it up with a reassuring nod. "Don't worry about me." He rolled his eyes. "See you at the vigil this evening?"

Dawson took my orchid into his hands and nodded.

I felt my chest expand as I shared a quick glance with Erin before making our way to the exit. I was eager to know what King couldn't tell me over the phone. His voice held something I had never heard before—not even on the day I was nearly killed by The Lady Killer. Something was up and I needed to know what it was.

Erin swiped today's paper on the way out the door and chased after me as I picked up my pace to get to King as fast as possible.

"Sam, I don't mean to keep bringing it up, but it's very clear that *The Times* will soon be out of business."

I didn't bother to shorten my stride. Erin was still fuming and she refused to miss her chance to argue why I should devote all of my energies to our own audience. Of course it was what I wanted to be doing, but I still had reservations that needed to be solved before I fully committed to our project.

"Good thing our website is picking up momentum," I said as I pushed my way out the door.

Erin barely looked up from the paper she read while she walked. "You should have published this piece on the website."

"I'm still employed here."

"It was beautiful."

I flashed her a skeptical look.

"Truly."

"Besides, you heard Dawson, he's encouraging me to keep blogging about our investigation in real time. That's what we should be focusing on. Bring our audience into the investigative process and show them how we decipher the clues made available to us."

"Of course that's what we should be doing. That's what I've been saying all along."

"Then what's the issue?" Stepping into the sun, I pulled my sunglasses off the top of my head and slid them over my eyes. "The way I see it, it's a win-win. Dawson is happy, and you're... well, you're content."

Erin hit the brakes, shaking her head.

I stopped and turned back. "I can do both."

"I'm not questioning your ability to juggle the demands of both jobs."

"Then what are you questioning?"

"I just know that if you didn't have your ankle tethered to the paper, we could give 100% of our energy to growing our own audience."

I turned my head away. Squinting into the sunlight, I said, "I'll tell you what. I'll quit—if I'm not let go first—when you show me the money."

Erin folded her arms across her belly, cocked out a hip, and grinned.

"Monetize the site and I'll leave the paper behind."

"You promise?"

I lifted my pinky. Erin stared at it for a second before she grinned and hooked hers around mine. "Watch out, Bell, I'll have the money rolling in before you know it."

My phone buzzed with a text message. Reaching for it, Erin asked who it was. "Mason."

*All good. Nolan is resting.*

A tremor of worry rolled over my stomach like lazy waves in the Gulf. "Nolan is resting," I relayed to Erin. "C'mon, let's not waste any more time."

Edging the building, I still thought that King could have found something that had to do with Mason. I needed to know, and cursed him for not giving me a little bit of a clue to what he'd discovered to at least settle my nerves. When we turned a corner, a man was leaning against my car.

I hit the brakes and Erin nearly collided with me. "Who is that?" she asked.

The man heard us and turned his head. Removing his sunglasses, he pushed off the car and strode over to us. Meeting him halfway, I couldn't place him but knew he was here for me.

"Excuse me, are you Samantha?"

His look told me I should know who he was but I didn't.

"You were just leaning against her car—" Erin huffed out a sigh of disbelief.

"Who's asking?"

"My name is Markus Schneider." He held out his hand for me to shake. "Gavin was my partner on the force."

# CHAPTER TWENTY-SIX

MARKUS SCHNEIDER LOWERED HIS HAND BACK TO HIS SIDE when I refused to shake it.

"I wasn't sure if you would remember me." Markus flicked a quick glance to Erin.

I dug out my car keys and handed them to Erin, telling her I'd be to the car shortly. Once I was alone with Markus, I said, "I'm sorry, have we met before?"

Markus took his eyes off Erin and rolled his gaze back to me. The friendly crinkles around his eyes ironed themselves out when he recognized the suspicion twinkling my eye. "I'm not sure if Gavin ever mentioned me."

Filing through my memory, I vaguely remembered Gavin saying he had a partner that he didn't get along with at one time. "You said you were his partner?" Markus nodded. "Then you'll know that Gavin died over a decade ago."

He lowered his gaze and scrubbed a hand over his goatee. "I heard. I'm sorry for your loss."

"Thanks, but that was a long time ago." I folded my arms over my chest, knowing Markus hadn't attended Gavin's funeral.

"You had a son with Gavin, right?"

I swallowed and debated whether or not to share details. "I did."

"Gavin always wanted a boy," he said, speaking as if he and Gavin had been best friends.

"What can I do for you, Markus?"

There was a glimmer in his eye as he looked around, stopping to tip his head back and smile at the sun. "It feels like a lifetime ago." He brought his gaze back to me. "I'm back living in Denver and thought I would reacquaint myself with old friends."

He should have gone elsewhere then. I didn't know him from a stranger on the street. "Are you still with the department?"

"Retired." Markus rocked back and forth on his heels as he grinned. "They said I would find you here."

Turning back to the obscure entrance of my new office, I couldn't help but feel confused by this sudden meeting from an old colleague of Gavin's. "Who told you I would be here?"

Markus shook his head. "It's just that I heard about what happened yesterday and I immediately thought of Gavin— and you, of course." He smiled. "Are you still living in that old house Gavin bought for you?"

Feelings of unease lifted the hairs on my arm. I thought it strange how he knew so much about me when I didn't know anything about him.

When I kept my place of residence a secret, Markus asked, "How is your son doing? Was he inside the school when it happened?"

I glanced to my feet and frowned.

"I'm sorry."

When I lifted my gaze, I saw Erin pointing to her watch. I held up one finger, acknowledging that I would be there in a moment. "I really should be going, Markus."

"I see you're busy. I'm sorry for taking up your time. I know how awkward this is for you—for both of us—but I was hoping maybe we could catch up sometime." He paused and met my skeptical gaze. "I'd love to share some memories about Gavin. Learn more about what happened to him."

Something about the way he asked made me believe him. "Okay, yeah. Maybe we could meet for coffee or something."

Markus pulled out a blank white business card with his digits scribbled on the back. Handing it to me, he said, "I'll be at the vigil tonight. Maybe I'll see you there."

# CHAPTER TWENTY-SEVEN

ERIN DIDN'T ASK ABOUT MARKUS UNTIL WE WERE BACK ON I-25 heading south to North High. "Care to tell me what that was all about?"

I was still disoriented myself. Having Gavin's old partner appear out of the blue—especially at a place as unfamiliar to me as it could possibly get—I wondered what kinds of stories he had to share about my husband and if they would be something Mason would want to know, too.

"That was my husband's old patrol partner."

"Gavin was a cop?" Erin's voice shot up in surprise.

I nodded and ran a hand over my hair without bothering to turn and look at her. Lost in my own distant gaze, my vision tunneled with cars racing past on both sides. Every new turn knocked me off my axis and I struggled to keep up with the pace.

"Then why the confused look?"

I flicked my gaze to Erin. "He seemed to know a lot about me and I don't know much about him."

"But you *do* know him, don't you?" She craned her neck.

Biting the inside of my cheek, I wasn't sure if I did. "I

can't recall Gavin ever mentioning his name. Then again, that was a long time ago. It's possible I just forgot."

"Partners are like marriages." Erin leaned back and brought her hand to her brow.

Turning my head, I said, "But if he is who I think he might be, then this partnership ended in divorce."

Erin turned with a furrowed brow. "What happened?"

I shrugged a shoulder. It had been forever since I had thought about it and, if Markus was who I thought he might be, they had worked together before my time with Gavin. "Gavin never seemed interested in speaking about it and I always assumed it was stress related to the job or just a bad fit." I flashed a quick glance. "Things like that happen all the time."

"Should we look into it?"

"He gave me his card. Said he would like to share stories about Gavin sometime."

"Seems harmless."

"That's what I thought, too."

Hitting the brakes, I turned the wheel and entered North High's student parking. Erin sat up and began looking for King.

"There he is." Erin pointed to the southeast corner.

Weaving the car in King's direction, I got us as close to the barrier as was allowed before parking. When I stepped out, King was already there. "Sorry for the delay. I got here as quick as I could," I said.

"Not a problem. Things aren't moving very fast around here." King greeted Erin but something about him still seemed off.

Digging my fingers into my sweaty palms, I felt my muscles begin to quiver with anxiety. I hated when he seemed to be keeping secrets from me. It only tangled my nerves further, making me feel like I couldn't keep my head straight when working under pressure.

When the breeze picked up, I brushed my bangs out of my eyes and felt the terror of yesterday rumble its way back into my mind. Without thinking, I reached for King's hand. Our fingers threaded and I kept my obvious need for comfort discreet.

"Sam, what I wanted to tell you needs to stay off the record," King insisted. "I can't let this get leaked. It will jeopardize the entire investigation."

I pulled my hand away. "What has you so tense?"

King looked to his left and swallowed. Then he swung his gaze back down to me. "Sam, there was a second shooter."

Erin and I shared a knowing look. "Are you sure about that?"

"We're still waiting for the ballistics report to come back, though the angle of the shot that killed the two officers is obvious enough for it not to have been taken from the school entrance."

Erin stepped forward with renewed interest. "Can you walk us through it?"

King blew out a heavy sigh.

"Erin suspected the same," I said.

King's brows shot up. "I'd love to hear how you came to your conclusion before we did."

Erin didn't hesitate in telling King about Nolan's wound and her theory that Timothy Morris didn't demonstrate the kind of marksmanship needed to have killed the officers. King nodded as he listened and Erin concluded by saying, "But what Sam and I haven't decided is if the shooting was designed to lure cops into range to be murdered, or if this was purely an attack on minorities."

King tucked his chin and held my gaze.

"There's something else, isn't there?" I asked.

King's brow wrinkled as he nodded.

I wasn't sure I was ready to hear more. Knowing that there was a second shooter was frightening enough. My thoughts once again drifted to Nolan tucked away in the nondescript hospital bed across town.

"Sam, Cook Roberts was one of the two officers killed yesterday."

My head swayed on its shoulders when I felt the blood leave my face. I swallowed down the bile rising up my throat. That was a name I knew, and knew well.

"You know who that is, right?"

I wished I didn't. It felt like I was on the edge of vomiting when I reached for King's shoulder to keep myself from falling.

"Who is he?" Erin asked.

Licking my lips, I exhaled a deep breath before saying, "Cook Roberts was a friend of Gavin's. Someone who was there for me when Gavin re-enlisted after September 11th." All this was new information Erin had never heard, and I could see her getting overwhelmed by the mystery of my past.

King's hand found its way to my waist and I lashed out. "Dammit, King. You couldn't have told me sooner?" My anger boiled over. It was all coming at me so fast. "As if you telling me Mason was a target wasn't hard enough. Now you're telling me one of Gavin's friends died yesterday, too?"

"You could be right, Sam." Erin's gaze locked with mine. "Maybe you are the common denominator."

King held up his hand. "I'm not so sure about that. As far as we know, yesterday was an isolated event."

"I'll be convinced of that once the second shooter is caught," I said.

King ironed his big hands down both my arms. "Don't worry, Sam. We'll catch this person."

As my mind scrambled to keep up, I pushed down the

fear I felt boiling up inside of me and thought more about Timothy Morris. "We spoke with the Morrises."

"When?"

"This morning."

"I heard they weren't speaking to the press."

"The police were there. What did they take into evidence?"

King rubbed the back of his neck. "I haven't heard."

My lips pinched.

"You got them to talk, didn't you?"

A glimmer sparkled inside my eye. "We're following some leads. How about you walk us through what you can share, and then I'll debrief you on our own discoveries."

We followed King across the parking lot, never once entering the building, and he told us in great detail how he and Alvarez came to the conclusion of the second shooter. It was all just as Erin suspected and I marveled with pride at how she managed to do it without having to visit the scene a second time.

"Firing from that distance," I said, looking at the hotel rooftop, "what are the odds the shooter has a military background?"

"I'd say pretty good," King said.

I turned to look at Erin. Then I proceeded to tell King more about Rick Morris. "Timothy Morris's father has a strong military background, as well as a zealous admiration for guns."

"Don't forget the family's intense sense of duty to God and country," Erin added behind us.

"Rick Morris posted something on his Facebook page a half-hour before the shooting began." When King asked what it was, I recited the bible verse.

"Putting it into context, there was something Nolan mentioned to us during our visit with him, something the shooter kept saying. Maybe he told you, too?" Erin asked King. "Something about being a patriot of God—"

King's eyes lit up.

"You know what it is?" I asked.

"Patriots of God?"

I nodded.

"I wish I didn't." King shifted his weight.

"What is it?"

King looked around, suddenly becoming very secretive as if not wanting anyone to overhear what he was about to share. "I'll tell you, but we can't talk about it here."

## CHAPTER TWENTY-EIGHT

My heartrate was through the roof as I followed King across the parking lot. The thrashing in my ears subsided once we stopped at my car but I was still holding my breath, wanting to know more.

King turned and looked back, double checking our trail to make certain we were out of earshot and away from anyone who might overhear him—including his partner, Detective John Alvarez.

Keeping his voice low, he asked me, "Are you sure Nolan heard Timothy say Patriots of God?"

I squinted my eyes. "He didn't mention anything to you?"

King shook his head.

"What is it?" I asked, thinking back to my conversation with Ginny Morris. I was convinced she was as ignorant to what her son was up to as I was, but something told me that Rick could be familiar with the term.

King scrubbed a wistful hand over his face and pulled in a deep breath. "I haven't heard that phrase in nearly two decades but I'll never forget it." He flicked his gaze back to the school and stared. A couple suits entered the building.

"Why would Tim say that?" I kept my voice low. "Does it have any relation to the bible verse Rick Morris quoted on his social media page?"

King could barely look me in the eye. "I'm not sure I have an answer to either of those questions. But what I do know is that the Patriots of God were a white supremacy group that sprouted up in Denver in the mid-90s."

Erin tilted her head and inched closer.

"The group wasn't even on the department's radar until a double homicide in Five Points led us to a couple of their members."

"It was a hate crime?"

"You could say that." King bounced his gaze between us. "Soon, as word spread about what happened, the black community was enraged. And deservingly so. When it finally got to trial, everyone was taking sides. It divided the city but, even more troubling, was how it worked its way into the department."

Erin gave me an arched look. I knew without asking what she wanted me to ask King. So I did. "Was Gavin involved in the case?"

"It was the kind of case impossible to escape. It was huge, and Gavin had just been promoted to SWAT officer. It wasn't until later, after the two white men were convicted of first-degree murder, that things really started to escalate. That's when things took a turn." King paused and stared. "Gavin wasn't the same after working the case."

"How come I didn't know about this?" I felt my pulse ticking hard and fast in my neck.

King's head was shaking when he said, "It happened before you two met."

"Okay," Erin started as my thoughts drifted to when I first met Gavin, "who are these led Patriots of God, and are they still around?"

"Political radicals," King said. "Like I said, I haven't heard their name for a very long time. However, they aren't afraid to take up arms in the name of purifying and saving traditional values."

I stood on wobbly knees, once again blaming myself for putting Mason in danger. It was my articles that put us in the spotlight. It seemed like every stone I overturned put my family at the heart of this investigation.

King kept talking but all I could hear were Nolan's words about Timothy telling him he was *cleansing the earth of its sins* while killing every black student he came across in the school. Then I snapped my head up when I heard King say, "They made it clear that everyone who wasn't Caucasian was inferior."

"We're still talking about the Patriots of God?" All the air was knocked out of me.

King nodded with strained eyes. "You recall the race riots of '98?"

"I do."

"You can thank the Patriots of God for starting them."

"I don't recall hearing that name." Erin's brows knitted.

"Every paper covered it. It was sensational news." King rolled his eyes. "Especially when a handful of white cops got caught on camera beating innocent blacks on a street corner."

Dropping my head into my hand, it was painful to hear even now, twenty years later. "Okay, we all know how it ended, but what happened to the group?"

"Fizzled away."

"That's it?" Erin whipped her head around. "Just disappeared?"

"It didn't end well for them."

"Was Cook Roberts part of the case?" Erin asked.

King shook his head. "Not directly. He was too young."

"Back up one second." I held up my hand. "What do you mean, it didn't end well for them?"

King took a deep breath. His eyes narrowed as he stared me directly in the eye. "Their leader, Douglas Davis, was killed at the hand of a cop."

I felt my heart skip a beat and I feared that, with the way King was looking at me, Gavin had been the one to pull the trigger. But before I could ask him about it, King said, "Their second in command is currently serving a life sentence."

"Now it's starting to make sense." Erin nodded. "This gives motive for revenge."

"It certainly does," I agreed.

Erin began thinking out loud. "The shooter, or shooters, were targeting both blacks and cops. What did Tim say to Nolan? Heroes will always be remembered, but a legend never dies."

"Babe Ruth," King said.

I nodded, then turned to King. "Any leads to who this second shooter might be?"

King shook his head, keeping one eye on the school.

"Could you even tell us if you did know?"

King's chest rose. "I'll share what I can."

Our conversation left me feeling queasy. Something told me that this militant group might be starting up again and, if it was political, I knew just where we needed to go next. "We have to visit the community college," I said to Erin.

King arched a brow.

"According to Timothy's parents, that's where he had found his passion."

"A political science course," Erin added for clarity.

"What's the professor's name?" King asked.

"Dean Croft," Erin said. "I found it when you were getting your box from your old office."

I was already making a mental list of questions I wanted

to ask Mr. Croft. If Timothy was, in fact, exposed to the Patriots of God inside his classroom, I assumed he would want to know about it. I knew I was certainly interested to learn the curriculum being taught and who was attending his classes. We had to check it out.

I made a move for my car but, before I could get too far, King clamped his hand around my elbow and said in a tense voice, "Sam, trust your instinct. If you feel like something isn't right, have the courage to walk away. Don't be a hero. If we are dealing with members of the Patriots of God, they're willing to not only die to protect their beliefs, but also kill anyone who stands in their way."

# CHAPTER TWENTY-NINE

THE BRIGHT ORB OF SUNSHINE DANGLED EVER CLOSER TO the peaks of the Rockies along the western horizon. The Sniper checked the time. It was getting close. Though still afternoon, soon the clouds sailing in from the west would brighten into an electric orange before darkness fell over the Mile High City.

Outside his black Honda Civic, children laughed and played around him, completely oblivious to his watchful eye. After all, this was their neighborhood, their playground after school. The place they came while waiting for their parents to come home after work.

School age girls were biking in circles while the boys tossed a football. They laughed and screamed at each other, acting as if yesterday's school shooting had never happened.

The Sniper watched intently, wondering if any of these children had older siblings attending North High. For these kids, life went on, just as it did for the Sniper. Another day. Another hour. One minute closer to acting out his next mission.

Fifteen minutes passed where nothing happened.

Suddenly, a pair of headlights turned onto the quiet street and caught the Sniper's attention. He flicked his gaze to the rearview mirror, wondering if it was the man he was waiting to see.

Squinting, he adjusted the mirror to get a closer look. When he noticed the vehicle was a patrol car, he felt his heart lunge into his throat. Panic made it hard to breathe and a million different scenarios rushed through his head. How did the police know he was here?

His heart hammered hard inside his chest and, despite his clenched stomach, he held steadfast. Casting his gaze forward, he didn't bother to slink down in his seat. He was either caught or he wasn't. Either way, he wouldn't go down without a fight.

Reaching between the seats, he gripped his 9MM semi-automatic pistol for added security, for the just-in-case scenario that might arise. Then he held his breath and waited.

The headlights drew ever closer.

Creeping up from behind, the Sniper swore he noticed the patrol car slow its approach.

*Did they know what car he was driving? Impossible. They knew nothing. He was a ghost to the world.* His ego boosted his growing confidence.

The Sniper's palms sweated as he stared, listening to his thrashing pulse grow louder inside his ears. With his finger feathering the trigger, the police cruiser passed by without even glancing in his direction.

His lungs released and he blew out a breath of hot air.

Laughing, the Sniper closed his eyes for a brief moment, pulled his lips into a smirk, and proceeded to turn on the radio to a low volume.

As much as he loved the unexpected rush of adrenaline, it was important he reminded himself that his involvement in yesterday's massacre was still unknown.

He listened to the news, had watched it when he could throughout the day. No matter who was reporting, they were still all talking only about Timothy Morris.

Glancing around at the quiet street, pride bloomed across his chest.

It was important he remembered why he was here, that none of this would have been possible if it weren't for Timothy's sacrifice. The Sniper considered him a martyr. If not for Tim, the Sniper wouldn't be able to fulfill his responsibilities to the much larger war they had waged together.

A minute later, a red Ford F150 pulled to the curb in front of the house the Sniper had been watching. He knew immediately that this was the man—and vehicle—he had been waiting for.

Glancing to the clock, it was nearly time for him to go. The vehicle's arrival was just as the Sniper had hoped.

Routine was everyone's worst enemy, the Sniper smirked.

Tempted to wave, greet the man stepping out of the pickup truck by name, the Sniper made a fist and kept himself from the easy delight, knowing he would have his chance for a personal meet and greet soon.

# CHAPTER THIRTY

King had me feeling afraid of what I might be walking into. But I couldn't let it go. I knew we were onto something. By the time I fell into the driver's seat, Erin was already on her smartphone, researching the Patriots of God.

Backing out of our parking space, I pointed the nose of my car southeast and started our journey to Community College of Denver to meet with Professor Croft.

"Says here the Patriots of God were blamed for instigating the riots, just like King said, but it also goes on to say that they refused to take responsibility and deflected the blame toward the Black and Hispanic communities." Erin shook her head. "Could you imagine if this happened in today's world with access to social media?" Erin lifted up her head and cast her gaze to the road ahead. "It would have been ten times worse."

"I remember seeing it on the news," I said.

"Me too."

"But I was too young to fully grasp the extent of what was really going on."

"And I certainly don't recall ever hearing the name the Patriots of God."

Neither did I. "Though they don't sound much different than any other militant group wanting to direct their anger toward the government."

Erin kept reading. "The second in command King referenced, his name is Kenneth Wayne."

I shook my head. The name didn't ring a bell.

"Mentions he's serving out his life sentence here in Colorado." Erin turned to me. "Maybe we could meet with him?"

I exited Speer Boulevard and merged onto I-25 South.

"I wish King would have told us that," I said, quietly debating with myself if I should just stop while I was still ahead. The last thing I wanted was for Mason to get hurt, or left without a parent to help him navigate this world.

"Maybe he didn't know?" Erin shrugged.

Once I settled into the flow of traffic, I instinctively reached for my phone. Checking for an update from Mason, I was disappointed when I didn't find one. Though I wasn't at all surprised. Mason had a habit of disappearing and wasn't the best at checking in. Telling myself, no news was good news, I let it go. At least until we stopped driving.

Erin must have seen what I was doing because she said, "You're going to tear yourself up constantly worrying about him."

I gave her a knowing look. Her natural instinct to always know what was going on was more impressive than I had originally thought. It was one thing I loved about her from day one, but she couldn't fully understand the extent of a mother's worry. "Did you really mean what you said back there?"

"What, that you're the common denominator?"

"Yeah," I breathed.

Erin spun her head forward. "Sam, maybe you didn't know your husband as well you thought."

A hot flash exploded from my core. "Don't speak about something you know nothing about. I knew Gavin better than I know myself."

"Then why was all that news to you?"

Tightening my grip on the steering wheel, I watched my knuckles go white. "We all have secrets hanging in our closets." I flicked my gaze to Erin. "But you missed a critical piece of what King was saying back there."

"I heard every word."

"I don't doubt that. But it's what he didn't say that left you in the dust."

Erin pinched her brow and gave me a confused look.

"The cop who killed the Patriots of God leader? That was Gavin."

"Are you sure?" Erin's face tightened. "I didn't get that from him."

Nodding, I said, "You don't know King like I do. I could see it in his eyes."

"You should have asked him straight up, even if you already knew."

"I didn't have to. Gavin was the best shot I've ever known. There was a reason SWAT recruited him. And, think about it, if Gavin was the one who killed the Patriots of God leader, that would give motive for Timothy to specifically want to target Mason, and the second shooter to murder Cook Roberts. Gavin and Cook were close."

Erin stared at me for a minute before asking, "Have you received more threats you're not telling me about?"

"I haven't checked." My voice fell flat. "I'm too afraid to find out."

Exiting off I-25, I slowed the car and merged onto Colfax.

"Nothing has been posted on our website," Erin assured

me. "Maybe we're just overthinking all this. Like King said, no one could escape their involvement in a case this big. This could all just be coincidence?"

As if that was supposed to ease my constant worry for my son. I flashed Erin a skeptical look. "Don't be naïve. You're better than that."

She stared back with her glowing blonde hair framing her face in the afternoon light.

"By the way, good job on identifying a second shooter before King did."

"I'm just glad that he let us in on his findings. Now we know we're on the right track."

"Speaking of which, any idea where we're going once we get there?"

"Somewhat." Erin was back on her phone. "Shouldn't be too hard to track down Professor Croft's office."

A few minutes later we arrived at the Community College of Denver, speaking of how distant our own college experiences seemed. Erin managed to get her bearings once we entered the building and she led me confidently through the halls as if she had been here before. Meanwhile, I couldn't stop thinking of Gavin and what other secrets he'd decided best not to share when I received a call from Dawson.

"Hey Dawson, what's up?"

"A man just called looking for you."

"Okay." I paused and shared a look with Erin. "Did you take a message?"

"Tried to but they weren't interested."

"Did you at least ask why they were calling?"

"I did. And that's why I thought I should call." Silence filled the line. "Sam, this man wanted to speak with you personally about the school shooting. Said you would find what he had to say most interesting."

"But he didn't leave his name?"

"Or a way to reach him. The call came from a blocked number."

A shiver moved up my spine, getting my neck hairs to stand on end.

"Something about it was off."

I took in a deep breath, reluctant to think too much into it. "If he calls back, try to get him to talk."

Dawson agreed he would do his best. "Stay vigilant, Sam. We are no longer seen as allies but viewed by many as enemies first."

"Thanks for the heads up," I muttered as I pulled my cellphone away from my ear, feeling queasy with everyone's warnings.

As much as I appreciated both Dawson and King wanting to look out for me, I found their need to tell me to stay safe more distracting than anything else. I had to stay strong and, in order to do so, I couldn't allow fear to seep its way into my thoughts.

"What was that about?" Erin asked as we started to move.

"Just missed a call at the office," I said, rounding the corner and coming within sight of Professor Dean Croft's office.

"Shit. It's closed." Erin rattled the door handle. Spinning on a heel, she asked, "What do we do now?"

Flipping through the sheets of announcements hanging below Professor Croft's nameplate on the wall, it didn't take me long to find what I was looking for. "According to his schedule, his office should be open now."

Erin pulled up her sleeve and checked the time. "Then where is he?"

Suddenly, the hallway filled with sounds of a horse trotting. I turned to find a middle-aged man stuffing what appeared to be a flyer inside his sport coat pocket, heading straight for us.

"I'm here. I'm here." He waved his hand through the air in the shape of a large rainbow.

"Professor Dean Croft?" I asked.

"Yes, that is me." He paused and cocked his head to the side when looking at me. "You're Samantha Bell. I know you."

"From *The Colorado Times*." I grinned. "Yes, that's me."

"Ahh... then I assume you're here to ask me about Timothy Morris."

Erin raised both her eyebrows and looked impressed. "How did you guess?" Erin introduced herself.

Professor Croft bounced his gaze between us. "He was in my class." He dug out his office keys and unlocked his door. Kicking it open, he said, "I've been waiting for the first reporter to show." He turned and smiled. "Congratulations. You won."

Following him into his tiny office, I asked, "You mean no one else has come to speak with you?"

"Surprising, isn't it?" He set a few things down and began sifting through stacks of papers. The place was a mess and lacked the organization I would have expected from someone in his position.

"Why do you say that?"

His head tilted to one shoulder as he lowered his chin, giving me a look of disbelief. "I've been following the news, Mrs. Bell. And, from what I understand, Tim killed himself."

"How did you react when you heard the news?"

His gaze traveled up and down both Erin and me. "I assumed the case would be closed but, I suppose with you being here now, that might not be true."

"Mr. Croft, we're only curious to learn what Tim was like inside your class."

"Quiet," the professor said, matter-of-fact. "But brilliant when he wanted to be." Mr. Croft turned his attention back to his desk, sifting through a stack of papers. "When he first arrived in my class, I assumed his shyness was only because of his age." Croft turned to look at us. "He was the youngest in the class, you know."

"Did Tim interact with other students?"

Without looking, Mr. Croft said, "Tim was an unassuming kid. He came and left, often times going undetected. I never saw him hang around much." As if hearing a class bell go off, Mr. Croft flicked his wrist and checked the time. Scooping his stacks of papers into his arms, he headed to the door. "I have class now."

"We'd still like to ask you a few more questions."

"Then you'll have to do it while we walk."

Following Professor Croft down the halls, I said, "Tim's mother seemed to think that something about this class in particular sparked an interest."

Croft dug his heels into the floor and came to a sudden stop. "She said that?"

I nodded.

A smile sprouted on his face and it was clear he was proud to have made an impact on one of his student's lives. He began walking, this time picking up the pace a little faster than before. "In today's political climate, and with so many hot button issues, we can't afford to sit on our hands and do nothing. It's an exciting time in our political history."

As soon as we entered his class, a half-dozen students were already sitting at their desks, another half-dozen filing in not long after us.

Croft headed for the front table near the whiteboard. Setting his things down on top, he continued, "Each of us has a chance to be part of history, create our own legacy if we so desire."

I saw Erin's head lift like a helium balloon out of the corner of my eye. She'd heard it, too. Croft's word choice couldn't have been by mistake. "Professor, we have reason to believe that Tim may have been part of a political group."

"Oh?"

The doors behind us opened and a young man trudged in with a backpack slung over one shoulder. Keeping one eye on him, I asked, "Has there ever been mention of the Patriots of God inside your classroom?" As soon as the words fluttered over my lips, the young man lifted his head and paused. I knew he was listening.

"Impossible," Professor Croft said.

I watched the young man make his way to the back of the room and, to my surprise, exited the classroom without making contact with any of the other students. Erin was watching a circle of students working on a project, making posters it looked like. Flicking my gaze back to Croft, I said, "You are aware of the group, though?"

"I am. That was a long time ago, Mrs. Bell. Many of my students were yet to be born."

Itching to catch up with the young man who'd left in such a hurry, I asked, "That may be, but is there any chance it might have found a place inside your class?"

Looking me straight in the eye, Croft said, "Mrs. Bell, I stand for the constitution. Not bigotry. If it has found a place inside my classroom, I would be the first to know about it."

# CHAPTER THIRTY-ONE

"SAM, SLOW DOWN." ERIN CHASED AFTER ME.

I couldn't leave fast enough. The student who'd arrived and left so quickly had my head spinning with possibility. His actions left me feeling like he knew something. I was determined to find out if my suspicions were right.

Lengthening my stride, I increased my pace until I was nearly running. The soles of my shoes hit the floor harder with each step. "Professor Croft is either part of it or ignorant to what may actually be happening inside his classroom."

We burst through the exit with heaving chests.

My head swiveled on my shoulders like a spool of unwinding yarn.

"What are we doing, Sam?" Erin followed my darting gaze, looking everywhere I looked.

"That kid." My eyebrows slanted as I scanned every bench, planter, and concrete wall I could find.

"What kid?"

I turned to Erin. "You didn't see him?"

Erin flicked her brows, continuing to act oblivious to the ghost I seemed to be chasing.

"The male with a black backpack slung over his right shoulder." I paused, hoping Erin would give me any sign of recognition. Rolling my attention back to the surrounding areas, I said, "He entered the classroom right as I asked Croft about the Patriots of God."

"I must have missed it." Erin sighed behind me.

*Where did he go?* Running out of options, I took my chances by heading right. Moving at a quick clip, Erin was one step behind.

"I'll tell you what I didn't miss." Erin raised her voice to make sure I heard as I briskly walked ahead. "Croft didn't seem to react to the news of Tim's suicide."

"It's was certainly a strange response, wasn't it?" I kept looking with fear hardening in my stomach that maybe I had missed my chance.

"Considering his student died? Yeah." Erin wet her lips. "He didn't seem devastated or saddened by the news."

"You think Croft isn't telling the truth?"

"Certainly makes me curious to know why he went straight to assuming the case should have been closed."

I brought my hand to my brow, shielding the intense low angle of the sun from my eyes.

"And what was that about creating our own legacy if we so desire? These are just kids. They shouldn't be worried about legacy at that age."

"Unless someone is telling them they should be." I squinted and I felt my heart pause inside my chest when I finally spotted the young man standing near an entrance on the corner of the building. "There," I said, pointing.

We took off, not wanting to let him get away a second time. Once I was within earshot, I slowed my stride. A thick white cloud spewed from his mouth. He was alone, vaping, and didn't see us coming.

"You're the student I saw in Professor Croft's class, right?" I asked as I approached.

He stood and stared without saying a word.

"My name is Samantha Bell and this is my colleague, Erin Tate." Erin flashed him her friendliest smile. "I was hoping we could ask you some questions about what it's like to be a student in Professor Croft's class."

He pulled another wop off his e-cigarette and blew thick plumes out of his nostrils.

"You see, my son was a student at North High. I'm sure you heard what happened there yesterday?"

The man raised his brows in a manner that led me to believe he was disinterested in anything I had to say.

"Anyway, I saw you stop in when we were speaking about it to Croft."

His head bobbed. "Ah, yes. Now I remember you."

Feeling my chest expand with renewed hope, I said, "I couldn't help but notice how you seemed to recognize the term Patriots of God."

The air between us went silent. We stared into each other's eyes but there was nothing.

"Are you aware of that term, or do you know what it is?" Erin asked.

He flicked his narrowed gaze to Erin and kept his Juul device gripped tightly in the palm of his hand. "I don't know anything about it."

"Why did you leave the moment you arrived to class?"

"I saw Croft was busy so I decided to have a quick smoke break before class."

"The boy, Timothy Morris, who shot up North High yesterday, he was in Professor Croft's class. Did you know him?"

"Tim hated it when people called him Timothy."

I shared a quick glance to Erin. She inched closer. "So, you knew Tim?"

He nodded. "I'm not surprised he did it."

The lines on my forehead furrowed. "Why do you say that?"

"Tim was an angry kid. He seemed to hate lots of people at that school."

"Did he tell you this?" Erin asked.

He nodded again and flirted with taking another wop off his machine but decided against it. "Tim had mentioned doing something but I never thought he would actually follow through."

My pulse grew faint. "Did you report this to anybody?"

The young man wrapped his lips around his wop machine and took a drag of nicotine. "Like I said, I didn't take his words literally." Smoke poured out of his mouth as he talked. "I just thought he wanted to appear tough while blowing off some steam."

I didn't want to fault this kid for doing nothing, but it was hard to believe he hadn't seen the warning signs.

"Do you think Croft's class inspired Tim to take action?" Erin asked.

"Let's just put it this way." His green eyes flicked to Erin. "In order to ace a paper, it's best you don't stray too far from Croft's personal views."

My lips parted. "You mean you just tell him what he wants to hear?"

The student squinted his eyes and pulled off his wop machine again. "It means Croft likes his fat little ego to be stroked." He turned his head and blew his smoke down his right arm. "If you ask me, politics is toxic and everything can be taken out of context or twisted."

"What do you mean by that?"

"What I mean is, Croft encourages us to get political.

Take on issues that are important to us. Some people get really into it."

"And you? What's important to you?"

He pulled out his cellphone and checked the time. "Do I look like I care about anything?"

"You look like a smart kid."

He huffed a disbelieving laugh. "I'm only here because it's a required credit." His eyes danced between Erin and me. "Look, I better get back inside before I miss too much."

I handed him my business card. "Contact me if you remember anything else you can tell us about Croft or Tim. We're trying to learn why Tim did what he did."

The student swiped my card out of my hand. Before he left, I asked, "Hey, what's your name?"

He hesitated for a brief moment before saying, "Chandler."

Then he headed back inside without another word. As soon as we were alone, I dug out my own cellphone. "Who are you calling?" Erin asked.

"Allison." I listened to the line ring. "She'll be able to track keywords and collect data in real time from the internet. If this group is reforming, it would be nice to know about it before something else happens."

# CHAPTER THIRTY-TWO

WE WERE DRIVING TO ALLISON'S OFFICE WHEN THE dullness inside my chest spread to each of my limbs. I couldn't get over how Tim's behavior prior to the shooting went unreported. When the bile in my stomach rose, I quickly swallowed it down. Then I scrubbed a trembling hand over my face and turned to Erin.

"Do you think Chandler might not be telling the complete truth?"

Without taking her eyes off her cellphone screen, Erin mumbled, "You heard what he said about politics being toxic."

"If what he said was true, Tim confessed to his plan." Keeping one hand on the steering wheel, I turned to Erin. "The school shooting could have been prevented if Chandler had said something."

"I understand what you're saying, but phrases like *I'll kill you* and *drop dead* get thrown around daily without it actually ever bearing fruit. No one takes those words seriously. How could you expect a man Chandler's age to think differently?"

"This is different."

"We don't know what Tim's exact words were. It's only different in hindsight."

"No, but Chandler said he wasn't surprised to learn that Tim was the one behind it."

"Do you really expect school administrators or the police to be able to sift through what's real and what's not?"

"Yeah, I do." My tone remained even. "If it means saving lives, then each threat needs to be treated as such."

Erin twisted her spine and angled her body to face me. "Then tell me this, do you still think Professor Croft might be more involved than what he's leading us to believe?"

Staring ahead, I said, "The fact that one student thinks he has to regurgitate Croft's personal views in order to ace a test is enough to make me think that Croft is doing more to push his personal agenda than teach the constitution."

Erin narrowed her eyes in deep thought. "King mentioned the Patriots of God fighting to protect traditional values."

"Yeah?"

"Then would that also apply to Constitutionalism?"

"Like the theories of John Locke?"

Erin nodded. "As well as the founders of our republic."

"Okay, I see where you're going. Let's say the Patriots of God did consider themselves modern day knights put here to protect the Founding Fathers' ideals. What does that have to do with Chandler or Croft?"

"When I first saw it, I thought it was a class project they were working on—all those posters—but now I'm thinking it wasn't that at all."

I flashed Erin an arched look.

"I bet it was protest signs." Erin stared and waited for a response. When I had nothing, she said, "Chandler's not wrong, you know. Politics can get toxic. If Croft wants to push his own agenda, standing up to protect the constitution the way he sees it, what better way to do it than to make your voice heard?"

"Chandler said Croft encourages his students to get political."

There was a sparkle in Erin's eye. "What could they be protesting?"

"What could they *not* be protesting? The election is nearly here and this governor's race has been anything but dull." I flipped on my blinker and made a right turn. "But I can't see how the Patriots of God relates to any of that."

We pulled into the back of Allison's small Tudor house she'd converted into an office space and parked.

"Either Croft knows and is keeping his involvement a secret, or his students are up to something and are using his class as an incubator for recruitment."

I sighed and felt my breath catch in my throat. The thought of it being either scenario prickled my scalp. Opening my door, we scampered around the house and entered Allison's office from the front.

Patty O'Neil, Allison's Chief of Operations, was the first to greet us. "Hey, Sam. I've been praying for you and your son. We all have been."

"Thanks." A soft murmur fluttered over my lips.

"Allison is in her office. She's expecting you."

"I'm here." Allison approached with a playful grin pulling at her lips. "Sam, how is Mason's friend doing?"

"He's doing well, considering."

"The office has been rooting for him." Allison glanced to Erin and winked. "Susan told me about wanting to meet up for drinks—"

I flashed her a questioning look.

Allison cocked her head to the side. "She didn't tell you?"

I shook my head.

"Well, I'm sure it slipped her mind. I got the impression

she's having an equally tough day and needs some girl time." Allison told me the details and I promised her we'd make it but I wanted to remind her about Pastor Michaels's vigil.

"Of course I'll be there," she said. "But that's not why you're here, is it?"

I shook my head. "I need your help."

Allison's smile evaporated into thin air. "I was afraid of that. Let's talk in my office."

We followed Allison to the back and found ourselves taking a seat the moment Allison closed her door. It was quiet while Allison took her spot behind her desk.

Allison leaned back and clasped her hands over her stomach. "Catch me up on your day and I'll see what kind of help I can be."

Over the next several minutes, I shared the details of our visit with Nolan before moving on to the discovery Erin made and King later confirmed.

"A second shooter, huh?" Allison's head shook with disbelief. "I assume this is something that needs to be kept secret? Because I haven't heard it being mentioned in the news."

"Top secret," I said.

"Then how can I help?"

"It's something Nolan heard the shooter say."

Allison's expression pinched.

I inhaled a deep breath before I said, "We need to know if the Patriots of God group is back."

Allison's eyes flickered like a candle in the night. Her shoulders tensed when she murmured, "I haven't thought about that in a very long time."

Erin tipped forward in her chair. "We have reason to believe that the organization might have regrouped."

Allison flicked her gaze to Erin. "And you want me to do what?"

"Confirm if Timothy Morris was a member," I said.

"Crawl the web and see if you can pick up any chatter that can also confirm if the organization is regrouping."

Allison rolled her gaze to the window. She stared with a nervous expression tugging her eyebrows awkwardly. If anybody understood the implications of a group like the Patriots of God, it was Allison. "It now makes more sense what Timothy was saying in his Facebook Live video." She turned back to face us. "His words mimicked things I used to hear my parents talk about when racial tension was high in this city."

"Do you remember your parents speaking about the Patriots of God?"

"Not much. They were good at making me believe the world was better than it is."

"Can you hack into Timothy's social media accounts?"

"If they're still active," Allison confirmed with a single nod.

"And if not?"

"It would be much harder."

"But you could still do it?"

One side of Allison's mouth curled as she bounced her gaze to Erin. The three of us smiled, hopeful that not all was lost and buried somewhere deep in cyberspace.

"We need to know what Tim has been posting leading up to the school shooting and if there are any obvious links to a second shooter. There is no telling if the shooter is planning anything new or if yesterday was it."

"I'm not sure how long it will take but I'll start working on it today." I pushed myself up, ready to leave. Before I could land fully on my feet, Allison said, "Sam, have you watched the news recently?"

"No. Why?"

Allison curled her fingers over her laptop keyboard and said, "There is something you should see before you go."

I was slow to lower myself back down into my chair. As soon as I sat, Erin reached over and took my hand inside of hers.

"This happened ten minutes before you arrived."

Allison flipped the computer screen in my direction.

I leaned forward and watched as Rick Morris spoke passionately to TV news crews. It was evident he was unable to take his wife's advice and keep his anger contained. Gripping a white cross in his hand, he looked directly into the camera lens and said, "Your children are not as innocent as you would like them to be. They are equally as guilty as the dark light you're casting my son in. And if you want to label Tim a dark villain, I will make certain you soon learn who the true villain really is."

## CHAPTER THIRTY-THREE

THE DOOR CHIMED AS THE SNIPER ENTERED THE SMALL GIFT shop. The clerk working the front register stared and greeted him as he entered with a single nod.

The Sniper grinned back and quickly looked away. He was on a mission and didn't plan to linger longer than he had to. It was too risky, even if his involvement hadn't been discovered. He was walking on thin ice, his strategy of deception a gamble to go all-in.

Strolling toward the gift aisle, nerves kept him jittery. He couldn't help but feel that the police were on to him—that they would see through his disguise of hiding in plain sight. His fears were all inside his head, of course. None of it was real. Even with his constant desire to nervously glance around, check to see if he was being followed, he kept his eyes pointed straight ahead, choosing confidence over fear.

He focused on his breath, listening to the blood thrash loud in his ears.

Weaving through the store, he kept searching for the item he needed—the item that would help remind him of his mission, the item that would signal to the world who he was and what he was fighting for. It would be his calling card, his beacon in the night.

Sounds surrounding him soon disappeared as he intently focused. His feet felt heavy as bricks. He wondered if he shouldn't have taken his chances at a larger box store instead of this little shop. He was here now, so he would take what they had on offer.

The Sniper kept looking. He would search this entire store before giving up. He wasn't a quitter. He fought on, got up when knocked over, and refused to be pushed around.

Then, suddenly, he caught sight of what it was he was after.

He felt his spine pull straight. Despite the urge to run toward it, he purposely slowed his approach with the hopes of not drawing attention to himself.

Feeling lightheaded, his head spun as his vision faded into a dark tunnel. Slowly he walked, staring at the flag. The colors of red, white, and blue were electric in the light but it was the shining object attached to the top that he was after.

Dropping to one knee, he reached for the white eagle perched above the American flag. Stroking it with his thumb, it was cool to the touch. It blasted him with a sudden surge of incredible power. He felt strong knowing many great men had fought and died for these colors. And, once he brought the white eagle to the white cross, the symbol of his heritage would be reborn.

A wave of heat moved beneath his collar.

His heartrate increased, along with his sense of power.

Standing, he floated back to the register like a ship set sail. The same man who'd greeted him when he arrived was still standing at the only open checkout. His dark eyes followed the Sniper all the way to the front.

The Sniper gripped the flag tighter inside his hand and lowered his brow as he studied the man's dark complexion.

"Find what you're looking for?"

The Sniper nodded without saying a single word.

Scanning the barcode, the price rang up. "It seems everyone wants to purchase these with this year's election. I suppose it's the rising patriotism that is encouraging the sales. Well, these and the little white crosses."

The Sniper swept his gaze up and stared into the stranger's eyes.

"After what happened yesterday." The cashier paused and hoped the Sniper would say something. "So sad." The man sighed and dropped the little flag into a plastic bag. "Ten-thirty-three."

The Sniper reached to his back pocket, opened his wallet, and pulled out a twenty-dollar bill. Handing it to the cashier, he kept his gaze pointed to the counter. It was important he wasn't recognized. He didn't want to be remembered.

"Your change," the cashier said.

Snapping out of his thoughts, the Sniper opened his palm and let the money drop into his hand. He left the store without saying a word and soon found himself tucked safely behind the steering wheel of his car, driving by North High.

He could still see TV news vans lingering at the scene of his crime. Police were working, combing the scene for evidence. Though it crossed his mind, he hadn't come here to tempt the authorities into learning that Tim hadn't acted alone. The Sniper had another location on his mind.

A minute later, he pulled into an empty parking space at Highland Park. Reaching across the middle console, he took both the flag he had just purchased as well as the little white wooden cross he had brought with him.

Stepping out, he walked through the park, listening to the dry grass crunch beneath his feet while clenching his two items close to his heart. The air was still and smelled clean. It

was the perfect autumn day, warmer than yesterday's flirta-
tion with winter.

Once in the middle of the park, he stopped and spun
around. He wasn't far from where he'd perched himself up on
the hotel rooftop and fired his two shots that killed Cook
Roberts and his partner to begin yesterday's massacre.

"Are you here for the vigil?"

The Sniper snapped his head around with sudden
surprise. He turned in the direction of the male voice. A boy
of 17 or 18 approached and seemed intent on speaking with
him. The Sniper kept quiet and stared, curious to know
where this would lead.

"I saw you holding the cross, so," the boy's eyes drifted to
the white cross near the Sniper's chest, "I assumed you were
here for the vigil."

The Sniper glanced to his hands.

"The community is gathering tonight at 8PM to both
mourn and celebrate the lives lost in yesterday's school shooting." The young man handed the Sniper a flier. "We're
encouraging all members of the community to attend."

The Sniper was slow to accept the flier. When he did, he
glanced to the text. A grin tugged at his lips when reading
Pastor Michaels's name, front and center.

The kid stood and stared.

The Sniper's insides twisted as he felt every muscle fiber
in his body flex with fear that the kid might be looking too
closely at who he was. Did he just see a flash of recognition?
He held steadfast beneath the light. Kept calm and planned
how he would respond to this curious intruder who insisted
to butt his way into the Sniper's life.

"We could really use your support."

The Sniper exhaled and cocked his head to the side.

"Even from you."

# CHAPTER THIRTY-FOUR

SUSAN YOUNG COULDN'T WAIT TO TAKE A BREAK FROM work. The drinks she was going to have with her best friends was hardly enough to get her through the last half-hour of her workday.

"I know a good lawyer who could consult on how best to handle this type of situation."

Susan's shoulders released upon hearing Philip Price's offer. She listened to her client's recommendation, feeling a bit odd about taking advice from the man who was predicted to unseat the same man who had started her day off with such a bombshell.

Ever since Governor John Scott's announcement earlier this morning to direct all donations to the school shooting victims fund to go to Susan's organization, Susan was struggling to contain her sudden onslaught of stress.

"I'm going to need all the advice I can get." Price gave Susan the name and contact details of his associate. "Thank you," she said, breathing a sigh of relief for the first time all day.

"I'll tell him he can expect a call from you." Price's voice was light, reassuring and completely supporting, and Susan couldn't have been more grateful for it.

Ending her call with well wishes on the candidate's evening, Susan dropped her face inside her hands and immediately rubbed the grit from her tired eyes.

It hadn't taken long this morning for the first calls from victim's families to start rolling in, asking when they could expect to receive the funds promised by the governor to pay for their child's medical or funeral costs. Susan couldn't believe how people expected her to move at the speed of light. She barely had a collection plate out by the time she was expected to divvy out the payments.

*How do we decide how much each victim receives? Not all medical costs are the same. Who gets what, when, how?*

Susan knew she had little choice but to take Price's recommendation and hire the assistance of a special attorney. Even if it ran the danger of getting political, Susan had little choice.

Price gave a recommendation when the governor did not. Governor Scott only nominated her company when he should have also assigned a team to help with the finer details. Since he didn't, Susan was left with only one option on how to proceed.

Her cellphone chimed with a reminder.

Glancing to the display screen, she thought about canceling on her friends. But even if she did, Susan wasn't going to miss the vigil. She'd promised Sam she would be there and, besides, she knew she would have to work into the night despite anything she did now. A break would do her wonders.

When she stood, her legs wobbled and her stomach grumbled. Realizing she had eaten very little all day, she reached for her purse and slung it over her shoulder before marching out the door. She had told her staff to go home an hour ago, and now she was the last to leave.

Exiting the building, she closed the door behind her and was locking up when she heard footsteps approach from behind.

"Are you Ms. Susan Young?"

Susan rolled her shoulders back and held on to her purse as she quickly assessed the man. He was well dressed, had his collar open, and appeared to be harmless. Easing a little, she said, "I'm Susan. How can I help you?"

Delving his hand into his inside jacket pocket, the man pulled out a single white envelope. "I was instructed to give this to you personally."

Susan stared at the thin envelope and wondered what was inside. "What is it?"

"A donation." He locked eyes with her. "For the victim's fund."

Sweeping her eyes up off the envelope, Susan said, "We prefer electronic deposits. All the information can be found on our website."

The man held the envelope closer to Susan. "Not this one. This has to be given in person."

Susan felt her heart knocking against her chest and her facial muscles tense. "I really can't..."

"This check is to be given to a specific family."

Susan felt her cheeks warm. Swallowing the lump down in her throat, she grew more nervous by the man's specific request. "What family is that?"

"Here. Take it." He held the envelope up to her. "The family's name is written on the outside. See for yourself."

Susan stared into the man's eyes. She held her breath as she pinched her fingers onto one side of the envelope and reeled her elbow into her side. Glancing to the name written in ink, her stomach dropped and suddenly she felt sick.

"That's right." The man grinned. "The money inside *must* be given to the Morris family."

# CHAPTER THIRTY-FIVE

ALLISON PUSHED US OUT OF HER OFFICE NOT LONG AFTER she showed us the clip of Rick Morris spouting his head off into the camera. She was anxious to get working on our behalf and I didn't want to be an unnecessary distraction so was happy to let her work in quiet. Two hours had passed and now we were back at my new desk, catching up on missed messages.

Staring into the screen of my laptop, I scrolled through my email. It was filling up quickly, mostly from sympathetic readers who had heard about my son being a student at North High. Though I appreciated their thoughts, I nervously anticipated the moment one person would reveal our secret I didn't want anyone to learn.

I fell back in my chair and clasped my hands over my clenched stomach.

I was having a tough time already, knowing Mason was a target who'd escaped unharmed. His vulnerability had me constantly worried that the man we were looking for might also be searching for my son.

"If you were Professor Croft, which issue would you

protest?" Erin had her feet up on the far end of my desk and
her laptop resting on her thighs. She still thought that Croft
was the voice behind the hate crimes and was determined to
begin tracking his movements.

"I guess I would have to first know if there were any
planned marches."

A glimmer caught in her eye. "Any guesses to where the
next big protest might be held?"

"Probably wherever Governor Scott or Philip Price is
scheduled to be."

Erin pursed her lips. "Hmm..." Her fingers tapped aggres-
sively over her keyboard. "Here we go."

I stopped what I was doing and swiveled my chair to face
my friend. I was curious to know what she was after. From
the look on her face, I knew she had found something of
interest.

"Planned protests happening within the week. Your
choices are," Erin raised her hand and pointed her index
finger to the ceiling, "LGBT, national security, the environ-
ment, racial justice, and religious liberty."

"Based on what we heard about the Patriots of God, I
would have to go with either racial justice or religious
liberty."

Erin bit her cheek. "Yeah, me too."

"So, my crime-solving friends," Dawson arrived at my
desk all smiles, "did Timothy Morris have an accomplice in
yesterday's shooting?"

Lunging to my feet, I reached my hand to Dawson's
shoulder and clamped my fingers around his neck, pulling him
down. Squatting in front of my desk with Erin straight as a
lighthouse looking out for possible spies, I asked Dawson,
"Have you told anyone our theory?"

He was giving me a concerned look when he muttered,
"No. Why? It's true isn't it?"

Erin cast her hardened gaze down and we locked eyes. I watched as she ran a hand through her hair before she swiveled her head around like an owl. Luckily, no one was around. If someone like Trisha Christopher—Ms. Gossip herself—overheard our secret, it would only be a matter of time before everyone knew and our whole investigation would blow up in our faces.

Jabbing my index finger at the tip of Dawson's nose, I said, "You can't tell a soul."

"Sam," he drew his brows together, "who do you think I am?"

I stared into Dawson's trustworthy eyes, knowing I could trust him with my darkest secrets. "Yeah, it's true. Tim had an accomplice."

Dawson's eyes grew into large coins as he pinched his lips shut.

"King and Alvarez came up with the same conclusion and are waiting for forensics to make it official."

Dawson's gaze drifted to the floor. "Shit. This is big news."

"It's huge. That's why we can't blow this investigation." Dawson's mind was churning. I could see it in his eyes. He wanted me to find a way to publish the story but I couldn't without tipping off the second shooter. "Someone is still out there and we don't know what they're planning, if anything."

Erin's hip flared as she hovered over us with crossed arms.

I turned my focus back to Dawson. "And that's why this needs to stay between us."

"Of course." Dawson's eyes suddenly flashed with a thought. "Could it be the person who called for you earlier?"

My lips abruptly went dry and I felt the ball of goo that had been floating around in my stomach all day suddenly harden into stone. Refusing to wear my fear on my face, I lifted my brows and asked, "Has anyone else called looking for me?"

"Not that I know about." Dawson flicked his gaze up to Erin.

When my calves began tingling I stood, pulling Dawson up with me. I caught Dawson up with our investigation without revealing too many specifics. Dawson was smart enough to know I was keeping something from him but he didn't ask, wanting to keep my sources protected. All I could say was this investigation was far from being over and I would have a great story waiting for him when it was.

"I assume you also saw the interview Rick Morris did?" Dawson was now sitting on the edge of my desk, rubbing his brow between two fingers.

Nodding, I tucked a loose strand of hair behind my ear.

"Do we have any idea who the true villain he's referring to might be?"

Erin and I were silent for a long moment as we hadn't discussed it ourselves. But I knew we had both given it thought. "I don't know," I said. "But I was hoping that maybe it had something to do with something Tim may have experienced."

"I can't get over the white cross," Erin said. "The way he held it, thrusting it into the air as he spoke."

"I thought it rather odd, too," Dawson said.

I didn't want to say it, but I knew it was what we were all thinking. "Maybe it has something to do with the Patriots of God." Dawson stared and I told him I had Allison crawling the web to see if she could get any hits that would indicate if the group was attempting to make a comeback.

"Did you decide on what angle you'll take for tonight's coverage?"

Reaching behind Dawson, I scooped up the printed sheets I'd made earlier. I had each of the school shooting victim's names printed off, along with a short synopsis on their life story. "I'd like to make Pastor Michaels a key highlight and somehow use his work when sharing the legacy each of the victims has left behind."

Erin rapidly blinked. She stepped forward, continuing to stare.

"I don't want their murders to go in vein."

Dawson turned his head and looked away when he heard his name being called. Pushing off my desk, he said, "Sounds fantastic, Sam." Stepping out of my small cubicle, he hollered over his shoulder, "I'll see you at the vigil. Keep up the good work and let me know if I can be of assistance."

As soon as it was just Erin and me, Erin put her nose to mine. "Sam, that's it."

I bounced my gaze with hers, feeling the crease between my brow deepen.

"Your story. It's what Rick Morris wants."

"I think it's the opposite of what he wants. Which is the point I'm trying to make. No one remembers the names of the victims, but everyone can tell you who committed the crime. I want this one to be different. It's been done and I'd like to do whatever I can to change that precedent."

Erin closed her eyes and shook her head. "By telling the victim's story, you're playing right into Rick Morris's hand."

"No, Erin. I have no interest in telling Tim's story."

"Look, just hear me out. Rick Morris was—and still is—a suspect. And now that we have learned more about the Patriots of God, don't you find it interesting that Rick chose to speak publicly while thrusting a cross high into the air?"

I felt my breath catch as I thought about the scripture Rick quoted from the bible and made public on his Facebook profile. "Okay, Rick is refusing to let his son leave the spotlight. But it's a strange way of keeping Tim's name in the news, don't you think?"

Erin's brows lifted. "Unless we're the villain he swore he'd expose if we didn't begin telling his son's story he wants people to know."

"What do we have to hide?"

"Maybe it's not our secrets we should be worried about, but those who are closest to us?"

A cold shiver moved down my spine and I was instantly reminded of my seemingly close relationship to the Patriots of God, Cooks Roberts, and Mason.

"Rick wants his son's name to live in infamy. I don't know why, but his actions leave me with little doubt that that's exactly what he is after."

The moment Erin paused, my thoughts drifted to the Morris household and the framed patriotism that filled their walls. Maybe Erin was right. There was no winning this. If I wrote about the victims like I planned to do, Rick would attack me for not giving his son the credit he thought he deserved. And if I *did* write about Tim, he would attack me for telling the things Rick didn't want to hear.

Erin's lips were pursed in thought. "Maybe it's time we ask Rick Morris what he knows about the Patriots of God."

"I agree, but that's not what I'm thinking is going on here at all."

Erin crossed her arms and tipped her chin back. "Then, tell me, what do you think is going on here?"

"I think the true villain Rick is referring to is Rick Morris himself and I'm afraid of what he might do to make his voice heard."

# CHAPTER THIRTY-SIX

ERIN AND I COULDN'T COME TO AN AGREEMENT BY THE time we arrived to the small restaurant off Federal Boulevard on the north side of town. We agreed to disagree and decided it best to let it come to a vote over drinks with the girls.

As soon as I stepped outside, the spicy scent of Mexican food made my stomach grumble. Poblanos and a tall margarita were on the menu for me, but what I needed most was to hear my son's voice.

I followed Erin to the entrance before stopping. Pulling out my phone, Mason still hadn't checked in. "I'll meet you inside," I said. "I'm going to call Mason."

Erin nodded, reached for the door handle, and stepped over the threshold of the double wooden door entrance. Her words were still rattling between my ears and I couldn't escape the thought that maybe she was right about Rick. What if he was coming after journalists and the people closest to us? It certainly seemed possible with what little we knew about him.

I pressed my phone to my ear and listened to it ring.

I didn't want Erin to be right. Not this time, anyway. It

would be much easier if Rick was only referring to himself as the villain he wanted to introduce to the world because, then, at least we had somebody to keep a close eye on. But if he wasn't the villain, we still had nothing. Either way, I was beginning to see Rick as a serious threat.

I exhaled a deep sigh just before I was about to give up. Then Mason answered.

"Mom, hey."

"Just calling to check in."

"I'm still with Nolan."

"Is everything going all right?"

"Everything is fine. Why?"

"I haven't spoken to you all day. Have you eaten anything?"

"I visited the cafeteria and have been picking from Nolan's plate."

"Mason." I sighed.

"He wasn't eating it. Anyway, I guess I should tell you now that I was planning to attend tonight's vigil."

"Good. I think you should go."

"Nolan wants me to go, too."

That made me smile. "As long as you'll be with friends and people you can trust."

"Of course, Mom."

"I'll be there, too, reporting." Mason didn't react. "Do you need me to pick you up and give you ride?"

"No, Natalie said she can take me."

My brows slanted. "She's going to leave Nolan?"

"Nolan asked her to attend for him. His dad said he would stay here, keep Nolan company. But I think Nolan is just going to sleep."

I asked Mason more about Nolan and he gave me a quick update. He said Nolan was tired, a bit sore, but his spirits were high. "Message me when you get there. I'd like to see you."

After Mason promised he would, we ended our call with my head swimming in self-reflection. I didn't want to hold my son back, and certainly didn't want him to stop living his life, but I was terrified about the fact that someone wanted him dead. I wasn't sure I would ever be able to let that go—at least not until this second shooter was caught.

I found Erin and Allison already huddled around a table in the back, curling their lips around their bright green straws. I slid in next to Allison on the booth and asked, "Anyone heard from Susan?"

"Running late but says she's on her way." Allison nodded and nudged my shoulder. "Hey, everything all right? You're looking rather glum."

I could feel my sour mood pulling my face down. "Just worried about my son."

Erin brought her elbows to the table and tipped forward. She didn't waste time in bringing up Rick Morris. After giving us context to her question, she asked, "What do you think Rick meant when he said, *I will make certain you soon learn who the true villain really is?*"

Allison tucked her chin into her neck and flashed me a questioning look.

Staring into her fudge colored eyes, I said, "I'm worried that Rick will cause further trouble."

"And I think he might want to increase the attacks on journalists." Erin's neck craned.

Allison came up with the same conclusions as we had, unable herself to decide on anything conclusive. "But what I can tell you is that I did some digging and read the scripture he quoted." Allison nodded once. "The guy seems like he might have a screw loose."

Thinking the same, I asked, "Did you find any links to the Patriots of God?"

"Not on Rick." Allison's lips pinched.

"But you did on somebody?" I glanced to Erin who was equally as curious to know what Allison would reveal.

Allison bounced her gaze between Erin and me. Then she nodded. "Now, just to be clear, I haven't been able to break past the firewall on Timothy Morris's social media accounts, but I did find a public post with him in it."

"What did it say?" Erin blurted out.

My knee bounced hysterically beneath the table as I held my breath, unable to control my anxiety.

"It wasn't what it said, it was what Timothy was *doing*."

Goosebumps filled my arms beneath my sleeves. "What was he doing?"

Allison lowered her brow and everything went still. "Tim was getting a tattoo last month."

"A tattoo of what?"

Allison raised her brows and I watched the whites in her eyes grow. "A white eagle medallion."

"The symbol of Patriots of God," Erin murmured as she fell softly into the back of the booth. "I saw it when doing research on the organization."

My mind jumped back and forth between Professor Croft and Rick Morris. "If it wasn't on Tim's page, where did you find it?"

"It was posted on the tattoo parlor's page."

"I guess they haven't figured out that they might want to disassociate themselves from a known mass murderer," Erin mumbled.

There was movement out of the corner of my eye and, when I turned, I found Susan stumbling across the finish line with the stooped posture of an exhausted marathon runner.

She fell into the booth with a thud and leaned into Erin. "I've had a day to remember."

We were all still in shock from learning what Allison found and we quickly caught Susan up to speed. "This is so bizarre." Susan lifted her head off Erin's shoulder.

"You don't have to tell us." Allison sucked from her straw.

"No. You don't understand." Susan suddenly seemed nervous.

We all shared a look, wondering what was going on.

Susan filled us in on the kind of day she was having and added, "As I was leaving the office to come here, I was presented with a donation which came with a stipulation."

"What kind of stipulation?" I asked.

"Can you actually do that?" Erin inquired.

Susan shrugged one shoulder. "The donor said the money had to go to the Morris family."

A collective gasp circled the table. This time, I fell back into the booth with my thoughts crashing to the front of my mind in tall, never ending swells. Suddenly, everywhere we looked the Patriots of God seemed to be making a comeback.

# CHAPTER THIRTY-SEVEN

PASTOR MICHAELS WAS IN HIS STUDY PREPARING FOR tonight's vigil when Youth Pastor Peter Mullen knocked on his door. Pastor Michaels's lips fluttered soft whispers as he finished reading the last line of text before glancing up.

"Sorry to interrupt, but it's time."

Pastor Michaels quickly noticed Mullen's shoulder bag already draped down at his side. "I need a few more minutes. Go ahead without me, I'll meet you there."

"Are you sure?"

Meeting his Youth Pastor's eyes above the rim of his reading glasses, Pastor Michaels nodded. "It's fine. I won't be long."

Mullen nodded and smiled. "We'll see you there then."

Pastor Michaels watched Mullen turn and leave his study in the same quiet manner he had entered. Casting his gaze downward, he went back to reading.

Pastor Michaels knew that his words tonight needed to be perfect. He couldn't afford to have any spin on his interpretation of what happened yesterday. He certainly didn't want his own anger to come out and be misconstrued as something other than what he truly intended.

He picked up a red pen, scribbled a couple of notes off to the side, and heard his staff leave the building. A calm silence swept into his office and Pastor Michaels felt the tension in his back release.

The pastor loved these moments of solitude and quiet. It was when he could think the clearest and, often, when he completed his best work. He had time to search deep within his spirit, to repent and plead for God to give him the strength he often sought. However much he sought all those things, tonight, time was against him.

Another fifteen minutes passed before the pastor was finally happy with the final product.

Pushing back from his desk, he gathered his things and left his office with a satisfied grin curling his lips. Completely alone, his ears piqued and he listened to the sounds of his heels clacking in a rhythmic mantra as he moved to the nave.

Inside the grand room, the sounds echoed off the ceiling and stained-glass windows. The lighting was dim and it was here he found companionship with Jesus Christ, his Lord and Savior.

"My Lord, please give me strength to conduct tonight's event in a respectable manner."

He stared up at his Lord hanging from the Roman cross. The pastor knew his community was as torn up about yesterday's events as his own heart had been feeling—completely shredded. Over the last day and a half, he'd poured so much energy and strength into helping others grieve that he had found little time to devote attention to his own suffering.

Dropping to his knees, he bowed his head and began to pray.

*Our Father who art in heaven, hallowed be thy name. Thy kingdom come. Thy will—*

Suddenly, a cold rush of air swept in behind him.

Slowly, Pastor Michaels lifted his head, turned, and faced the front entrance.

With his heart pounding, he watched the big door creak back and forth on its hinges.

Tugging his eyebrows together, he convinced himself it was nothing. Pastor Mullen had probably simply forgotten to latch it shut when he had left nearly a half-hour ago. But no matter what he told himself, inside his heart he knew it could be something different.

The pastor stood and walked to the door with all feelings of serenity vanishing with the wind. Now, as he made his way to the back of his empty church, a wave of fear crawled beneath his dark skin.

A wind gust slammed the door wide opened.

The pastor jumped back with surprise as he gripped his racing heart.

He stepped forward and lunged for the door. Catching the edge inside his hand, he went to quickly shut it before all the heat in the room escaped. Before he could, something caught his eye.

With one foot out the door, he darted his gaze around. The sidewalks were empty. No one was there. His breath clouded in front of his face as he stared down at the shiny metallic object laid out on the top step like a gift.

His world started to spin.

Everything inside of him froze.

Bending at the waist, he plucked it from the ground and knew immediately what it was. A white eagle medallion, the symbol of a far uglier time he had hoped he would never see again.

Standing tall, he took one glance around before retreating safely back inside his church.

# CHAPTER THIRTY-EIGHT

AFTER FINALLY GETTING BOTH FOOD AND A MARGARITA into my system, we arrived as a wolf pack to the vigil an hour later. It was just the four of us at first, but I soon locked eyes with Pastor Michaels.

"I'll catch up with you in a bit," I said, excusing myself from the group.

With my hands buried inside my jacket pockets, I skirted the sidelines and kept one eye on the lookout for my son. People seemed to be coming from all directions but none were Mason. Pastor Michaels met me halfway and immediately asked me about my son.

Gripping my phone tight, I was waiting to hear from him myself. "He should be here soon."

"It would be great to see him," Pastor Michaels said.

"I'll be sure he finds you tonight." The pastor grinned. "Hey, I wanted to apologize about not being able to help spread the word about tonight. Apparently, I was too late for my publisher to sign off on the approval."

The pastor clasped his long fingers in front of his chest and looked around at the impressive turn out. A grin sprouted on his lips. "I think the Lord spread the word for us."

"So, I'm forgiven?"

"We can only give our best efforts."

"Sometimes that's all I have." I glanced to my feet and kicked the grass around with my toe. "I was assigned to write a column on tonight's gathering." I lifted my head and the pastor rolled his gaze back to me. "I was hoping I could highlight you and the work you do for this community."

"Highlight the victims." He nodded. "It's their stories that need to be heard."

I told him my angle, how I had the same plan, when we were abruptly interrupted.

"Excuse me, Pastor, but it's time."

Pastor Michaels held up a finger to indicate he would be there shortly.

"We're already running behind schedule."

Pastor Michaels acknowledged his staff's request, then turned to me and chuckled. "I tend to forget time exists when there are so many friends I would like to greet."

"It's been good talking with you."

The pastor's brows slanted. "Sam, there is something I would like to speak with you about. Tonight. In private."

As my watery gaze danced inside his aging eyes, I could see something serious was on his mind. His mood had flattened, along with his lips.

"Will you find me before you leave? It's important."

"Yes, certainly," I breathed.

The glimmer of light came back to his eyes when he reached for my shoulder. "Now, if you'll excuse me, the Lord's work is calling."

I watched him leave, unable to peel my feet off the grass floor. He'd left me feeling completely unsettled. Something had him spooked.

As I looked for the girls, I teetered on the balls of my feet. Thoughts bombarded me about how vulnerable we all were, standing out here in the open, waiting to be picked off by the second shooter I knew was still out there somewhere.

Two arms were waving overhead, fifty yards to the north. I felt my mouth curl as I noticed the familiar face. But it was the flutter in my heart at the sight of King that had me excited to see him. And, when Mason popped up behind King a second later, I dug my toes into the dirt and sprinted toward both of them.

Leaping into Mason's arms, everything else became blurry. I heard nothing but his breath. Felt nothing but his lungs breathing. By the time I had Mason blushing in complete embarrassment, I released him and turned to King. As soon as I latched on to him, I could feel how tense he was.

"Hey." His voice was crushed gravel.

The moment my heels hit solid ground, I asked, "Are you all right?"

I didn't expect him to answer. Not in front of Mason. But I could see it in his eyes, and I knew he was thinking the same thing I was. Having the vigil outside made for the perfect ambush. We were all sitting ducks—even with the police securing the area.

Not voicing my concerns, I asked, "Did you look further into the Patriots of God?"

King was looking everywhere but at me. "Sorry, Sam, too much work at the school. The place is a war zone."

A woman approached, passing out candles. We each took one and our conversation was quickly drowned out by the sounds of a microphone.

Pastor Michaels and his team were on-stage, leading the crowd in prayer.

I caught sight of Nancy Jordan and we shared a quick glare before joining the choir in singing the first hymnal. Not long into the song, another woman passed around small white crosses. As soon as I took one into my hand, I thought of Rick Morris.

Squeezing King's hand, he lowered his head. Standing on tip-toes, I whispered into his ear, "I think you should look into Rick Morris."

He twisted his neck and arched a brow.

I told him more about the two running theories Erin and I had about his statement and what he meant by it, who the true villain might be.

"There's no crime in him speaking out," King said.

The mood was sad, peaceful. Everyone seemed to be coming together as one. Students of all races and genders were linked at the arms in a show of unison. Some held signs with messages including *Books not bullets; I want to live; No fear;* and *I'm not scared.* I wanted to smile, I really did but, more than anything, I wanted King to see what I was seeing inside my head.

"No, I know," I said. "But did you hear what he said to the media today?"

King hadn't and I briefed him as best I could.

"Rick was holding a cross just like this. Wouldn't you like to know if he has any past affiliation with the Patriots of God? He could be the person we're all looking for." But as soon as I heard myself say it, I knew how ridiculous is sounded. If a white cross was all I had to go on, then tonight, everyone who held one was as guilty as Rick.

*That thought was quickly followed by questions: Who'd paid for these? Could it have been planned to take our eyes off one of our two prime suspects? Was Croft, then, the man we should be chasing?*

As if on cue, the air filled with shouts of anger. A burst of commotion followed a second later and, when I followed the noise with my eyes, I could see what had caused the disturbance.

My pulse ticked so hard I could feel it in my throat.

King gripped my hand at the same time I latched onto Mason's coat with my other.

I couldn't believe what I saw next. What had begun as a peaceful gathering to mourn the dead had turned into aggressive activism by a small group of passionate protesters.

# CHAPTER THIRTY-NINE

THE SNIPER STARED AT THE FLIER, WONDERING IF HE HAD made a mistake. He couldn't stop wondering what the kid in the park had meant when he said, *Even from you.*

Taking the rearview mirror into his hand, the Sniper angled it onto himself. He stared into his own glimmering eyes, questioning whether the sparkle he saw was suspicion or excitement. Perhaps a little bit of each.

*Did he know who I was?* It wouldn't be that hard to connect the dots. He'd talked to people he shouldn't have. Said things he probably shouldn't have. These were the same people he knew were trying to connect anyone to Tim. And, instead of hiding, he'd kept to his daily schedule hoping to hide in plain sight.

Living on borrowed time, the Sniper knew he had to act.

He turned his head and flicked his gaze out his window.

The sounds of sirens wailed somewhere off in the distance. He listened intently as the sound grew faint, heading away from where he was parked.

Since visiting Highland Park—the place of tonight's vigil—his heart hadn't stopped racing. Everything sent it into a frantic rhythm and he thought it might explode. Despite his self-imposed will to relax, tonight that was proving to impossible. He had grown increasingly sensitive to noises that surrounded him, spooked as easily as a cat. Some minutes he felt the walls closing in on him, while other times the adrenaline he felt pumping through his veins gave him a false sense of confidence—and his cue to go.

Convinced his location hadn't been blown, he took the paper flier into his hand once again and lifted it into the light. The vigil was to begin at 8PM, fifteen minutes from now. He could only hope that Pastor Michaels had received his gift.

Inhaling a deep breath of air, his chest expanded fully and the Sniper knew that he had done his due diligence to get him to this point. He had planned and obsessed over every last detail. Now it was time to move to his next location and prepare to send this city into chaos.

The Sniper opened his door and moved to the trunk of his car. The street lights flickered on overhead. He glanced around and made sure he wasn't being watched before opening the back. Parked between a rusty old pickup and a two-door sedan, he remained hidden.

The trunk bounced open and the Sniper reached inside, going for his new jet-black baseball cap. Tugging it low, he next slid his arms through a matching jacket. It was thin, but adrenaline promised to keep him warm. Finally, he reached for his trusty guitar case and prepared himself for war.

Slamming his trunk shut, he turned on a heel and trotted down the sidewalk. A couple blocks later, he stopped and stared at the house he had scoped out last night. Standing on the opposite side of the street, he watched as the family inside went about their evening—assuming nothing of what their evening would become.

A tingle of excitement flushed through his body.

Flicking his wrist, he checked the time and knew he had to keep moving.

Taking an obscure and round-about route in order to cover his tracks, he finally found himself staring up at the fire escape of the Park Hill Branch Library. It had closed for the day two hours earlier and the parking lot was now deserted.

Heaving his guitar case to the top, he shimmied his way to the roof. Settling near a vibrating and loud air vent he settled in, knowing it would be perfect to silence the sound of the single shot he vowed to take in a few short minutes.

Kneeling on both knees, the Sniper clicked open his case, assembled his rifle, and lay down on his stomach before tossing a white blanket—the same color as the rooftop—over his back for both warmth and camouflage.

With his rifle securely on the ground next to him, he dove his hand beneath his collar. Pulling out the chain around his neck, he kissed the white eagle medallion perched above the colors he swore he would die to protect, no matter the cost.

Now he waited in the dark, undetected.

With one eye open, he held his rifle in his hands and scoped the area toward his target. The crosshairs—the shape of the cross—acted as a reminder that Jesus, the son of God, was on the soldier's side.

Then, his watch started beeping with the alarm he had set earlier. Alerting him to the time, he reached for the burner phone at his side and dialed 911.

"Hello, this is 911, what is your emergency?"

"I'd like to report shots fired."

"Sir, what is your address."

The Sniper revealed the location and quickly hung up the phone.

# CHAPTER FORTY

DENNIS HALL WAS SITTING DOWN FOR DINNER WITH HIS wife and two young children when he noticed his white walls begin blinking a bright red and blue.

He shared a concerned look with his wife before pushing back from the table. His wife's hand landed on his arm, gripping it tight. There was fear flashing over her brown eyes but, not wanting to spook her children, she spoke with only a look.

"I'm just going to see what this is about," Dennis told his wife.

She reluctantly released her grip and snapped at the children to quiet it down.

"Mommy, what is going on?" the older of the two boys asked.

"Just eat your dinner," Dennis heard his wife say as he moved toward the front of the house. Peeking through the front window curtains, a sudden coldness hit his core when he saw two police cruisers parked in his lawn.

Dennis's youngest came running toward him. "Stay in the kitchen!" He snapped his fingers and pointed. He watched his child's eyes pop wide open before he darted back to the dinner table. Dennis turned back to the window. *What the hell is going on?*

"What's going on, Dennis?" his wife asked.

"I'm about to find out." With his heart pounding, he reached for the doorknob. *This has got to be a prank.*

"Don't go out there, Dennis," his wife pleaded.

Determined to get some answers to what this was all about, Dennis held his palm up to silence his wife and opened the door.

As soon as it cracked open, the police began shouting for him to come out and put his hands behind his head. Hiding behind the door, Dennis felt his limbs begin to shake. Four officers stood in a wide stance with their hands gripping their holstered handguns.

"I'm not coming out until you tell me what this is about," Dennis yelled.

His heart shot into his throat when he saw four guns being drawn and pointed at him. Blood thrashed in his ears and he started to hyperventilate. *This is a mistake. They have the wrong house.*

"You have thirty seconds to come out or we'll come in after you," an officer shouted.

Dennis thought about his family, knew he was innocent of any crimes, and had only one logical choice—he had to face the cops.

Sucking a deep breath of air into his lungs, Dennis first showed the officers his empty hands while keeping his body hidden behind the wall. Slowly, he revealed more of his large body, inch by inch, until he was staring into the blinding spotlights pointing at him.

The police screamed for him to slowly approach, clasp his hands behind his head. "Now get on your knees!" they yelled.

As if moving in slow motion, Dennis bent his knees when,

suddenly, a hot searing pain tore open his left lung, hitting him directly in the heart. He gasped as the velocity of the bullet that knocked him onto his back.

The dark sky above swirled as he lay on the cold concrete steps, coughing up hot blood. He heard his wife wail and, when he blinked next, she was there hovering over him.

"Dennis. Dennis." She pinched his cheeks with tears falling from her eyes.

There was no pain. Only confusion. "I love you baby. You and the kids—" A bright flash of light filled his vision. Then a loving calm swept over Dennis as everything went black.

# CHAPTER FORTY-ONE

EVERYONE SEEMED AS STUNNED AND CONFUSED AS I WAS. We hadn't moved, our feet glued in place. The songs and prayers had stopped as our jaws dangled at the sight of the two opposing sides now facing off.

"Mom, what is going on?" Mason whipped his head around as he stood taller.

"I'm not sure." I squeezed King's hand.

"Don't they know we're here to pray in peace?" Mason kept insisting it was wrong. And I agreed, but there was nothing I could do to stop this from happening.

Chaos swirled around us in a dizzying array of tornadoes. Conversations were swept up in the wind storm and strong words were lobbed like grenades.

I whipped my head to the right.

A new charge of people ran toward the protestors.

Snapping my focus to the left, other people retreated to nearby pine trees for safety. Dogs barked and children clung to their mothers as they cried.

"This is going to get ugly," King said.

"Why aren't the police doing anything?" Mason bounced

on his toes as I waited for him to decide he had to join the fight.

"What can they do?" King's tone was loud enough to be heard over the shouts. "The protestors have as much right to be here as we do."

"This isn't right." Mason breathed heavier.

I liked that Mason listened to King. He wasn't wrong, even if I understood what Mason was saying. None of this seemed right.

When the sea of people parted, I caught sight of Natalie Dreiss. She was stunned, not sure what to do as she watched the peaceful event she'd come to support suddenly turn into something much different.

"Natalie," I yelled, waving my white cross high above my head. When she didn't hear me, I called her name again, finally getting her attention.

She blew out her candle and trotted over to us. I slung my arm around her shoulders as soon as she joined our group. "Can you believe this?" she said to me. "How dare they choose tonight to protest?"

Linking arms, we formed a wall. Me, King, Mason, and now Natalie holding onto each other to keep the others from falling.

As the energy of the two sides intensified, a blind man could see that this wasn't just about what was right or wrong, but a clash between black and white. And as the white protestors shouted about racial injustice, the blacks telling them to take it somewhere else, it was the shirts the protestors wore that sent a chill down my spine.

Each of them had the slogan *Soldiers in Arms for a More Prosperous America* printed in bright bold red colors across their chests. They raised their picketing signs like pitchforks and a few wore helmets as if expecting things to turn violent.

Frisking the crowd with my eyes, I was just waiting to see Rick Morris.

Soon, the girls found their way to us and Erin sidled up to my side. "Sam, this is Croft's doing."

Nodding, I grinded my teeth thinking how Croft had played innocent with us. He knew what he had planned for tonight—the protest he was most likely assisting his students with. I couldn't wait to confront him about this and close my fingers around his neck.

A loud roar erupted near the podium where I had last seen Pastor Michaels standing. Arms swung wildly through the air as large bodies dog-piled on one person. I couldn't make out who was who, only that things seemed to be getting out of control quick.

I heard Susan gasp and, when I glanced at her, she was staring with her hand covering her mouth in disbelief. I didn't know what I could do without putting myself in danger. I kept shaking my head. *How could this be happening?*

A handful of uniformed officers rushed the people fighting. More punches were thrown, more violent words tossed at the opposing side. Soon, the police had a couple people in cuffs but things only seemed to intensify when, suddenly, I recognized a face from our visit to the community college.

"Erin, look," I said.

Erin lowered her brow. "I knew it," she growled.

"But where is Croft?"

Erin turned and gave me a look. Against King's advice, we took off in search of the professor.

"We just need a photo to place him here," Erin said, pushing her way through the crowd.

We stuck together, not wanting to lose the only safety net we had. But Erin was right, we needed something—anything —to link Croft to this protest so we could build our case that he was in fact using his classroom to resurrect the Patriots of God.

Erin hit the brakes and swung her head around. Turning back to face the crowd, we couldn't find Croft anywhere.

"He's not here," I said, pushing my fingers through my hair. *And neither is Chandler.*

"Who are you looking for?" a familiar voice said from behind.

I turned to find Nancy Jordan flanking us. "Don't you have somewhere you need to be?"

"Don't you?" She quirked a painted brow.

"Come on, Sam." Erin reached for my arm. "We don't have time for this."

"He's not here," Nancy barked. She flicked her gaze to Erin. "Professor Croft isn't here."

"How do you know that's who we're looking for?"

Nancy's eyes drifted to the protestors. "Isn't it, though?"

"Have you been following us?" Erin stepped up to Nancy and glared down into her flashing eyes.

"I know what you're up to," Nancy sneered. "It would make one hell of story, too."

My stomach clenched as I stared into Jordan's eyes. I wondered how much she knew, how much was meant to get me to react simply to reveal my cards.

"What do you say? Work together on this, Sam?"

Erin was shaking her head as I let Jordan's words bounce around my mind for a brief moment. "I'll tell you what, you send me what you have and I'll think about it."

Nancy Jordan held out her hand. "Shake on it?"

"Just send me what you have." I turned and scampered off with Erin.

"You can't be serious." Erin sounded disgusted.

"Maybe she has something we don't."

"I can't stand that woman. There's no way I'll be able to work with her. You don't really trust her, do you?"

"I just want to know what she has. If she knows as much as we do, I don't want her to risk tipping off the man who might have instructed Tim to kill my son."

King was on his cellphone by the time we regrouped. His brow was furrowed and the bags beneath his eyes were darker than when I had left him only a minute ago.

"I'm on my way now," I heard him say.

King lowered his phone to his side. "Sam, something has happened." I felt it before he said it. "There has been a police shooting."

"What? Where?"

"Park Hill."

"Is it the second shooter? Did they get him?"

King cast his gaze downward, his fingers going cold inside my hand. "I'm not sure what happened, but it sounds like a police officer may have killed an unarmed black man."

## CHAPTER FORTY-TWO

DETECTIVE ALEX KING ARRIVED ON SCENE WITH HIS stomach in knots. The last thing the department needed—no matter if the suspect was guilty or not— was for a black man's life to be taken at the hand of an officer.

Emergency lights flashed, illuminating the night sky in a flickering red and blue.

He drove as close as he could get before parking his sedan. The block had been cordoned off and the roars from the neighborhood cracked the air like a whip as soon as he stepped out.

Suddenly, he was engulfed in a flame of chaos.

His muscles tensed and, by his own assessment, King swore the entire neighborhood was here thrusting their closed fists into the air. It was ten times the energy of what he'd just witnessed at the vigil, though eerily similar.

"You murdered my brother!" a man shouted toward the house.

"Police can't be trusted!" another woman bellowed at the top of her lungs.

King heard everyone cursing the police and, as he

approached the line, it didn't take long for him to be called out for being on the wrong side of the line. "You fucking pig!" A woman spit in King's face but missed.

King kept pushing his way to the police line and flashed his badge to the uniformed officer standing on duty. Ducking beneath the tape, King tracked down Lieutenant Baker.

"Don't worry, they're abusing anyone who wears the color blue, not just you."

"And here I thought it was just because I was white."

The whites in Lieutenant's eyes glowed in contrast to his dark complexion.

"What happened?"

Lieutenant rolled his head toward the front of the house where he watched the tech team label evidence. "Received a call of shots fired. Four officers responded and, before we know it, we're on the scene of what the ME is calling a homicide."

"Let me guess, the officers were white?"

"Over there." Lieutenant flicked his gaze in the direction of where four uniformed white officers were being debriefed by Detective Alvarez. "According to the wife of the deceased, he was unarmed."

King slanted his eyebrows. "Was he?"

"Appears so." Lieutenant sighed.

"Do we have a positive ID on the victim?"

"Dennis Hall, age 34." Lieutenant sucked his lips into his mouth. "His record was clean. The vic doesn't even have a moving violation." Lieutenant glared at the crowd from under his brow. "I've never seen a situation so fucked up as this."

King twisted his spine and turned to face the crowd. "Word spread fast. Any witnesses?"

"That's where the story takes a turn."

King returned his focus to his superior officer with both eyebrows raised.

"Even stranger is that none of our officers fired a weapon."

King felt the air get knocked out of him. He stared into Lieutenant Baker's chestnut eyes for a brief pause before flicking his gaze back to where the victim had been shot. He feared this was the second shooter—the cop killer. He felt guilty for not being able to connect the dots before another tragedy struck. But it had only been hours since he and Alvarez decided on that theory themselves.

King scrubbed a hand over his face. "This might be connected to yesterday's shooting at the school."

"The second shooter?" Lieutenant shared a questioning look which King confirmed.

"Everyone had their sights on tonight's vigil, and maybe our suspect anticipated that to be the case."

Lieutenant Baker flashed King a skeptical look. "Why here? And why Dennis Hall?"

King stared at the front door of Dennis's house, shaking his head. "If this is the second shooter from yesterday, I guess we now know he's not just a cop killer."

"How does this help me, Detective?"

"Because chasing a cop killer might be easier."

"Easier?" Lieutenant's brows furrowed and was looking at King like he was crazy.

King glanced behind him once again, staring at the angry crowd. "Now he doesn't have to target cops himself when he has the city's African American community to do it for him."

"You mean to say he's trying to turn them against us?"

"If he is, I'd say he's doing a good job of it."

"You were at Pastor Michaels's vigil, right?" Lieutenant asked and King nodded. "Then tell me, what does that have to do with this?"

King realized then that Lieutenant Baker hadn't heard about the protestors cutting the vigil short. But he did know about the second shooter at the school yesterday, and that was enough to make the connection. "The vigil ended early when it erupted in protest."

"Decency doesn't exist, does it?" The muscle in Lieutenant's jaw twitched. "Who were the people protesting, and did they have a permit from the city?"

King thought back to earlier in the day when Sam brought his attention to the Patriots of God and, as he looked around tonight, there was no doubt in his mind that Sam was right. "I don't know who they were but I can tell you what they were saying."

"I'm all ears," Lieutenant said.

King repeated a few of the slogans he'd overheard and their theme of racial injustice. "But it was what a survivor heard Timothy Morris spouting off as he marched through the school yesterday that has me truly worried."

"I'm still following." Lieutenant's patience waned.

"Timothy Morris mentioned being a Patriot of God."

Lieutenant lowered his brow and muttered a few curse words under his breath as he looked around, finally seeing for the first time what was actually taking place within his city. "I hope you're wrong, Detective. If what you're saying is true, then God help us all."

# CHAPTER FORTY-THREE

MY WORLD SPUN AROUND ME IN A DIZZYING ARRAY OF colors. King's words that an unarmed black man may have been killed by a cop had knocked me off my axis. And, as I stood there not knowing what to do next, I couldn't stop wondering what, and where, Professor Croft and Rick Morris were up to now when the fabric of our city seemed to have suddenly come undone.

"We can't stay here." Susan rolled her shoulders back, firmly gripping her purse straps slung over her left shoulder.

"Neither can I," Natalie echoed. "My time is better spent with my son."

We quietly nodded our heads, pretending like we understood Natalie's grief but, the truth was, none of us could even come close to feeling the anxiety I could see lining her face. Wishing her our best, Mason turned to me with clenched fists as soon as Natalie was gone. "Mom, you have to do something."

My heart was still racing as I tried to come up with a solution for what I should do next. Erin and Allison were looking at me as if my decision would also influence their own. Maybe it would have, but I still had to write Dawson a story. I had to stay. Find out more about this group of protestors and why they'd decided to target the candlelit vigil. And if they were somehow connected to the Patriots of God.

"Mason's right, we have to do something," I said.

"What, Sam? What can we do?" Susan argued, flinging her hand toward the unruly crowd.

"Look around." I spread my arms out wide and craned my neck. "We can't leave when there are so many people suffering."

"Sam——" Susan frowned.

Flinging my arms down to my side, I dropped my chin and sidestepped to stand next to Mason. "I have work to do."

"Then I'm not leaving either." Erin stepped forward.

"And neither am I." Allison grinned along with Erin.

Susan bounced her gaze around the circle and, by the look on her face, I could see that she was succumbing to peer pressure. I felt a flood of gratitude bloom across my chest when Allison linked arms, and I was hit with warmth when Susan finally conceded to the group's demands.

"We stick together," Susan said.

"Always and forever."

Closing our circle, we all huddled together feeling the power of friendship radiate through our smiles as we swayed back and forth on our heels. Our eyes were bright and determined. Even Mason was there, staring and grinning at our silly giggles.

"How can we help you, Sam?" Erin asked.

"All we need is to confirm that our suspicions about Croft are right." I looked into everyone's eyes, catching up the girls on the theory we were working. "Because I have a feeling that this story might make front page tomorrow and I can't afford to get it wrong."

"Mom, look."

I lifted my head and found Pastor Michaels trudging his way to our little circle. "Mason, come with me." We moved swiftly to the pastor and quickly said, "What happened?"

"I had a feeling something like this might happen."

His words were as shocking as when the protestors interrupted our songs. I stepped closer, feeling my eyebrows tightly knit as I stared up into his brown eyes. "Did you know this was going to happen? Is that why you asked to speak with me after?" I felt my body tense as I worked myself up.

"Samantha," he lowered his voice, "you know me better than that."

I ran a hand over my head and forced myself to relax. "What are you saying, then?"

"There is something I need to show you. Something that could explain all this." He flicked his gaze to the crowd, watching the police fight to maintain civility.

"Okay. Show me," I said breathlessly.

"Not here." The pastor looked directly into Mason's eyes. "Son, how are you doing?"

"Fine." Mason shifted uncomfortably on his feet.

"Your mother told me your story from yesterday." The pastor paused. "How is your friend?"

"He's doing much better. Healing."

"I'm praying for him."

"What is it you have to show me?" I interrupted, knowing that I didn't have time to beat around the bush.

"Not in front of the boy."

I told Mason to wait by the mature tree nearby and, once it was just me and the pastor, he pushed his hand deep into his jacket pocket and pulled out a medallion. "I received this gift tonight." He opened his palm and we both stared at the object. "A white eagle medallion."

"The Patriots of God," I exhaled.

Pastor Michaels tipped his chin back and dropped it into

my hand. "You said Mason was on the school shooter's hit list?"

I swallowed and nodded. "The school shooter mentioned Patriots of God during his rampage."

A burst of shouts exploded behind us. We turned to watch the crowd grow further enraged.

"You said it was a gift; who gave it to you?" I asked.

"I'm not sure."

I narrowed my eyes.

"It was left on the top step of the church's front entrance just before I came here."

He told me the story in great detail and I felt lightheaded by the time he was finished. I cast my gaze back to the medallion. Deep inside, I knew that this was the reason why Mason was on the kill list. This group, this symbol, and the racist philosophy behind it explained everything.

I brushed my thumb over the medallion, thinking of the tattoo Timothy Morris got recently. Then my thoughts drifted to how, against all odds, I seemed to have found myself in the middle of an investigation so closely linked to my family, how a decision Gavin made years ago may have finally come back to haunt us all.

I lifted my gaze and met the pastor's eyes. "There is something I need to tell you, but I need you to promise me that it will remain between us."

"Your secret is safe with me."

I thought about King and my promise to keep this information top secret, but I knew that I had to tell the pastor in hopes of it leading me to find the person who was behind this. "It's highly likely that there was a second shooter yesterday."

"At the school?" The crease between his eyes deepened.

I nodded. "And his two targets were the two officers killed."

The pastor stared with thoughts churning over. "I heard both officers were black."

"It's true." I felt my pulse grow weak. "And you knew one of them well."

"Who?" The pastor's head tilted to one side.

"Cook Roberts."

Pastor Michaels pressed the flat of his hand over his heart. I watched his gaze drop to the white eagle medallion as I tried to give it back.

"No." He closed my hand, wrapping the medallion inside my fingers. "You keep it."

"And do what with it?"

"Find out if the group is back or not."

"I'm afraid I already know it is, and something tells me you do, too." I heard my voice shake and it sparked enough fear inside of me for my knees to quake.

A sullen look fell over the pastor's face. "If it's true, then lots of old feelings will resurface and a simple nudge would be all it takes to plummet our community back into the race war many of us haven't forgotten."

"Like what happened here tonight?" My voice grew shrill as I pointed to the protestors.

"Yeah." He breathed, his eyes turning to slits. "Exactly like what happened here tonight."

My thoughts traveled to King and the call he'd received from Lieutenant Baker. An unarmed black man had been killed and I was just waiting for the next explosion to rock our city. "Any ideas who might have left you this memento?"

"No." Pastor Michaels leaned close and lowered his voice. "But I can see in your eyes that you do."

"I have an idea but I can't say for sure."

"You're one of the best reporters I know, Samantha. If anyone can figure it out, it would be you." He straightened his spine and stood tall. "But please stay vigilant. Gavin was a vocal opponent of this group, and if they find out you're snooping around God only knows what might happen."

My heart pounded harder. "Gavin was a vocal opponent of the Patriots of God?"

The pastor nodded. "He had enemies, even within the department who wished he wouldn't have taken some of the positions he did. If the Patriots of God are back, and know about you, Samantha, you could be in danger for what your husband did."

# CHAPTER FORTY-FOUR

A SHARP PAIN PULSED ACROSS MY CHEST. MY MUSCLES WERE tense, though my knees threatened to give. Inside, I crumbled with fear and confusion, not sure I knew what was going on anymore. The pastor's warning didn't line up with what I knew of Gavin. Even as I tried to sort it out inside my head, for every question answered two more were born.

Mason came running back to me. "Mom, what was that about?"

I stared at Pastor Michaels and watched him work his way back to the front lines. The crowd roared, heating up like an inferno about to explode. His battle was here, tonight, to bring peace to the crowd that had come to gather on his watch. But why did he leave me with the extraordinary task of having to learn of my husband's secret?

"What did he give you, Mom?"

I dropped the medallion into my pocket and turned to Mason. Not wanting to scare him any more than I knew he already was, I kept the medallion hidden. Our eyes danced and soon I felt mine begin to blur with tears.

Mason reminded me of Gavin. Gavin had given him so

many of my favorite traits, it was as if Gavin was here with me now. I clamped my hands around both of Mason's arms and didn't want to let go.

"Just something for my story," I said with blood sloshing between my ears.

There was more to my husband than what I knew and it left me feeling breathless. This medallion confirmed we were chasing a group thought to have been killed off. What had Gavin said about them to find himself making enemies within the department he worked?

A loud roar erupted behind us.

Mason and I turned to look.

Things were taking a turn and violence seemed imminent. "We have to go, baby."

"What? No," Mason pleaded. "You have to stay, tell this story. Just like you said you would."

I shook my head. This wasn't my place. Not anymore. "I got what I needed." My words were firm. "Now let's go." I tugged on Mason's arm.

It wasn't worth putting Mason in more danger than what I had already done. He'd escaped one attempt on his life, but would he again? The thought alone sent a cold shiver up my spine. I'd give my life to prevent him from having to live through another shooting.

Together we marched to where the girls were still huddled. The jab of regret stitched my side and I couldn't stop thinking about the secrets Gavin had kept from me. He'd told me everything. Why didn't he tell me about this? Did he think I would never have to know?

"Everything all right, Samantha?" Susan asked as soon as I arrived.

"We're leaving," I said.

Susan's brows shot up, surprised.

"Go to the car, Mason. I'll be there in a minute." I tossed

him the keys and pointed to where I'd parked before he trotted off.

"What's going on, Sam?" Erin had a quizzical look on her face.

I dove my hand inside my jacket pocket and revealed the white eagle medallion. "This."

Erin's eyes widened and flashed with a terrified curiosity. "Where did you get that?"

"What is it?" Allison asked.

Handing the medallion to Allison, she recognized it immediately. "It's the same as the tattoo Timothy Morris got."

I glanced over my shoulder toward the crowd and then shared with the girls what the pastor had told me. "The Patriots of God are back and they wanted the pastor to know."

"Jesus, we were right." Erin gasped. "Why give it to the pastor?"

My insides tied another knot. Shrugging, I said, "Maybe because whoever is behind this knows that Pastor Michaels is the leader of the black community."

"This is serious." Allison sighed.

I inhaled a deep breath, staring into the crowd. I didn't have the answers but something told me it had to do with whatever Gavin had done years ago. "We know more about what is happening than anybody else—maybe even more than the cops."

"Tell us what to do, Sam, and we'll do it." Susan inched closer.

I flicked my gaze to Susan. I knew she had an extremely full plate with the donations hitting her business's bank account and was itching to get back to the office. "I need you to think really hard about what the man who gave you that donation tonight looked like."

"You think it could be the same person who gave Pastor Michaels that medallion?" Susan's nose scrunched.

"It's worth looking into. I don't know the details of how you'll distribute the donations from the victim's fund, but if you have to give money to the shooter's family, please make it discreet."

"I'll do my best."

"Allison." Allison swept her gaze up to mine. "Break through Tim's firewall. We need to know who radicalized him, what he was saying in the days leading up to the school shooting, and how he chose his targets. Something tells me that will get us closer to who might be behind this."

"You got it." Allison nodded.

"I'll speak to his family again, ask about the tattoo." I whipped my head around. "Erin, figure out where the professor was tonight. We need to know why he chose this specific time to protest when emotions were already high. We know these are his students and we know he's a constitutionalist—"

"But is he a Patriot of God?" Susan asked.

I shrugged. "That's what we need to find out."

"What are you going to do, Sam?" Erin asked.

"Take Mason home and wait to see what King says about the call he received tonight." My head bobbed. "Then I'm going to find out where Rick Morris was tonight."

"The true villain," Erin whispered.

I nodded once. "He made the threat and then this happens? Seems too big of a coincidence for me not to think he might have somehow influenced tonight's activities."

Once we were all assigned with our next task, we group-hugged and made sure to tell each other how much we loved them when suddenly Allison's cellphone started ringing. She answered and was off the phone within seconds.

"Anything important?" I asked but didn't have to. Her face told me everything I needed to know.

"Where did you say King went?"

I felt the blood leave my face. "Park Hill. Why, was that him?"

She shook her head no. "But it sounds like the neighborhood in Park Hill is about to riot."

# CHAPTER FORTY-FIVE

AFTER SPLITTING FROM THE GROUP, I CALLED KING ON MY way to my car. Relief swept over me the moment he answered. "Hey," I said.

"Hey."

"I know you're busy—"

"Is everything all right?"

"Not really." I choked up. King had a way of making me weak. I could be myself, be vulnerable to him by not having to play tough girl. I loved that he had that effect on me, even when we were miles apart.

"Is it the protest? Did it get worse?"

I gave him a quick update on what was happening, promising him it was nothing too alarming, and said, "Tell me what's going on with you."

"I can't really talk about it, Sam."

I grinded my teeth, frustrated by his inability to talk about his job, but I understood. Our relationship was anything but conventional in the sense that a detective was dating a reporter. But I could trust him and he could trust me and that was enough to keep it feeling like we weren't totally keeping secrets from one another when we had to keep our answers short.

"Allison received a call and said something about Park Hill possibly rioting," I said with a furrowed brow.

"It's ugly, Sam." I felt my chest tighten when hearing King's words. "The emotions are high but, so far, people are choosing to keep their anger contained."

"Alex," I paused to gather what little strength I had left inside of me, "Pastor Michaels received a gift tonight I think you might find interesting."

The line went silent but I could still hear him breathing. I went on to tell him about the medallion, where the pastor had found it, and how he knew what it was. "Any chance that the protest at the vigil was a distraction from what you're working now?"

"I don't know about the protest, but without looking at the medallion myself, I'd say you're not too far off." King had to go and promised to call me later once he was finished canvasing the neighborhood.

"Be careful," I said as I ended our call.

By the time I joined Mason in the car, my son was busy scrolling through his social media accounts. "They stole the show, Mom. No one is talking about yesterday's victims anymore."

"Unfortunately, I think that was their intention, honey." I took the keys off the dash and slid them into the ignition.

"Why are they talking about racial injustice when they were white?"

"What are you reading?" I asked.

"Nothing. I'm watching videos of tonight's protest. They're already posted online."

I stared out over the hood of my car, not sure I had an answer. When a knock on my window kick-started my heart,

I startled and gasped. His sharp eyes shined through the glass and I recognized his face immediately.

"What is he doing here?" I mumbled as I opened my door.

"Mom, who is that?" Mason leaned over the center console and stared.

Pushing Mason back with the sharp part of my elbow, I said, "Stay in the car. This will only be a minute."

"Is that Mason inside?" Markus Schneider bent at the waist, attempting to sneak a peek at my son. I stood in front of him and blocked his view.

"I'm sorry, Markus, but now is not a good time."

Markus straightened his spine and stared. I tried to be polite but the timing couldn't have been worse. With my head still swimming in questions about the medallion, my concern for King, and the work I still had to do for Dawson, Markus being here now was nothing short of suspicious.

"I overheard what Pastor Michaels said to you."

My heart stopped. I crossed my arms over my chest and stared without blinking.

"You what?" I asked, thinking back to my conversation with the pastor.

I swore we were alone. How did Markus overhear? Where was he hiding? *Why was he snooping?* I swiveled my neck around on my shoulders, looking to see if we were alone. My friends were gone and, if I had to scream for help, no one would hear me over the sounds of the distant roars. I couldn't have been more vulnerable and was thankful I had Mason with me.

"I know, I know." Markus took a step back and showed me his palms. "I should have said something but I didn't want to interrupt." He paused and held my gaze. "It looked like you were having a serious conversation."

Pastor Michaels's words bounced around my head. All I

could hear was his warning that Gavin had many enemies, even inside the department. Could one of them have been Markus? I knew nothing about him, yet he seemed to know an awful lot about me.

"What are you doing here, Markus? When did you arrive?" This wasn't how I imagined us getting together and talking about Gavin. Now I wasn't even sure I could, after pulling a stunt like this.

"Supporting the community after yesterday's loss, just like everyone else. I've been here since the beginning." He squinted his eyes at me. "You're here working a story, aren't you?"

"I'm a reporter. I'm *always* working a story."

"Not just any story, though."

His words were too playful and confident for my liking. "What are you getting at?"

"What I'm trying to say," he huffed an uncomfortable chuckle, "is that I think you're wondering what all this has to do with the Patriots of God."

I snapped my lips shut and, once again, went stiff.

He wagged his finger in my face and smiled. "Don't worry. I won't tell, but you should know that it's not the first time I've heard that name."

"You don't know what you're talking about."

"No? Then how is this? There is a rumor floating around that Timothy Morris mentioned the group during yesterday's shooting."

"Where did you hear this?" I snapped, feeling my anger swell.

A glimmer caught his eye. "So, it is true."

I felt like a fool for falling into his trap. Maybe he knew, but maybe he was only baiting me to confirm a theory he was working himself. It was a technique I used—one Gavin had taught me long ago—and it was a good skill to have. But to be a victim of it? It didn't feel so hot.

"You don't have to answer. I know it's true." His eyes drifted over my shoulder to Mason. I once again blocked his view. "It isn't hard to learn as long as one knows where to look."

As I listened to Markus gloat about how great a detective he was, I couldn't recall ever seeing him at any point during tonight's vigil. Yet now here he was, confronting me when I was most susceptible to his abuse.

"Okay, so you're a decent detective. What does this have to do with what you *think* you heard Pastor Michaels say to me?"

Markus chuckled and leaned closer. "What you have to know, Samantha Bell, is that Pastor Michaels isn't as innocent as he appears."

I listened to the faint beating of my heart. I couldn't look away, no matter how hard I tried. Markus had my undivided attention and I was ready to hear him out—even if I was afraid to learn what he had to say next.

"You see, the pastor has a secret he is not telling you. I think it is something that could save your life."

# CHAPTER FORTY-SIX

My jaw unhinged and dangled off my face. I wasn't sure I was even breathing. What Markus just shared was shocking and, if proven to be true—and something inside me told me it would be—than everything wasn't what I thought.

"Mom, who was that?" Mason yelled through the window glass.

Keeping my eyes on Markus, I watched him skirt the edge of the crowd still gathered in the park before disappearing into the shadows. Mason was still talking to me but I didn't respond.

A tremble rocked through my bones and shook my limbs as fear took control.

Could what Markus said about Pastor Michaels be true? Did I know the pastor like I thought I did? My head squeezed with sudden pressure. There was too much information to keep up with, too many players who all seemed to want a part in the growing conspiracy surrounding me and my family.

"Mom, what are you waiting for? Let's go," Mason grumbled.

I pressed the flat of my hand to my heated forehead and felt the energy radiating from the crowd buzz louder.

When pressed, Markus insisted he was here to support the community in mourning the loss of the students but he couldn't tell me what time he arrived. That was a big question mark I couldn't get past—a gaping hole that left too much unknown. He had mentioned he would be here tonight when he first caught me outside the newsroom this afternoon, so maybe I was thinking too much into his presence.

I darted my eyes from side to side searching for the pastor but couldn't find him anywhere. The longer I stood there thinking about what Markus just shared, the more tonight's protests made sense.

"Can we go now?" Mason grumbled loud enough for me to hear.

Spinning around, I flung the door open and fell into my seat with a bang.

"Who was that?" Mason didn't bother taking his focus away from his phone.

"Someone your father used to work with," I murmured as I started the car. Pulling away from the curb, I pointed the car east. Turning to Mason, I asked, "Do you have clothes at Grandma and Grandpa Bell's house?

Mason's head flinched back slightly.

"Do you or don't you?" I raised my voice, feeling like I was running out of time.

"I do," Mason stuttered.

"And a toothbrush?"

"Everything, Mom." He squished his eyebrows together and spoke in a meek voice.

Keeping one hand on the wheel and an eye on the road, I swiped through my list of contacts in my cellphone and put a call in to Gavin's parents. After a couple of rings, Gavin's mother, Irene Bell, answered. "Hey Irene, it's Sam. I have Mason with me and was hoping he could sleep there tonight."

"Is everything all right?" It wasn't Irene's normal first response to be so concerned, but after yesterday, everyone was on edge.

I flicked my gaze to my son. *No. Everything is far from being fine.* "Everything is fine. It's just that I'm working on a tight deadline and would prefer if Mason wasn't left alone while I completed it."

"Yes. Yes. Of course. Roger and I are home watching television."

"Great. Thank you." I told Irene we would be there in under ten minutes and, as soon as I hung up the phone, I relaxed knowing Mason would be sleeping somewhere safe.

"Mom, what's happening in the world?"

I readjusted my grip on the steering wheel and swallowed. "I'm not sure I know myself."

"Nolan told me something that Tim said just before he shot Nolan."

My eyes grew wide as I held my last breath in my lungs until it burned. Mason stared but I couldn't look him in the eye. I knew what he was about to tell me.

"Nolan said he was looking for me."

My lips were dry and there was a thickness in my throat that made breathing hard. I knew I should have been the one to tell Mason earlier but I'd been afraid. Maybe it was best he heard it from his friend instead of me.

"I know I look different, but I never thought it would be a reason for someone to want to kill me."

I took my right hand off the gear shifter and reached to Mason. Pushing my fingers through his thick head of hair, I said, "Baby, the world can be a cruel place."

"I know, Mom. But I guess what I'm trying to say is, was

that why those people came to protest tonight? Because they don't like people of color?"

"It could be." I turned down the street Gavin's parents lived on. "You know, when your father and I started dating, people said all sorts of things."

"Because he was black?"

"And I was white." I nodded. "But you can't let their words stop you from living your life."

I slowed to a stop, parking in front of the house along the curb. Mason stared into his lap and was quiet for a long while before turning to face me. "Mom, am I safe?"

I shuffled my feet and sighed. "Do you feel safe?"

Mason cast his expression downward as he shook his head no. "Not always."

I reached for his hand. "Now are you feeling safe?"

"I don't know," he mumbled. Then he glanced at me out of the corner of his eye. "Do you feel safe?"

I froze. My tongue was tied. *Of course I didn't.* "C'mon, get your stuff. Grandma Bell is waiting." I pointed to the front door where Irene stood on the front stoop beneath the porch light in her night gown.

We scampered up to the house, arriving to open arms. Irene wrapped Mason up inside her old arms and squeezed him until Mason was embarrassed. Then it was my turn and, when I hugged her, I whispered, "Thank you."

"Sam, I've been watching the news. Something big happened in Park Hill. This doesn't have anything to do with yesterday, does it?"

My muscles were still weak when I nodded. "I think it might."

Irene gasped and covered her mouth with one hand.

"I'm hoping to learn more when I meet up with Alex King."

Irene pulled back and looked me in the eye. There was a

familiar sparkle that made me feel at home. "Mason told us about you two."

"I'm sorry," I frowned. "I've been meaning to say something."

"Don't bother, honey." Irene tipped her chin back and smiled. "You deserve to be happy. And, in case there is any doubt, Alex would have been Gavin's choice, too."

# CHAPTER FORTY-SEVEN

COOPER WAS CURLED UP AT MY FEET AS I SAT ON THE couch with my legs stretched out and my laptop perched on my thighs. I was researching the medallion that left me freaked out while keeping one eye on the news.

As soon as I'd said a quick hello to a tired Roger and said my goodbyes to Mason and Irene, I headed straight home. The entire drive, I thought about Irene's comment about me now dating Alex. But, more than anything else, I thought about how I couldn't answer Mason's question about whether or not I felt safe.

I felt awful about it. Not wanting to lie to him, Mason didn't have to wait for an answer because he already knew what I was going to say. I didn't feel safe. But what really left me feeling unsettled was the fact that I couldn't put a finger on the danger I felt lurking.

Cooper lifted his head and gave me his sweet puppy dog look as if reading my mind. I swore he could sometimes. "I know, buddy, you'll keep me safe." I scratched behind his ear with my toe.

Cooper lowered his head and went back to sleep. Even

with him here, the house was far too quiet for complete comfort.

The TV screen flashed in the corner of the room and, as I read the headlines from the continuous coverage of what was happening in Park Hill, my thoughts were with King.

I hadn't heard from him since the last time we'd spoken on the phone. As the minutes turned to hours, my thoughts kept me in a perpetual state of uncertainty. But at least I knew where he was and that he wasn't alone.

A surge of emotions resurfaced and I could no longer keep my blood from boiling over.

I closed out my internet browser and booted up a new Word document. My fingers went straight to work, pounding at the keys, as my thoughts poured out of me.

I rehashed my day, relived my night, the words spilling onto the page easily. What was originally planned as a story to call for peace and unity quickly turned into something that sounded more like a far-fetched conspiracy. As soon as I mentioned a second shooter still on the loose, I knew I couldn't put it to print.

Two hours had passed by the time I checked my phone. It was now after midnight and there was still no update from King.

*Hey. Just thinking of you. I'd love to see you tonight. I'm home.*

After sending my message, I set my laptop down on the coffee table and sank deeper into the couch. Exhaustion pulled at my eyelids. As I drifted to sleep, I suddenly found myself wide awake when remembering something Markus had said earlier.

Pushing myself upright, Cooper raised one brow. "It's all right, boy. Just struck with a thought."

I reached for my laptop and quickly typed Pastor Michaels's name into the search bar. As my screen populated, I flicked my gaze to the white eagle medallion.

*Why did you give that to me?* I asked myself.

I didn't want it. Maybe he was hoping that it would be enough reason for me to search for what I was now looking for.

When I rolled my gaze back to my computer screen, Pastor Michaels's face filled my search results. A flood of memories came rushing back. The day he officiated my wedding ceremony with Gavin and how Gavin insisted it had to be him. I remembered Mason's baptism and the smile on Pastor Michaels's face as he held the crying child; the countless Sundays I attended his service. We had a long history and yet, now, as I stared into his picture on my computer screen, I wondered if I knew him at all.

Digging deeper into the pastor's online life, my heart beat wild with anticipation.

My eyes scanned the text and I read as fast as I could, only slowing down when landing on specific details I didn't know.

Pastor Michaels was an activist in the mid-1990s and apparently an outspoken critic of what he called "institutionalized workplace suppression," or his way of saying the policy of affirmative action wasn't working.

I didn't find this all too surprising. I knew Pastor Michaels fought for the rights of the African American community—he always had. But it was another piece that stole my attention.

According to the article, Pastor Michaels organized marches to rally against racial injustice during the same years King mentioned the Patriots of God coming onto the scene. The irony of the same thing happening at his vigil tonight didn't pass me.

I kept reading.

And what I saw next lifted the hair on the back of my neck.

Backing away from my computer screen, it was just like Markus said. I couldn't believe I hadn't heard anything about this until tonight. My head floated as stars flashed across my vision. This was huge, and yet there was no reason for me to know. But, even so, I hated the feeling like I had been purposely left in the dark over something this big.

I reached for the medallion and plucked it off the table.

Stroking the piece of metal with my thumb I muttered, "That's why you were given the medallion. *You're* their next target."

# CHAPTER FORTY-EIGHT

Erin Tate pushed her way through the knots of protestors, snapping photos with her cellphone along the way. She needed to record everything she could tonight because somebody here knew more about the Patriots of God and who was behind its resurrection than what she knew herself.

She ducked beneath racial slurs. Snapped photos of screaming men and woman. And spun her way around, making sure to get as many faces recorded as possible.

"Are you a student at Community College of Denver?" she asked a young man, receiving no response. She asked another, then another. Her words, time and again, fell on deaf ears. When no one responded, she started to feel like she was a ghost who they couldn't see.

Erin came to an abrupt halt.

Standing on the tips of her toes, she scanned the sidelines with hopes of spotting Professor Croft.

Nothing.

She'd been at it for hours and she still had no leads.

The police had managed to control the crowd from the initial violence that erupted earlier and were now telling everyone they had to leave the park or face arrest. Few listened and time was running out for Erin.

Going back to work, she asked a young woman, "Why did you come here to protest tonight?"

"Read the sign, woman!"

The woman shoved her shoulder into Erin's chest and pushed her out of the way. Erin winced and gripped her ribs as the air was knocked out of her. Gasping for breath, Erin managed to refill her lungs seconds later. When she stood back up, she froze.

Markus Schneider stared with unwavering eyes.

Erin felt her pulse speed up when suddenly she was knocked over again. The crowd of people around her swallowed her up and, by the time she resurfaced, Markus was gone.

Whipping her head around in all directions, Erin couldn't find him.

She wondered if Sam had seen him, thinking he was most likely looking for her. She shook off her thoughts and went back to searching for more information that could link Croft to tonight's protest.

Erin backpedaled, withdrawing from the crowd, and tried a new strategy to target the people hanging to the back. Again, no one was interested in speaking, and certainly didn't want to go on record.

Feeling defeated, Erin was about to give up when a young woman stepped up to her and said, "You're asking if we are from the community college?"

Erin blinked and stared. "Yes."

The woman gave Erin a quick sideways glance. "I saw you today."

"You did?"

"Professor Croft's class." She smiled.

"Is he here?" Erin asked. "I'd really like to speak

with him."

"Look," the woman stepped closer, "I'll make you a deal."

"What kind of deal?"

"If I'm going to allow you to interview me, then you need to make sure my name is front and center in whatever paper you get your story published in."

Erin shifted her weight to her opposite leg. She thought about her website and podcast with Sam and said, "I might be able to do that."

"Oh," the woman wiggled her eyebrows, "and tag me in all the social media posts, too." She grinned. "I want to go viral."

Erin resisted the urge to roll her eyes at the ridiculous request but decided to play along. After having a night like this one, she was about to do anything to learn what Croft said to get his students to come here tonight—and be so passionate about it, too.

"I think I can do that."

"Great. My name is Heidi Strauss." The woman perked up. "What do you want to know?"

Erin jotted down Heidi's name. "Is everyone here from Professor Croft's class?"

"Nah. Not everyone." Heidi pointed to the current students and then picked out a dozen faces she said were from prior classes Croft taught. "We might not be all from the same class, but we did all come here to make sure our voices could be heard."

Erin did a quick once-over of Heidi. She was well dressed, seemed to come from a well-to-do family. Erin couldn't possibly understand why a white middle class, suburbia-raised child, like she assumed Heidi to be, could be so worked up about being treated like she was a minority herself.

"Why here? Why tonight? Why target a community who is grieving?" Erin's questions flew off her tongue at the speed of light.

"Simple." Heidi bounced excitedly on her toes. "Professor Croft encouraged us to come here tonight for extra credit."

"And the people who aren't currently enrolled in his class, what do they get out of it?"

"Media coverage." Heidi turned and faced the cameras. She smiled and waved before spinning back around to Erin. "Croft knew they would be here. He's never wrong, you know?"

Erin didn't know what to think as she stared over Heidi's shoulder toward the satellite vans and TV news crews.

"Oh, he said something else, too."

"Who, Croft?"

"Yeah. Said something big was going to happen." Heidi's eyes drifted down Erin, thinking that her being interviewed by Erin was the big thing Croft had mentioned. But Erin knew the girl had completely missed the point. "Looks like he was right."

## CHAPTER FORTY-NINE

COOPER'S BARKING PULLED ME INSTANTLY FROM MY DEEP sleep. His ears were tucked back and his tail stiff as an arrow. Rubbing my eyes, I swung my feet to the floor and said, "Coop. What is it boy?"

He stared at the front door, growling.

Flipping my hair over my shoulder, I perked an ear and glanced around the dark house. Remembering I was alone, my heart knocked harder. I turned my attention back to the front door, glad to see the deadbolt still locked.

A subtle knock sent Cooper into a frenzy.

"Coop, easy!" I stood, moved to the door cautiously, and checked to see who it was.

My lungs released at the sight of King.

Grabbing Cooper by the collar, I opened the door and pulled him back. "Hey, sorry. I fell asleep on the couch. Come in."

Cooper's tail wagged as King bent to greet him. Rubbing his ears, King met my sleepy gaze. "I got your message. It's not too late, is it?"

I pushed my hand through my messy hair and turned

toward the couch. "You should have called." When King didn't respond, I glanced over my shoulder to find him giving me a look like I was crazy. "You did call, didn't you?"

He raised both his eyebrows and grinned.

I rubbed my forehead with feelings of shame squeezing my temples. "Sorry," I said squishing one side of my face.

"Is Mason home?"

I shook my head. "I dropped him at Gavin's parents' house." King stood but kept his hand on Cooper's head. "I saw the news, Alex. What happened? Did the police really murder an unarmed black man?"

King kicked off his shoes, removed his jacket, and moved to the couch. "It's bad, Sam." He flicked his gaze over to me. "Tension between the community and the police hasn't been this high—"

"Since the mid-90s?" I finished, falling into the opposite corner of the couch.

King stared for a moment before nodding. "We've requested to put a rush on the ballistics tests, but I'm certain we're dealing with the same shooter as yesterday."

I inhaled a deep breath, staring at the floor where Cooper was lying at my feet. A dark cloud fell over me as my thoughts tangled into a web of knots. I had so much I wanted to ask but didn't know where to begin. Without looking in King's direction I asked, "Did Gavin have any enemies within the department?"

King's spine peeled off the couch cushion. Resting his elbows on his knees, he turned his head and looked at me with a quirked eyebrow. "This has nothing to do with Gavin."

I locked eyes, wanting to believe King. It would have been so much easier if it was true but I couldn't get the pastor's warning out of my head—couldn't stop linking my entire family to this group I knew nothing about until today.

"I need to show you something," I said.

Kings lips slightly parted as he watched me retrieve the medallion from under my notebook on the coffee table. Handing it to him he asked, "Where did you get this?"

"You know what it is?"

Kings eyes rounded like saucers. "I do."

"Do you remember the name Markus Schneider?"

King's brows knitted tightly together. "I do, but how do you know it? That was a long time ago. And, if memory serves me correct, before you and Gavin got together."

"You have a good memory." My smile was small, feeling flustered by a less than ideal situation. "Markus is back in town."

King inhaled a deep breath and cast his gaze downward to his hand still holding the medallion. "Did he give this to you?" King's voice grew urgent, protective. He snapped his neck and faced me. "Tell me, Samantha. This isn't just a medallion but a symbol, a call to arms. If Markus gave it to you, I need to know now."

A wave of heat traveled beneath my shirt. I was completely breathless when I asked, "You think it could be him?"

King's blue eyes hooded and his voice dropped to a whisper. "Depends if he gave this to you or not."

Rubbing my hands over my thighs, I stood, stepped over Cooper, and crossed my arms. "He didn't give it to me, but someone left it for Pastor Michaels to find."

King shot up off the couch, rooted his hands on his hips and, when I turned to meet his gaze, he quickly looked away.

Over the next several minutes I told King how Pastor Michaels found the medallion waiting for him moments before he was to join tonight's vigil. King stared wide-eyed, hanging on to every word, deciding not to respond with any follow-up questions until I was completely finished.

"Did the pastor seem afraid?"

I watched King's chest rise and fall as I thought about the big secret Markus revealed to me about Pastor Michaels. I drew my brows together and said to King, "You know?"

King tucked his chin and flashed me a questioning look.

"You know the pastor's secret." I felt my blood pump fast as I closed the gap that kept me separated from King. "How he was a key witness in the trial of Kenneth Wayne."

King kept his eyes on me as he tipped his head back.

"I've done my research, Alex. I know how important Pastor Michaels's testimony was to have the Patriots of God's second in command convicted of murder. But is it true?"

King lowered his brow. "Is what true, Sam?"

My heart knocked so fast I thought I might pass out, face-plant into the floor. "Did the pastor commit perjury?"

King's cheeks hollowed. "It's a long story, and one that no one should be speaking about."

Clenching my fist, I held my chin high. "Why hadn't you told me that Pastor Michaels was a key witness in a double murder trial?"

"Sometimes you have to break rules in order to see justice served."

"Christ Almighty, Alex." My muscles quivered with the sudden shock of confirming the story's truth.

"That trial, Kenneth Wayne's conviction, put an end to the Patriots of God, Sam. That was the goal. The reason Denver didn't completely burn to the ground."

"But he lied?"

"Would it be different if he wasn't a man of God?"

"No." I hated King for being right. It didn't matter who lied about what. It served a greater good, I understood that, but something about it still felt wrong. "And you couldn't have mentioned this to me after I told you about Tim spouting off about being a Patriot of God?"

King's Adam's apple slid up his throat when he visibly swallowed. "I don't know what to tell you."

"Markus is telling me more than you are."

"What else did Markus say?" King's jaw twitched. "And where have you been meeting with him?"

"He said the pastor's secret isn't safe."

"I'd say he's right if somebody is giving him that." King pointed at the medallion.

I wrapped my body in my arms, not feeling like myself. Suddenly, the house was much colder. King stepped forward and pulled me into his chest. I latched my hands around his waist and rested my ear against his heart, stealing all his warmth. "I'm worried about Pastor Michaels."

"You should have told me about Markus as soon as he tracked you down."

"Until tonight, I didn't see reason to." Tipping my chin back, I looked into King's dark gaze. "Who is he and why are you talking about him like he's a bad guy?"

King's eyes narrowed as his voice dropped down to a raspy breath. He hooked my chin with his finger to make sure I didn't look away. "Sam, Markus is no good, and certainly no friend of Gavin's."

I felt disoriented and knew there was a reason I'd sent Mason to Gavin's parents tonight. "I know their partnership ended in divorce, but that's as much as Gavin ever shared. Gavin never spoke of it and, like you said, it was before our time." King's eyes frowned. "Tell me what happened, Alex. I need to know. Erin and I are uncovering more dirt than we anticipated and I can't be caught off guard when chasing somebody—or something—that poses so much threat to my family."

King threaded his fingers through mine and led me to the couch. He told me to sit. Despite being as stiff as a board, my insides fluttered with eagerness. King's eyes were pointed down at our fingers dancing with each other. There was a long pause before he started up. "Markus and Gavin were one of the few mixed partnerships in the department. At first, they seemed perfect together. Both competitive, motivated, extremely smart."

"So, what happened?" I asked when King paused.

King blew out a heavy breath and started up again. "Markus started to resent people of color after being passed on a promotion to detective." King lifted his eyes and stared. "The person who received the promotion was black."

"One of our victims?"

King shook his head. "But you do know him."

My head tilted to one side.

"Lieutenant Kent Baker." King paused to allow me a moment to catch up. Once he saw I was ready, he continued. "Markus got caught up in the movement. In those days, everyone was talking race, picking sides. That's why Gavin refused to speak of him. Markus wouldn't shut up. To him, it was everyone's fault but his own that he didn't move up the ladder. Eventually, Gavin had enough and requested he be assigned to a new partner. You know Gavin. He was a patient man until he wasn't."

I laughed, remembering Gavin exactly how Alex phrased it.

"Gavin was focused on his job. There were no gray areas with him. Markus thought DPD was discriminating against whites and left the force, not on good terms, either."

"So why is he back?"

King tugged on my fingers as he shook his head. "Truthfully, I can't believe he is."

"Was Markus a known member of the Patriots of God?"

King swept his ocean blue gaze up to me. "Not to my knowledge but, again, that was a long time ago."

I chewed the inside of my cheek, thinking how just when

my suspicions were pointing me in the direction of Rick Morris and Professor Croft, I found myself spun in a completely new direction. Turning my focus to the medallion, I asked, "Is Markus the second shooter?"

"His timing certainly seems suspicious." King shrugged one shoulder. "He's also a trained marksman. An excellent shot, if I remember right."

I thought more about the facts and how whoever was behind this had to be smart. We weren't just chasing an average career criminal but somebody who was well-versed in the history of what happened between the city and the police force. It had Markus's name written all over it. But was it him?

"You said a black cop killed Douglas Davis, the leader of Patriots of God?"

King confirmed with a single nod.

My palms began to sweat. "It was Gavin wasn't it?"

"No."

"No?" My brow furrowed. "I could have sworn that's what you were telling me at the school this morning." King was still shaking his head when I asked, "If not Gavin, then who?"

"Sam," King was slow with his words, "Lieutenant Baker was the one who took the kill shot."

## CHAPTER FIFTY

SUSAN YOUNG SMILED AS SHE WOKE AND NUZZLED HER nose deeper into her big fluffy pillow. The musky masculine scent surrounding her had her waking easily.

Pushing her hand beneath the covers, her fingers searched for the hard body she'd had her limbs wrapped around last night but it was gone. Hearing the television flicker on, Susan tucked her elbow beneath her head and curled up on one side, finding the man she had been looking for. Benjamin stood at the foot of the bed, tying his tie while staring at the screen.

"You're not leaving, are you?" Susan was afraid he'd been called in to work.

Turning his head, Benjamin flashed her his award-winning smile. It was bright and full and everything Susan needed to start her day off right. He turned on a heel, purposely leaving his tie dangling loosely around his neck as he crawled back into bed.

Susan rolled onto her back. Reaching for his tie, she took it between her fingers and pulled the big man on top of her.

The mattress crumbled beneath his weight as he fell to one

side. Keeping his head propped up on his bent elbow, Benjamin tucked a long lock of Susan's hair behind her ear. With seduction drooping his eyelids closed, he leaned in for a kiss.

Susan's heart knocked and, though she wanted nothing more than a repeat of last night, she quickly turned her head away. "Not with morning breath," she said, covering her mouth.

Benjamin didn't seem to care. He peppered kisses over Susan's neck, smoothing his hand up over her fluttering bare stomach before landing on a breast. Things were moving fast between them, but Susan knew Benjamin was unlike any other man she had been with before. And she wasn't going to miss an opportunity so good.

"Careful, don't start something you can't stop." Susan's body tingled with anticipation.

Benjamin had been her escape from the stress of work, her way of forgetting the fear she felt after everything she'd experienced in the last forty-eight hours. Even with the amount of work she knew was waiting for her at the office, she could delay the start of her day if it meant being with her new boy-toy for just a little while longer.

She hooked one leg over the back of his and asked in a raspy breath, "I have time, do you?"

Benjamin chuckled. "Kiss me and I might find the time."

"Benjamin! No." Susan giggled, her body squirming beneath his. "Let me brush my teeth first."

"If you leave this bed," his hand ironed down her side, "I'm not coming back."

Susan turned her head and pointed to the soft spot behind her ear. "You can keep kissing me here."

"Like this?" Benjamin's lips brushed the exact place Susan pointed.

"Just like that," she purred.

Things were heating up and Susan was close to giving in to his demands, when suddenly both their attentions were stolen by what they heard the news anchor say on the television.

"Did you know about this?" Benjamin asked without looking at Susan.

"I was there." Susan's mind traveled to last night's vigil.

Shaking his head, Benjamin rolled off the bed and approached the TV with both hands planted firmly into his hips. "I worked on those kids who were shot." He pointed to the television, expressing his disgust. "They will never be the same. And people are protesting a candle light vigil?"

"Turn it off," Susan requested.

Benjamin turned back to the television and sighed. Reaching for the remote, he flicked it off. "I'm sorry."

Susan got out of bed and approached him. "It's awful, I know."

Benjamin lifted his arm and let it fall over Susan's back. Holding her tight, he said, "It just seems like no one has any empathy anymore."

Susan stood on her tiptoes and pecked at Benjamin's lips. "I'm going to take a shower and, after I'm dressed, I would like it if you would take me to work."

Benjamin kissed her again, the mood lost to the tragedy, as he nudged her toward the shower.

After Susan left the girls last night, she'd gone straight to her office. She worked a couple more hours, still unsure how to handle the strange request she'd agreed to when she accepted the envelope addressed to the Morris family. And, to complicate things even further, it wasn't just a small sum of money. Inside the envelope, she had found a check written for ten grand.

Showered and dressed, Susan found Benjamin in the

kitchen of her condo finishing a glass of orange juice. "Ready?"

"You look beautiful." He looped his hand around her waist and kept it there all the way to his car. Opening the door for her, Susan again thought how today was beginning so much better than yesterday.

During the short drive to her office, they talked about this weekend's Bronco game and plans for dinner. By the time they were parked out front, Benjamin caught Susan's hand. "You do great work. Remember that when things get tough."

"Thank you." Her face beamed. "I know."

Benjamin took her face inside his hand and kissed her goodbye. "I'll call you later."

Susan watched Benjamin drive away and, once he was out of sight, she turned on a heel and hurried up the sidewalk. Her cheeks were flush with memories lingering and she could still feel the way Benjamin's lips made her body tingle. He was so perfect, she thought. *How did I get so lucky?*

"Susan Young?"

Susan swept her gaze up and nearly smacked into Rick Morris. "Yes." Rick introduced himself, but Susan knew who he was from Samantha. If it hadn't been for Sam, Susan would have recognized Rick from the news clips she had seen. "What can I do for you?"

"I would have called but I thought meeting in person would be better." Rick kept his hands buried deep inside his jacket pockets and shifted uncomfortably back and forth on his feet as if he was riding ocean swells on a boat. "I was told you have money for me."

"Who told you that?" Susan's eyebrows squished.

"I can't really say."

"I'm sorry, Mr. Morris—"

"Please, call me Rick."

"Rick," Susan paused to meet his intense gaze, "I'm going to have to ask you to direct your questions to our attorney."

"To your attorney? What is this?" Rick's face ripened apple red. "I thought you were accepting donations to the victim's fund."

"You're correct."

"And my son is a victim," Rick snapped, taking an aggressive stance.

Susan stood, unsure how to phrase her words without causing further damage. "I'm sorry for your loss, Mr. Morris. But I'm afraid I can't speak about specifics."

"It's simple. Either you have the money or you don't. And I know you do."

Susan felt smaller than she was as Rick towered over her. "Mr. Morris—"

"No. I told you to call me Rick. You're not listening. No one is listening," he fumed. "We are victims, too. My son deserves what the others are receiving."

Susan stared, her gaze bouncing between his wild eyes. "Again, I'm sorry for your loss. Please contact our attorney. Now, if you'll excuse me."

Susan ducked and stepped around Rick. Jolted by his hand clamping around her arm, Susan's heartrate spiked. Feeling terrified, Susan thought about screaming for help but instead said, "Let go of me or I'll call the cops."

"I expect to get an answer from you by tomorrow about how much my family will receive. I know you have the funds," he sneered. "If I don't hear from you, just think how the white community will react to you playing favorites."

Susan's thoughts flashed back to last night. She remembered the words of hate she'd heard being screamed at both sides. The community was already divided. If Rick acted on his threat, Susan could only imagine how she would be blamed for further dividing her own community between racial lines.

Rick released Susan's arm when Carly stepped out and asked, "Susan, is everything okay?"

Susan's fingers tingled with pins and needles as the blood rushed back into her arm. Without looking, she knew it would bruise. "I'm fine." Her voice cracked as she nodded enthusiastically.

"Tomorrow," Rick whispered close to Susan's ear before walking off.

As soon as he was gone, Susan rushed into her office, shut the door behind her, and immediately reached for the phone to call for help.

## CHAPTER FIFTY-ONE

DRAPED IN THE COMFORT AND PROTECTION OF KING'S arms, I smiled at nothing in particular. All my uneasy feelings were washed away when King agreed to stay with me overnight. It was the first time I shared a bed with someone who wasn't Gavin. With Mason out of the house, it made it easy to not think too much into what I—what *we* —were doing.

I was hyper-aware of the way King held onto me. He made me feel safe, and I knew he cared. Though he never said it, I knew he worried about my safety—Mason's too.

Latching both hands onto his forearms, I closed my eyes and inhaled his sweet scent.

I loved everything about him. We hadn't been dating for long, but our relationship was mature. We were two consenting adults knowing exactly what we were doing. There was no need to beat around the bush or play any games. This was meant to be. While I knew Gavin would approve, it didn't hurt to have Irene tell me the same thing.

When King stirred, I twisted around in his arms and faced him.

His eyes were heavy with sleep but, as soon as he saw me, he cracked a smile.

Taking my face between his rough hands, the pads of his thumbs stroked my rosy cheeks. Our eyes swayed back and forth and King could see something was on my mind.

"Did you get much sleep?" he asked.

"Alex, why did you never marry?"

He rolled onto his back, tucked one arm behind his head, and stared up at the ceiling.

I tucked my body against his side and traced lazy circles over his chest with the tips of my fingers. "I'm sorry, too early for those type of questions?"

He didn't react. "There was someone close once."

I was jolted with surprise. This was news to me. I liked that there was still something mysterious about him that I didn't already know. "What happened?"

"Her name was Angelina." His words came out in a soft whisper. "But it fell through not long after I made Detective."

Silence fell over us and I knew the story all too well. The job of detective was a demanding one and King's schedule was rigorous. Having to be on call twenty-four-seven was only half the reason dating a detective was difficult. It was the other half of him witnessing the gruesome leftovers by the sickest members of our society that proved disastrous. It wasn't a lifestyle meant for everyone but I knew it better than anybody—experienced as much as he had.

"I'm glad you haven't found anybody," I murmured.

King lifted his head off the pillow and looked me in the eye.

"And Gavin would be happy, too."

King brushed his fingers up and down my arm, holding me tight.

"It's not weird for you, is it?" I asked.

King's hand stopped moving and he took his time to

answer. "Gavin was one of my best friends. I know he would rather it be me than anybody else. It's not weird. I just don't want to pretend like I can fill Gavin's shoes."

"No one is asking you to," I said, sharing Irene's words. I crawled up King's body and pressed my lips against his. "Can I make you breakfast?"

"You can make me anything you'd like."

We kissed again before he tossed the covers and disappeared into the shower. As soon as he was gone, I made the mistake of turning on the television.

The news cycle was already going.

I stared with disbelief filling my eyes.

The screen filled with images of cars flipped over, fires burning, shops vandalized. *What happened?* Overnight, Park Hill erupted as news spread about the shooting of innocent Dennis Hall. The people blamed the white officers who were first on scene, but I knew that was a lie. The cops weren't responsible. It was this second shooter we were hoping to find—the one no one could talk about—and as the sickening feeling in my stomach spread, I knew that this was the exact response this asshole wanted.

King's cellphone beeped with a series of messages, most of which I ignored. A second later, King walked out with only a towel wrapped around his tight waist.

"Look at what happened," I said, pointing to the TV.

King's face tensed as she stared. "Bloody hell." King muttered a few curses beneath his breath. "This was what I was afraid might happen."

"You weren't the only one."

King reached for his phone. "It's an update from LT," he said after catching himself up on his backlog of messages.

"Still have time for breakfast?"

When his eyes landed on me, I watched his shoulders relax. "Yeah. But I might have to eat and run."

I let King have some privacy when getting dressed and headed into the kitchen, not wanting to miss my chance to feed him before we both headed off to work. Taking the eggs and sliced bread out of the fridge, I was embarrassed by how little food I kept in the house. But there was still the Chinese Susan had brought the other night. Though I knew King wouldn't mind eating that if we had to, I decided on sticking with my original plan.

After turning on the burner, I checked my own messages. There was still nothing from Nancy Jordan. I was starting to doubt she had anything new on Professor Croft that Erin and I didn't already know. But there was still a chance she knew something else. And that was what had me worried most. If she jumped the gun on telling this story first, she might be the reason the second shooter would be tipped off that we were on to him.

I fed Cooper and then called Mason.

Irene answered after the second ring. "Just calling to check in," I said.

Irene was quick to jump into telling me they were safe and last night's activity stayed close to the commercial zones. There wasn't anything to worry about. "Here's Mason, darling." The phone rustled. "Good talking with you, Sam. Be careful out there when you're working."

When Mason got on the phone, I said, "Hey sweetie, did you sleep well?"

"I'm still tired."

"Grandma Irene said you were watching the news."

"Not really, but I know what's going on. Is that why you're calling?"

Plopping the sliced bread into the toaster, I held my phone to my ear with my shoulder. "I have a busy day of work ahead of me. I just wanted you to know in case anything came up and you were wondering where I was."

"I know, Mom. You're always working."

My entire body ached with the truth of his words. I didn't have a choice. "Anyway—"

"Mom, I want to visit Nolan today."

I paused and stood still. "I'll tell you what, if I can catch a break, I'll come pick you up and we can go together."

"I'll believe it when I see it."

I could just see Mason rolling his eyes at me. "Mason, you saw what happened last night, heard what's happening in Grandma Bell's neighborhood. It's dangerous out there and I'm trying to figure out what is happening to keep us safe."

"I knew it," Mason grumbled. "It's always about you."

"Mason—" I heard the phone line click and knew I had lost him.

I spun around and felt my body close. Heat flushed up my spine. I didn't know what to do about my teenage son. He could be such a pill sometimes.

Cracking an egg, I watched it sizzle in the pan as my thoughts churned, filing through the case, reminding myself of everything I knew. I couldn't stop thinking about Markus and how he seemed like a likely suspect except for the fact that he was being so brutally honest with me. Did he not know that I would learn of his past? He didn't seem that arrogant. However, he did have enough arrows pointing his way for me to wonder if he was the mysterious second shooter.

First, he knew Pastor Michaels's secret connection to Kenneth Wayne's conviction. Second, he probably held enough resentment against Lieutenant Baker to want to take action. Those alone were enough for me to believe he had reason to justify the killings.

Either way, it was clear to me that both the lieutenant and the pastor weren't safe.

The toast popped and the egg yolks were running—just

the way I liked them—by the time King snuck up behind me and wrapped his big, strong arms around my body.

He gathered my hair inside his hands, nuzzled his nose in my neck, and said, "I can feel your mind is already drifting to work."

"And what does that feel like?"

"It feels like this." He massaged my stiff neck, my shoulders almost instantly releasing their stress. Despite how great his hands felt working out the knots in my back, I found it impossible to stay relaxed knowing how close this case was coming between me and my family. "Relax," he said.

"I can't." King spun me around and I tipped my chin back to look him in his eyes. "I keep thinking about Markus and his determination to wedge his way into my life. It's like he's following my shadow, wanting me to know he's not far from where these crimes are being committed."

"I'll look into it." King gripped my hips and yanked me closer. "I promise."

I knew he would, but King's words last night had me feeling spooked. Had Markus fooled me into believing he was here because of Gavin? Or did I have it all wrong?

King lowered his brow and moved to the plates of food. Taking them both into his hands, he said, "I'd like to know myself." He flicked his gaze to me. "Ask him why he came to say hi to you and not me." He winked, getting me to laugh, but the moment of joy was short-lived.

"If Gavin had enemies inside the department—people who are your colleagues now—you would tell me, wouldn't you?" My muscle fibers quaked.

King came to a dead stop and stared into my eyes. I saw a twinkle of truth sparkling in his blues when he said, "Of course."

King sat at the table and I followed him but I still couldn't shake the nerves out of my system. "My face has been published everywhere lately. Anyone can find me. I make myself an easy target every time I publish an article someone doesn't agree with." My worries were coming out as fast and straight as an arrow. King was my target, and I felt bad for shooting him with all my concerns.

King draped his hand over mine, looked me in the eye. "I'll check Markus out."

When he squeezed my hand, I knew I had to let this go—trust him to do everything in his power to check out this potential danger. He released my hand when his cellphone rang.

"It's Alvarez," he said, glancing at the screen. Excusing himself from the table, he took the call in the living room.

My stomach was still unsettled as my thoughts kept tumbling inside my head.

I couldn't stop thinking how Lieutenant Baker not only was promoted to detective, but now sat high on the totem pole of command within the police department. If Markus resented him then, I could only imagine how he was feeling about him now.

If only I could confront Markus without tipping him off that we were onto a second shooter, then maybe I could learn enough to give us an idea what he'd been up to since coming back to town. But, first, I needed to warn Pastor Michaels that his secret was out and that is life could be in danger.

My own cellphone rang and, when I picked it up, Erin said, "Sam, are you home?"

"I'm home." My blood rushed to my toes.

"I'm coming over. You're not going to believe what I discovered."

# CHAPTER FIFTY-TWO

THE SNIPER SET DOWN HIS PEN AND RUBBED HIS EYES. HE stared at the letter he had rewritten a half-dozen times, thinking he had finally gotten it right.

The news flickered on the television in the background. He hadn't got much sleep since his journey began. He sat there, alone, thinking how Kenneth Wayne would be proud of him and his crusade. After all, the Sniper was doing it for him—for the future of *his* community.

Wayne had sat behind bars for far too long, and the fact that the Sniper knew he had been convicted under false pretenses left him with a sour taste in his mouth. The Sniper swore to bring revenge to the people who'd wronged Wayne. He promised to do anything to get people to remember the man who was wrongly convicted of a crime he didn't commit. It seemed as the world had forgotten, moved on, and was okay with putting an innocent man in prison. But not the Sniper. He would never forget.

Reaching for his coffee mug, the Sniper brought it to his mouth. It was empty so he stood and went to make another pot when he stopped to stare at the television.

Turning up the volume, a smirk sprouted at the corner of his mouth.

The morning anchor spoke of riots and unrest. The Park Hill community was reacting exactly as the Sniper had hoped. *Yes, Dennis Hall was shot by those evil white cops.* The Sniper laughed hysterically.

But then he stopped when he heard the news anchor say, "The police are investigating whether there is a connection between the riots and the protests that erupted into violence at last night's candle light vigil for the school shooting victims of North High."

With his heart knocking loud against his chest, pride filled his lungs. His skin was raw. He was devious in his master plan as he considered it a stroke of genius. The Sniper even considered thanking Pastor Michaels for his assistance. If it were not for his vigil, the Sniper wouldn't have had the perfect distraction that had allowed him to sow the seeds of doubt.

Laughing his way to the coffee maker, he knew that ballistics would come back and clear the names of the two officers. But, for now, he had the community believing *him*. The Sniper dumped the ground beans into the back of the machine, flipped the switch on, and checked his watch for the time.

He had his next target already in the crosshairs. With the city's unrest, the Sniper was granted easy access to complete his mission and let the city of Denver know that the Patriots of God were back. That Kenneth Wayne deserved to be set free.

# CHAPTER FIFTY-THREE

As soon as I was off the phone with Erin, I immediately put a call in to Allison.

"I understand that, Sam. I'm trying my best." Allison was as tense as I felt. The urgency to hack into Timothy Morris's accounts was wearing on us all.

"I know you are, sweetie." I pressed my hand flat on my forehead, not wanting to add to her stress. But time was running out.

"You need to warn him, Sam."

My stomach clenched as my thoughts locked on Pastor Michaels. "I will."

"Like, right now." Allison left little room to argue. "If he hasn't connected the dots..." Her words trailed off to nothing but anxious breath.

She knew about Pastor Michaels being gifted the white eagle medallion and after I mentioned how the murder of Dennis Hall wasn't as it seemed, Allison jumped to the same conclusion I had. Pastor Michaels's life was in danger. Though I debated whether I should have further explained to Allison that he had a secret of his own, in the end I decided against telling her about him committing perjury. I didn't want to be the one to taint his reputation—especially when the community needed him.

"Just get inside Tim's accounts. Oh, and be on the lookout for the name Markus Schneider," I said to Allison the moment I heard King step back into the kitchen. I turned to face him and stared into the deep contours mapping out his face. There was something he wanted to tell me. I could see the urgency flickering in his eyes.

"And who might that be?" Allison asked.

"I'll tell you later."

"I don't like secrets, Sam."

"You have to trust me on this." I told Allison I loved her and then ended our call, promising to check in as soon as I could.

King scrubbed a wistful hand over his face.

"What is it?" I asked.

"The ballistics came back."

"And?"

King gripped his waist just above his belt. "The bullet that killed Cook Roberts was fired from the same rifle as the one that killed Dennis Hall."

My breath remained even. "What does your gut tell you?"

"That Markus has every reason to be the one killing these people." King blew out a heavy breath as if surprised by his own conclusion.

There was a knock on my door just before Erin came spilling over the threshold. She had her hair tied up into a messy bun and her coat hung open like she had left in a rush. I called out to her, moved to King, and pressed my lips against his. "I'll call you later."

"Wait? You're not even going to finish breakfast," King called after me.

"Lock up when you leave." I hooked my arm through Erin's and dragged her to her car.

"Did he sleep over?" Erin had a knowing glimmer in her eye. She was dying to know if King and I had finally slept together.

"Mason is at his grandparents' house and I didn't feel safe home alone," I said, falling into the passenger seat.

Erin hurried around the front of her car and jumped behind the wheel. "I'm not trying to put my nose where it doesn't belong."

I flashed her a skeptical look.

"It's fine if you two are sleeping together. I was just surprised to see him, is all."

"Really?" My cheeks burned with embarrassment.

"Really." Erin's face was deadpan. "I thought King would have been out all night. I saw the news. Park Hill is rioting. Didn't you see?"

I flicked my gaze forward, a pressure headache forming. I wanted to tell Erin everything that I'd learned since I'd last seen her, but I didn't know how. "I saw."

"Can you believe those cops killed an unarmed black man?" She cranked the engine and blasted the defrost.

"They didn't." My eyes dulled to a half-mast.

Erin paused, turned her head, and stared.

I rolled my gaze and stared back. "The cops didn't kill Dennis Hall."

Recognition flashed over her eyes. Her lips parted, then quickly snapped shut.

"It's him, Erin. The second shooter. He set this all up. King just confirmed it with ballistics."

Erin swallowed hard. "My God, another black man dead and the entire community is rallying against the department."

"Tell me you found something on the professor?" I kept my theories about Markus to myself, not wanting to take

Erin's focus off of whatever urgent news she couldn't wait to share.

"Croft never appeared last night but I did catch a break."

I felt my body lean closer to her, my stomach eagerly fluttering to know what she'd found.

"Once I got home, I did some research and was able to find some information that I thought might be useful." She pulled away from the curb and continued debriefing me, telling me that a student of his did confirm that he was behind last night's march on the vigil. "Croft was a protestor in the 90s and, get this," she paused and glanced to me with eyes glowing, "Markus Schneider was his student."

"Holy shit." The trap doors in my stomach opened and my insides dropped to the floor.

"Yeah. Big. I know." Erin nodded and rolled her eyes back to the road. "I don't know what it means, Sam, but something tells me you might."

My thoughts spun into a tight web of possibility. I wondered if we were wasting our time chasing Croft or Rick Morris when suddenly everything seemed to be pointing directly at Markus.

"Are you sure about that?" I asked, making sure we weren't chasing our own tails.

"Positive." Erin didn't even flinch.

I didn't pay attention to where we were driving. Didn't really care. The walls around me were crumbling and I couldn't help but feel like I was drowning in a big conspiracy to attack the police department Gavin once worked for.

"I saw him, Sam. I saw Markus last night."

"He told us he was going to be there," I was quick to counter.

"You saw him, didn't you?" Erin didn't wait for me to respond. She already knew that I had. "What did he say to you?"

My head was still spinning, trying to make sense of the facts we had. Croft never showed at the protest he'd organized. Dennis Hall was shot about the same time the protestors arrived. "Maybe Croft and Markus are working together," I muttered.

The car went silent and I could feel Erin's muscles tense.

"Markus only showed his face after the vigil had been disrupted. Croft could have been in Park Hill knowing everyone's attention was in the park." I paused and felt my pulse race. I turned to Erin with big saucer eyes. "Markus overheard my conversation with Pastor Michaels."

"The one where he gave you the medallion?"

I nodded.

Erin's brow furrowed with confusion. I quickly caught her up, telling her how Markus told me Pastor Michaels committed perjury in order to have Kenneth Wayne convicted of a double homicide. Erin listened with a slack jaw as I continued rambling on. I was hearing everything I was saying and still couldn't believe it myself. By the end of my story, Erin knew everything I did, including that Lieutenant Baker was promoted to detective years ago and that had sown the seeds of resentment Markus had for the whole department.

"If Croft and Markus are working together, what does Croft have to gain from this?" Erin asked.

"I'm not sure I have an answer. But Croft has a platform to spark debate; maybe that's all Markus needed?"

Erin grimaced and shook her head. "But Croft was the one missing from last night."

She wasn't convinced, and I still had my own doubts. Between all three of our suspects, Markus had the closest ties to Cooks Roberts, but Markus and Rick both had reason to feel like their community had let them down. I couldn't see a reason for Croft to pull the trigger, but I did for Markus.

Erin slammed on the brakes. The tires squealed as I jolted forward in my seat, bracing my hands on the dash to minimize the impact. Once the car had come to a complete stop, Erin stared with an unwavering gaze that had me nervous. "Are you sure the pastor lied under oath?"

Markus had brought it to my attention. But if it hadn't been for King's confirmation, I wouldn't have been certain. Nodding, I said, "I'm sure. King confirmed it."

"That's what this is about then." Her eyes were bright as lightbulbs. "Look, Sam, we're certain this second shooter is a Patriot of God." I nodded. "And if the pastor lied under oath to put Kenneth Wayne behind bars, that's the reason to attack the same people working for the justice system that unfairly sentenced him."

I stared ahead, looking at nothing in particular. The sound of the engine was purring and I understood what Erin was saying except it didn't explain why they chose to begin their battle by targeting a school.

Erin was still gripping the steering wheel with both hands when she asked, "Could you sit in prison knowing you were framed by the police?"

"You're talking like Kenneth Wayne is behind the terror attacks."

Erin raised her brows. "Maybe he is orchestrating it from the inside?"

"He's been dormant for nearly two decades. Why start up his fight now?"

"I don't know." Erin shrugged. "But maybe we should learn if any of our suspects have been visiting him recently."

Erin was onto something. Wayne was here in Colorado. It would be easy to pay him a visit. I agreed we should, but added, "The pastor doesn't know that his secret is out."

"Call him, Sam." Erin smacked the wheel with the palm of her hand. "Tell him now. He needs to know."

I dug out my cellphone with my heart hammering and made the call. The line rang twice before clicking over to voicemail. I ripped out a string of curse words. "Pastor, it's Sam." Erin dropped the gear and pointed her car into the sea of traffic. "Your secret isn't safe. You know the one I'm referring to. The one you've been living with for close to twenty years. I know about it and so do others. Listen, I'm coming to the church now. Don't talk to anyone. Your life could be in danger."

# CHAPTER FIFTY-FOUR

RED BRAKE LIGHTS STARED BACK AT ME LIKE LITTLE DEVIL'S eyes laughing at our sorry attempt to speed to the church. I slammed my fist down on the dash. The sound of it cracked the air. Erin's knee bounced and she couldn't sit still.

It seemed we hit every road block imaginable, including traffic. It was slow moving and I grew extremely frustrated by our inability to get to where we needed to go. Every second counted and Pastor Michaels still hadn't responded to my message.

Finally, we funneled past the accident that had caused the delay and Erin put her foot down to the floorboard and sped off. A minute later, we were zipping into the church parking lot and coming to a dead stop near the front entrance.

I had my door open before the wheels stopped turning. My feet hit the ground running. Rushing inside, I was afraid that we might have been too late. Scared of what we might find, we couldn't know when the second shooter would strike again, but were betting that he would. Erin kept pace and, as soon as we entered the big room, we ran up the aisles until digging our heels into the ground when seeing the pastor alive.

Pastor Michaels came out of nowhere and, when he saw the two of us, he raised his eyebrows and smiled. I sucked back a deep relieved breath, wanting to keel over and die with embarrassment.

"Don't act so surprised to see me." The pastor chuckled. "I practically live here. You, on the other hand," he angled toward us, "probably have work to do."

"Did you get my message?"

He responded with a questioning look.

"I left you a message." Erin nudged me to move along, step closer to the man we had come to see. My feet dragged over the floor as I walked, my heart heavy as if afraid of getting too close to the eyes I once thought of as pure.

"I'm sorry, Sam. I must have missed it." The pastor gripped his bible between both hands and brought it to his chest. "Unfortunately, another funeral request came to my desk. As if I didn't have enough already to conduct this week."

"Dennis?" My whispers grew louder as they echoed off the chamber walls.

The pastor frowned and nodded once. "What is it that couldn't wait?"

Wiping my palms on my thighs, I asked, "Is there somewhere we can talk in private?"

The pastor flicked his eyes to Erin. "We are alone and beneath the eyes of God." He leaned forward and stood on the tips of his toes. "Whatever it is you came to say can be told in the presence of Jesus."

I felt my neck pulsating, a throbbing ache stitching my side. "I have some questions I wanted to ask you about the Kenneth Wayne murder trial."

The pastor's face flushed pale. "You're right." His eyes

sank deep into his skull. "We better have this conversation in my office."

We followed Pastor Michaels through the corridors and into his office. Shutting the door behind him, we each took a seat. I watched the pastor stare at the wooden cross hanging on his wall. He had the sagging look of a man riddled with a life of guilt. The room spun and the air buzzed with anticipation. His shoulders curled forward when he broke the silence saying, "I have feared when this day would come."

Struggling to keep my own emotions from boiling over, I told him how I'd learned of his secret. "But what I want to know is how Markus Schneider knows."

The pastor was still staring at the cross. His lips fluttered soft whispers only he could hear. Erin nudged him into spilling the truth by saying, "Markus was with the department when you were made a witness, isn't that right, Pastor?"

Breaking his trance, the pastor cast his gaze to his threaded fingers, closed his eyes, and smiled as if finding peace in prayer.

"Markus overheard our conversation last night," I said with a rolling stomach. "Was he the one you were warning me about?"

The pastor opened his eyes, turned to me, and asked, "Do you have the medallion with you?"

I pushed my hand deep into my pants pocket and retrieved the medallion.

"Can I see it?" His eyes were so soft I wondered if he hadn't already made peace with himself for the danger he had put himself in long ago.

I dropped the medallion into his open palm. Pastor Michaels inspected it for a moment before saying, "I know Markus was there last night." He lifted his gaze and locked it on mine. "And, yes, Markus was the one name I was thinking of when I warned you about Gavin having enemies."

The hair lifted off my nape and I momentarily stopped breathing to consider the weight of what he had just said. Markus was Gavin's enemy, yet he was here, trying to be friends with me. *Why?*

"Do you think Markus left that for you to find?" I asked.

Pastor Michaels set the medallion down on top of his desk and pushed it back to me. "I knew this day was coming. My day of judgement." His smile never hit his eyes. "There hasn't been a day that has gone by since I testified in Wayne's trial that I haven't felt death breathing down my neck. The fear I've lived in since then has been punishment from God for what I did."

"We need to protect you." I gripped the edge of his desk, watching my knuckles go white. "Let us take you to the police. It's clear your life is in danger."

Shaking his head, he refused. "I can't run away from this. I'm not going to hide, either."

"You could die, you know that?" My heart drummed so loud I swore everyone in the room could hear it.

Without flinching, the pastor looked us in our eyes and said, "We will all face that moment of truth when the Lord calls our name."

"So, if Markus knows about your perjury, who else knew?" Erin asked.

The pastor swiveled in his chair and brought both elbows to the table's surface. "Gavin knew. So did Lieutenant Baker." Before Erin could present him with a follow up question, he said, "But they would never speak out."

I wondered if he could be so certain about that. We all had our breaking points. Maybe someone had reached their limit. "That doesn't explain how Markus knew."

The pastor peeled his gaze off the cross. "He should have never known."

"Who revealed your secret. And why?"

There was a soft knock on the wooden office door. The pastor called out to his visitor, inviting her inside. A middle-aged woman peeked her head into the small study and said to the pastor, "It's time."

Pastor Michaels nodded. "Thank you. I'll be out in a moment." As soon as the door shut, he turned his attention back to us. "My community is in turmoil and needs me to attend to them."

"Your community is taking their fight to the police under false pretenses." I told him how Dennis Hall wasn't killed by the white officers like everyone had thought. As soon as I said it, I knew I'd let too much of my own secret escape.

Pastor Michaels stood and ironed his hands down his front. With wisdom filling his eyes, he said, "That doesn't erase the fact that Dennis is dead and hearts are broken."

# CHAPTER FIFTY-FIVE

ALEX KING SAT AT HIS DETECTIVE DESK DOWNTOWN reading up on the trial of Kenneth Wayne. He wanted to remind himself of the details, the timeline of events. It was a different time, a lifetime ago. So much had happened since that even his outlook had changed. King was one of the few white officers who knew the pastor's secret. Gavin had let him in on it. Though Gavin hadn't approved of the strategy himself, it hadn't been his decision to make. Nor was it King's.

King had Wayne's photo pulled up on a second browser and he printed off Wayne's criminal record for reference. He couldn't stop thinking about Markus or the legacy of Wayne and the Patriots of God that had been left behind the day he was sentenced to a lifetime in prison.

Someone knew the pastor's secret and was making a point to let him know, but who?

Searching old files in the police database, King couldn't find anyone from those days who wasn't already locked up or six feet underground. Yet someone from the movement was working hard to reignite the tension between neighborhoods. *Why?*

King dove back into the stacks of reports he had printed off on Wayne.

According to the prison warden, Wayne had a reputation for good behavior. His last report even mentioned Wayne's work to assist other prisoners toward a successful path of rehabilitation.

King's knee stopped bouncing when he lifted his gaze off the text.

What did that mean? Did Wayne have the capability to organize from within? If so, that meant he had someone working for him. Could the second shooter be a released inmate Wayne had worked with on the inside? King was determined to find out.

Moving his hands back to his computer keyboard, King began pulling up whatever records he could on Markus. It didn't take him long to find what he was looking for. King knew Markus had left the department, but what he didn't know was that Markus had soon found employment in Boise, Idaho where he finally rose to the rank of detective.

King paused and scratched his head.

None of this made any sense to him.

Markus got what he wanted—he'd become a detective. So, if he was the one behind these murders, why was he still bitter at the department he'd left?

The smell of black coffee drifted into King's brain before Alvarez set a paper cup down on his desk. "Here's your coffee." King didn't respond. "I had a hell of time with the elevators so it's probably cold."

King never bothered looking at his partner. His head was still scanning for a connection—a reason for Markus to be the second shooter.

"Didn't make it home last night?"

"Huh?" King snapped out of his thoughts.

"You're wearing the same suit." Alvarez lifted his coffee cup and pointed at King with his pinky finger.

King glanced down and turned his attention back to his computer screen. "It was a long day and an even longer night."

Alvarez swirled around in his chair, still giving King a look of suspicion. "I'm not here to tell you who you should and shouldn't date—"

"Then don't." King cut him off before he said something he would regret.

Alvarez sipped his coffee. "Samantha is a smart and attractive woman—"

King shot Alvarez a glare from the corner of his eye. "Are you sure you want to go down this road?"

Alvarez showed King his palms. "All I want to do is remind you that she's a reporter and reporters are only out for themselves."

"You clearly don't know Sam." King double checked a note he'd made earlier and kept working while he talked. "She wants what we want."

"But if she mistakenly reveals something she shouldn't and risks tipping off our suspect—"

King turned his head and looked Alvarez in the eye. "We don't even have a suspect."

Alvarez quirked a brow and nodded. Facing his own desk, Alvarez added, "All I'm saying is we can't risk tainting a future jury pool because you think she's one of us."

King pushed his coffee away just to make a point. Changing the subject, King brought up the ballistics report that had come through early this morning. "Even if the captain was to release a statement to the press, no one will believe that the bullet didn't come from one of the officer's guns."

"Seems like the perp's intention." Alvarez smacked his lips.

"Any leads on who might have made the call that brought cops to Dennis Hall's house?"

Shaking his head, Alvarez said, "The call couldn't be traced; came from a burner."

"The shooter made the call," King muttered under his breath. "A way to lure the cops to his target."

"Seems likely." Alvarez sighed.

King leaned back, angled his chair to face Alvarez, and said, "My fear is that if this is the shooter's way to lure cops in, there is no safe way to decipher his calls from those who actually need our help. Our guys are sitting ducks until this jerk is caught."

Alvarez gave King a knowing look. Then his eyes rolled to King's computer. He sat forward when noticing the image of Kenneth Wayne and asked, "Still thinking this asshole we're looking for is connected to the Patriots of God?"

King's fingers extended to his knees. "You ever hear the rumor that evidence was planted against this guy?" He pointed to Wayne.

"Him and every other guilty asshole out there." Alvarez laughed. "But, on a serious note," he glanced around to make sure they were alone, "yes." Alvarez craned his neck. "You don't believe it?"

King arched one eyebrow. "Do you?"

"Pastor Michaels testified. He was a witness to the murders."

King stroked his chin, staring into the eyes of Kenneth Wayne.

"You don't look convinced." Alvarez rolled his chair closer to King.

King met his partner's eyes and lowered his voice.

"Depending on who you ask, some say the pastor lied in order to get Wayne convicted."

"A lie like that would destroy a man in his position. Ruin his career."

"Let's just say that it's true," King's heart hammered inside his chest, "and that someone learned of the pastor's lie. Wouldn't that be reason enough to want to toss this city back into the race wars Wayne first started?"

It was silent for a long minute between them before Alvarez asked, "You have someone in mind who might know the pastor committed perjury?"

King cocked his jaw and opened his eyes. "You remember the name Markus Schneider?"

Alvarez pulled back and stared with a ghost face.

"He's back."

# CHAPTER FIFTY-SIX

ALLISON WASN'T ONE TO SHY AWAY FROM WORKING UNDER pressure. Under normal circumstances she embraced the challenge. But this request from Sam was different. The stakes were higher. Not only was what she was attempting to do illegal, but Allison also considered that maybe the FBI could be trying to do the same exact task in the very same moment.

Shedding her fleece jacket, beads of sweat formed on her upper lip. Her fingers tapped fiercely as she hunched over her computer monitor in her dimly lit room, wishing she kept a stick of deodorant at the office.

Allison could have told Sam no. Said this didn't feel right, that she didn't want to take the risk of getting caught. She felt all those things today. Instead, she'd kept her mouth shut hoping karma had her back.

If it were not for seeing firsthand what happened at North High and knowing that her community was hurting after last night's murder of Dennis Hall, she might have considered passing this on to someone else. But she could feel the emotions surrounding her turning into anger.

Allison knew she had a small window of opportunity to

get into Tim's accounts. If she didn't succeed, an actual race riot might break out. It was up to her to make sure it didn't.

Her plan was simple. All she needed was Timothy Morris's correct phone number or main email address. Then, once she had that information, she would install the software she had written and use the *forgot password* link to divert the SMS to a private phone accessed by only her. That would give her the one-time passcode to enable her to hack into Timothy's accounts, giving her unfettered access to all his past posts, both private and public.

But, first, she needed that phone number or email.

Using a robustly built artificial intelligence program, Allison wrote out a set of instructions, giving the AI software parameters to follow before releasing the bots to crawl the vast web of online information.

When it was finally all set, she said, "Here goes nothing."

She clicked *Enter*, sat back, and crossed her arms, feeling her heart hammer in her chest.

Allison sipped off her can of soda, waiting to receive an alert. After fifteen minutes of nothing, she checked to make sure things were still running. When still nothing came back, she reminded herself what was at stake for the umpteenth time.

The Patriots of God were back, and this time they had a plan to get the city to take action based on a set of lies. Her gut flexed and she felt her own anger bellow up inside her.

The news played softly on the radio behind her. Everyone was taking their fight to the police. Pointing fingers at anyone but themselves. Allison felt the same bile rise in her throat as when she saw the white eagle medallion for the first time last night. The taste was just as sour and proved to be an equally agonizing reminder that what she did today had implications for tomorrow.

Her eyes landed and locked on the sticky note she'd

written to herself after speaking with Sam. *Markus Schneider?* was all it said. She would find whoever influenced Tim to shoot up that school. And, when she did, she would pass the information along to Sam, who then would tell Alex King.

Her computer dinged with a pop-up message.

Allison spun her chair around and read the text. Smiling, the bot had come back with both a phone number *and* email address linked to Timothy Morris. Now, all Allison could do was cross her fingers and hope that her plan would work.

# CHAPTER FIFTY-SEVEN

"What do you mean there is nothing you can do?" I heard a heavy metal door slam shut. King might have been whispering but I could hear the way his words growled with anger into my ear. He had moved to somewhere he couldn't be heard.

"Sam, if I get caught attempting to hide what the pastor did, I could receive severe repercussions." He paused and dropped his voice deeper. "Maybe even lose my job."

My ear was riddled with the spit I imagined flying from his mouth as he clenched his teeth when he talked. "Someone will kill him if you don't do something." I held my ground.

"He lied. Under oath, Sam." A swooshing sound rushed through the line. "The only way I can protect him is if I arrest him."

I pushed my fingers through my hair and turned my eyes back to the church. I stared at the brick building wishing Pastor Michaels hadn't opened his doors for the community today. He wasn't taking the threat seriously and no one seemed to care but me. "They will get to him."

King went quiet and I questioned if maybe I had lost our connection. "I wish there was something I could do."

Erin tapped her wrist, signaling it was time. I nodded. She started the car and began driving. With the pastor stubbornly ignoring my warnings, it was useless for us to stay here.

"Well, did you at least look into Markus?"

"I have," King said.

"And?"

"There's not enough to bring him in for questioning."

"Then call me back when there is enough." I killed the call, slamming my skull back into the headrest. I was beyond frustrated with King and hated the hoops he was making me jump through. That was what would get the pastor killed. If not the pastor, it would be someone else. At this pace, the second shooter kept the advantage.

"You two *are* sleeping together."

There was a sparkle in Erin's eye that I ignored. "Just drive."

The journey to the community college gave me enough time to cool off from my conversation with King. I never stopped worrying about the pastor but he was already looking over his shoulder. He knew what was coming—had felt it nearly half his life. I could only do so much, and Croft was next on my list of suspects to tick off.

"According to the schedule online, class is starting now." Erin parked near the front of the west end of the building and removed the keys.

I kicked the car door open and followed her into the building. Together we rushed through the maze of corridors, bursting our way into Croft's classroom. We slammed on our brakes when a handful of students turned their heads to look at us like we were crazy. And maybe we were, because Croft wasn't anywhere to be seen. *Did we get the wrong classroom?*

"You don't think he canceled, do you?"

As soon as I was about to say something that would implicate him in the murders of Dennis Hall and Cook Roberts, I heard the professor's voice echoing off the outside walls. Following him with my ears, I stepped into the hall, ran to the corner, and caught sight of him heading into his personal office. "Croft," I called after him.

He opened the door to his office before turning his attention back to me. "You should be reporting what's happening in the streets, not questioning me."

I pulled back, my mind spinning with disbelief. Remaining vigilant, Erin shot back first. "And we would be if you weren't giving your students extra credit for picketing places people come to mourn."

"Who told you that?" Croft's face went red.

"It doesn't matter." Erin rolled her shoulders back and took one step closer to Croft. Narrowing her eyes like a snake, she hissed, "You and I both know it's true."

"At least they're brave enough to make their voices heard." Croft puffed out his chest, going toe to toe with a woman. "It's more than you can say, I'm sure." His judgmental eyes drifted down her front.

"Professor, we know you have a track record of provoking certain issues," I said, hoping to cool the tension raging between Erin and Croft.

Croft's eyes were slow to leave Erin's, but eventually they made their way to me. "When you incite emotion, you know you are on to something worth your while." His lips curled upward at the corners. "That is not a bad thing, Mrs. Bell." Croft snapped his head and quickly looked away as if suddenly remembering he was talking to a couple of reporters. He stepped fully into his office. "Though, I suppose you two might know that better than even myself; knowing when you're onto something good."

Butterflies were in my stomach as I watched Croft move

around his office. I couldn't stop questioning myself, thinking that maybe he was the second shooter. I had my doubts, but that was because I was still uncertain about Markus.

"Quite the stunt you pulled last night," I said.

He raised one sharpened brow and looked at me out of the corner of his eye.

"It would have been nice of you to at least extend the curtesy of inviting us to the rally you planned."

"Mrs. Bell. Ms. Tate." His eyes bounced between us. "There is something you must understand about me."

I bit my lip and transferred my weight to the opposite leg.

"I only facilitate. The students are the ones who make the final decision. It's our right. *Their* right to speak out about policies they feel are wrong."

"Funny, I didn't see you facilitating last night." I turned to Erin. "Did you see him facilitating?" Erin shook her head. "In fact, we didn't see you anywhere near the vigil."

"I see what you did there." Croft dropped his nodding head into his chest. Looking at us from under his brow, he began to softly laugh.

Erin and I didn't share the same enjoyment. "By claiming something big will happen to them?" Erin began drilling him. "What did you do? Promise them that if they went, they would have their moment of fame? A chance to be interviewed by big shot reporters? Get their face plastered all over TV?"

"Where were you last night, Dean?" I dropped his first name to make sure I got his full attention.

His smile vanished from his mouth, erased from his eyes. Dean Croft stood there huffing heavy breaths out of his nostrils, looking like a stick of dynamite about to explode.

"At home." He spun swiftly to his desk and jabbed his stocky index finger hard into a block of papers. "Grading papers. Finals are only a couple weeks away and I can never keep up this time of year."

"I hope you're being honest because let me paint a picture of what it looks like to us." A surge of adrenaline topped me off with the confidence I so desperately needed. "A candle light vigil, a coming together for the community to mourn the loss of innocent teenagers murdered by a madman is suddenly interrupted by a dozen of your students—past and present—at the exact moment another innocent husband and father was murdered in Park Hill."

Croft's chest didn't move and, though he was still standing tall, I knew he wasn't breathing.

"What Mrs. Bell is saying, Professor, is, why is it that you used your students as a distraction to kill Dennis Hall?"

"What? I didn't kill anybody. The police shot him." Croft was jumpy as his words left his mouth at a hundred miles per hour. "I saw the news. I know what happened. That man's death has nothing to do with me."

Reaching my hand inside my jacket pocket, I felt my fingers close over the white eagle medallion. I set it down on the professor's desk and stepped back. "I'd believe you except for your track record for inflaming racial division."

"Whatever you're suggesting is a lie." He barely looked at the medallion.

"You knew about the race riots of the 90s but failed to mention you were part of the protest when we spoke yesterday."

"Because it's irrelevant."

"Affirmative action was a hot button issue back then. Care to share what else you might have objected to during that time?"

"In those days we marched to open doors. We didn't have access to social media, nor did we have the luxury of hiding behind our computers and pretending to be patriots. No," he shook his head, "we fought in the streets. Took our griev-ances straight to those we were fighting. Making such large assumptions about my involvement in something you know little about is a dangerous approach. One that could get you in trouble."

My heart was beating so fast, I was happy I had Erin by my side. I wasn't sure I would later remember everything the professor said but knew that, together, we would. "You recog-nize that medallion, don't you, Professor?"

He inhaled a noisy breath through his nose and I watched his facial tics round his face. "It's time for you to leave."

I shared a knowing glance to Erin. Then I turned back to Croft. "I think it's fair to say that if what you're teaching inside these walls comes back to any of these murders, you could be charged as an accomplice."

Croft glared but didn't move.

I reached behind him and snatched the medallion off his desk. And, just as we turned to leave, Croft said, "I'm a patriot. And sometimes patriots become martyrs for the causes they believe in."

My heart stopped as I stared wide-eyed at the white wall in front of me, feeling my muscles tremble with fear from what I was hearing.

"The moment we become complacent, Mrs. Bell, is the day we trade our freedoms for enslavement."

"We'll see about that, Mr. Croft." I rolled my neck and glanced over my shoulder. "The truth always has a way of rising to the surface."

# CHAPTER FIFTY-EIGHT

WE WEREN'T MORE THAN FIFTY FEET OUTSIDE CROFT'S office when I told Erin, "We need to find Chandler."

Erin's blonde hair lifted off her shoulders as she galloped to catch up with me. "You think he knows something about Croft?"

"I think he knows a lot. But what I'm most curious about is if he knew Timothy got that tattoo." I slowed to a near stop, turned to Erin, and held her gaze inside my own. "These young kids like to brag about their new ink. I'm sure it was big news at the time."

"Wait," Erin's expression pinched, "did you ever hear back from Nancy Jordan?"

I shook my head.

"I knew it." Erin flicked her gaze down the hall. "She must not have anything, otherwise she would have contacted you by now."

Suddenly, I was curious again. I glanced at my phone just to double check I hadn't missed anything. Still nothing from Nancy. I kept walking.

Erin's boots clacked behind me. "If we're going to speak

with Chandler, it wouldn't hurt to know why he wasn't interested in last night's extra credit."

Searching for signs to point me to the registrar's office, I said, "Maybe he didn't need it. Or he didn't think it was worth involving himself in something he considered toxic."

"It's a soft approach. A way for us to break the ice. C'mon, Sam, we have to use the information we have to get us closer to asking the tougher questions without risking scaring him off. He's currently our best chance at understanding exactly what has been happening inside Croft's classroom. We can't lose him."

"And we won't." I swiveled my stiff neck around, trying to locate any directory. "There," I said, pointing at the far wall.

Digging my shoes in to the polished flooring, my soles squeaked as I took of jogging. My palms slammed into the wall and I dove to the sign, looking for a number. "Here it is." I turned to Erin.

"Croft's class list?"

Excitement flashed over my eyes as I nodded. We kept moving.

"We can check Croft's alibi, too. Make sure he was home last night grading papers like he said. That was a thick stack of papers. I'd like it if someone could vouch for his whereabouts." Erin kept her gaze forward as she nodded along. With each step, my pace increased. "He's left important details out before. We can only assume that he did again today."

We turned the corner like a couple of race horses and hit the brakes as soon as we came to the office door. Erin hung back. "I'm going to call Ginny Morris; ask her if she knew about Tim's tattoo."

"See if you can get her to hint at what her husband has been up to, too."

Erin gave a single nod of confirmation as I stepped

through the registrar's threshold. Blood sloshed in my ears as I approached the front desk. I was still fuming about the way Croft acted so arrogant toward the entire situation. He seemed like a man pissed off at the world. I wondered what caused that kind of resentment and if it gave him enough reason to want to kill.

I stopped at the front desk. A round woman sitting behind it swept her gaze up and batted her long lashes. "Hi. I'm Samantha Bell from the *Colorado Times*—"

"What can I do for you, Samantha?" She smiled before letting me complete my sentence.

"I'm doing a story on the school shooting at North High and I was hoping I could get a list of students currently enrolled in Professor Dean Croft's Political Science course?"

"You're in luck." The woman half smiled, half frowned. "I've been getting lots of requests for this lately."

It wasn't all that surprising considering it was the biggest story in the state, maybe the country. Cops, reporters, hell, everyone was trying to connect the dots to why someone would shoot up a school.

"Here you go." She handed me a single sheet of paper. "Anything else?"

"That's it for now," I said, muttering a quick thank you on my way out the door.

"No one is answering," Erin said, her face flustered with growing frustration. "I'm going to call again." She hit redial, pressed her phone to her ear, and paced the hallway corridor with fingers drumming on her side.

Gripping the class list with both hands, it didn't take long for me to lock in on a familiar name.

"I got their voicemail again." Erin sucked her bottom lip into her mouth, clenching her cellphone at her side. "What is it?" Her brow furrowed.

I lifted my gaze. "Turner. Chandler's last name is Turner."

"Does that mean anything to you?"

"No. But now we have a last name, which could lead us to a home address." I handed the paper to Erin. "C'mon, let's get out of here."

"But shouldn't we stay and find Chandler?"

My phone rang. I felt my arteries open up. When I saw it was Susan, my lungs released.

"Sam, Rick was here. At my office." Susan's words flew at me fast. "Ambushed me outside on the street. He attacked me, Sam."

"Are you all right?" The cords in my neck strained. I couldn't believe what I was hearing. Worry knotted my belly.

"He knew I had money donated specifically for his family."

"How did he know that?"

"I don't know. But I told him to contact our attorney."

"And did he?"

"Doubtful. He didn't even give me a chance to give him our attorney's name. And it just so happens, the attorney is on his way here now."

I stared at Erin with my heart pounding. She stared with curiosity twitching her brow.

"But here's the thing," Susan continued. "Rick said that I have until tomorrow to decide what his family gets, and if I don't give him his fair share, he said, 'Just think how the white community will react to you playing favorites.'"

"He actually said that?" My jaw unhinged.

"And I still don't even know who gave this check to me."

"Rick Morris is clearly trying to pour gas on the situation."

"Sam, be honest with me. What's the chance that Rick is the one behind all this racial tension?"

"I'm not sure, but let's not make it any worse by giving in to his demands."

"I don't know what to do, Sam. What if he comes back?"

The room spun around me and I could feel the tension building on all sides. The air buzzed with an electricity that raised the hairs on my arm straight into the sky. Something big was about to happen, and I didn't feel any closer to zeroing in on any one target to stop it before lightning struck. "You need to call the cops before that happens. Rick Morris could be just as dangerous as his son was."

# CHAPTER FIFTY-NINE

HE FLICKED HIS WRIST AND FLUNG HIS HEAD. THE DIGITAL wristwatch frantically beeped. Slapping his free hand over the time piece to silence its alarm, the Sniper lifted his gaze and glanced around to make sure he wasn't being followed.

It had been fifteen minutes since he had seen Samantha Bell and her blonde sidekick parked near the entrance to Pastor Michaels's church. Their presence had caught him by surprise. His gut told him that they were well on their way to learning his true identity.

He double backed around the block, cursing under his breath the entire way. The pastor had been talking. The Sniper's anger and resentment swelled with each step as he reminded himself of the mistakes he had made. He knew he should have killed the pastor first instead of the man the news was calling Dennis Hall. It was the pastor who deserved to die, not Dennis. Dennis was a means to an end. It just so happened his luck had run dry.

With his heart drumming loud inside his hollow chest, the Sniper hid behind a thick cottonwood, keeping one hand securely attached to his guitar case. From behind the tree, he stayed on the lookout for any other unexpected surprises before making his next move.

When his eyes stopped on the landing of the church steps, he thought about the medallion he had left for the pastor to find. A smirk tugged at his lips but, inside, he was mostly filled with regret. Today, he didn't have anything clever to give the pastor. Only a bullet that would end his life.

With Samantha Bell gone, the Sniper pushed away from the tree and marched up the sidewalk. He kept his head down, visualizing inside his mind what he would say before taking the life of Pastor Michaels.

His blood pulsed as he moved into position. His body buzzed with excitement knowing how close he was to ending the life of the person who pretended to be a man of God. The Sniper knew better. And, soon, the entire world would learn of his secret, too.

The entrance drew closer. Just as he was about to turn and gallop up the front steps, he caught a flash of light out of the corner of his eye that made him pause. In that split second, he was forced to make a quick decision to not head into the church.

Without visibly reacting, the Sniper cursed to himself as he pulled his baseball cap visor further over his eyes and kept walking.

The police car slowed as it approached the church. The Sniper's heart nearly stopped but he kept his eyes forward and his stride even.

*No. This can't be. I'm not finished. I must finish what I started!*

Inside his head he was running while he moved at a slow and even pace to not draw attention to himself. His palms sweated and his heart swelled uncomfortably but he kept moving. If he was stopped and questioned, he was doomed. It would have been impossible for him to assemble his rifle and pop off a couple of shots before he'd be hit with one first.

Adrenaline kept his nerves jumpy and only did they start to settle once he turned the corner and disappeared around the block. Blowing out a shaky breath, he could feel that his days were limited.

Closing his eyes, he paused to remind himself what he was once told about being a martyr.

*Martyrs are the true patriots who serve others by making the ultimate sacrifice to ensure a better future for all.*

The Sniper dug his heels into the concrete and suddenly stopped. He picked up his head and glanced over his shoulder. His thoughts churned as he stared at the parked patrol car. A dozen different scenarios played out inside his head, and then, an idea came to him.

## CHAPTER SIXTY

SUSAN STARED OUT HER WINDOW, PINCHING HER LIP between her fingers. Her pulse was slow but she was still breathing. She hadn't moved from her chair since getting off the phone with Samantha. Her words were still rattling around Susan's head and she wished her friend had given better advice than to just call the police.

Susan sucked back a deep breath and sighed.

She didn't know what she wanted her friend to say to her, what other options she had. The city was on edge and Rick Morris's words kept her stomach feeling jittery.

When Susan ironed her hand down the arm Rick had grabbed, Samantha's warning whispered into her ear.

*Rick Morris could be just as dangerous as his son was.*

Susan flinched, shivering in the cold chill that sent a wave of fear up her spine. Those departing words Samantha left her with managed to steal her entire focus. It was bad enough that the attorney was running late, but this was proving difficult to shake.

A part of Susan wondered if that wasn't Sam's objective—

to keep Susan vigilant when danger was knocking on her door. She could have just said it if that was her intention.

Susan startled when she heard a set of knuckles tapping lightly on her office door.

Rolling her neck, she stepped out of her web of thoughts and found Carly standing with a concerned look creasing her brow. More bad news, Susan thought.

"Is he here?" Susan asked about the attorney.

"No sign of him yet." Carly dropped her hand from the door and let it dangle at her side. "People are beginning to speculate how much money has been donated to the victim's fund."

"Okay. Let them speculate." Susan leaned forward and pretended to work. Another quake rolled through her body. She knew she would never be able to meet Rick Morris's insane demand by tomorrow. "We'll release numbers soon enough, but now we keep our mouths zipped until a more appropriate time."

"I understand." Carly's chest rose as she nervously bit the edge of her lip.

Susan knew the money her organization had received was incredible, but they were still undecided about a realistic timeline of when the victims could expect to begin receiving their allotted sums. Susan was hoping that was something the attorney could sort out with them.

"What is it, Carly?" Susan was short, feeling irritated.

Carly visibly swallowed when she inched closer. "The media is speaking to the victims' families." Carly paused and Susan stared. "They're upset, asking what we're waiting for."

Susan fell back into her chair, threading her fingers over her stomach. "What *we're* waiting for?" It had barely been 24 hours since the governor had unexpectedly opened a victims' fund at Susan's company. Donations were pouring in at a rapid pace. They couldn't be expected to send money out until the fund was closed.

Carly nodded. "The reason I'm bringing this to your attention is because soon we'll be forced to release a statement ourselves."

Susan understood perfectly well what was coming. "What else are the families saying?"

"They're saying all sorts of things. They're asking how can we drag our feet when they don't have the choice to push back their child's funeral. Medical bills are adding up and will be sent out soon. Susan, people are anxious and don't know how they will cover these costs or if they'll ever receive the money that was promised to them. They think we should just pass it straight through our bank account in an instant. That we shouldn't hold on to it at all since it isn't ours."

Susan's heart went out to each of the families. While she was looking forward to helping them out, there was nothing she could do to speed up the process. "Prepare a statement to be released after we meet with the lawyer."

"But there is something else."

Susan shot Carly a tension-filled expression, resisting the urge to roll her eyes. "Go on."

"There is also a rumor going around that we're stealing the money to pay down the business's debt. That that's why we're not giving it away as soon as we have it."

"That's ridiculous." Susan guffawed.

"But people believe it."

"Where the hell is this guy?" Susan stood, turned to face the window and quietly cursed the governor for selecting her organization to take on this extraordinary role with no outside assistance.

Susan's desk phone rang. Both women stared. Susan reached for it and gave Carly a look. "Some privacy please?"

Carly trotted out the office, closing the door behind her. "Susan Young speaking," she answered.

A local reporter from 9News introduced himself and didn't stop to pause before firing off the first question. Susan responded professionally, mostly directing him to her attorney who she had yet to meet personally. Then he caught Susan off guard when he asked, "It has come to my attention that your organization is also planning to give Timothy Morris's family an equal share of the donated funds. How much are you planning to give and will you make that public?"

Susan lowered her brow and softly asked, "Where did you hear that?"

"Are you confirming it's true, Ms. Young?" She could almost hear him smiling.

A bubble closed over Susan when she muttered, "We'll be releasing a statement soon. Until then, you can direct all your questions to my attorney." Susan slammed the phone down in its cradle, hung her head, and screamed.

# CHAPTER SIXTY-ONE

ALEX KING ENDED HIS CALL WITH SAM FEELING PELLETS OF sweat stream down his back. He lowered his head and pushed his fist into his mouth. Biting down on his knuckles until the skin broke, he stifled a loud growl of frustration. His hands were tied. Without a known threat on the pastor's life, there was nothing he could do. But maybe he could go after Markus?

Slamming the heavy metal door wide open, King exited the stairwell and marched back to his desk with Alvarez giving off a vibe that said *I told you so*. He dropped like a dead-weight into his beat-up old chair and proceeded to leaf through his piles of papers. He couldn't stop thinking about Sam and how his gut told him there might be more to Markus than what she was telling him.

Alvarez leaned back with a perp's profile in his hand. "If Markus was Gavin's partner, he could have learned what the pastor did from Gavin."

King turned to his partner. "It makes sense, doesn't it?"

Alvarez gave a single nod. "What's Samantha saying about all this?"

"I thought you didn't want to work with a reporter."

Alvarez quirked a brow.

King rolled his chair to his partner's desk and lowered his voice. Over the next several minutes, King filled his partner in on everything he and Sam currently knew about Markus.

Alvarez listened, saving his follow-up questions for when King was finished. Maybe there was more to Samantha's investigation than he'd originally given her credit for.

King told his partner about Markus's sudden reappearance after all these years and how it coincided with the first shots fired at the school. It was King's theory that Cook Roberts was Markus's way to retaliate against the department that betrayed him, and now he was back to balance out the world order he believed had been knocked off its axis.

"This is messed up." Alvarez scrubbed a heavy hand over his face. "Have you checked to see if he's visited Kenneth Wayne?"

King held his partner's gaze and shook his head no. "The only connection I know of is with the pastor and Markus's past hatred against Lieutenant."

Alvarez's eyes flashed when he turned to look at Lieutenant's office. "Has he made contact with either of the two?"

"Only the pastor that I know of."

Alvarez was still staring across the room when he asked, "Have you seen Lieutenant today?"

King's gut flexed. "No."

Both men shared a quick glance, jumping to their feet at the same time, having come to the same conclusion. Together they jogged across the floor, between the desks, with their shoes squeaking like soles on a basketball court. Bursting into Lieutenant Baker's office, his desk was empty. King's heart raced. Pushing past Alvarez, he didn't want to waste a second. They looked everywhere but kept coming up empty. No one had seen Lieutenant, and King's worries grew.

Then the captain arrived like divine intervention.

Sprinting to their superior, they came to a skidding halt. "Cap, have you seen LT?"

Captain was poised as he stood tall, rooting his hands into his sides. "You boys look frantic."

"We came across something." King's ribs squeezed.

Captain gave an arched look. "Lieutenant Baker is monitoring the situation in Park Hill."

"When did you last hear from him?"

Captain glanced to the clock. "Twenty minutes ago. You want to tell me what is going on?"

King debated what he could share without completely humiliating himself. He wanted to only give Captain information he knew was the absolute truth, but even that was in short supply. "There is a rumor going around that Pastor Michaels lied in the trial of Kenneth Wayne."

Captain narrowed his eyes. "And this has to do with Lieutenant Baker, how?"

King dropped his gaze and shook his head. "Something tells me that it's not a rumor and what the pastor did is true."

"That's enough, Detective." Captain sliced his hand through the air, sharp as a knife. He stared at King long enough for King to get the point. "Whatever you're have heard never happened."

The room went silent. The captain bounced his squinty gaze between the men.

"Cap," King held up one hand, "I wouldn't be bringing this up if it wasn't relevant to the case."

"Kenneth Wayne's case is closed." His eyes traveled over King's left shoulder.

"But Cap, I have reason to believe the person who is spreading the rumor might be the guy we're looking for."

Alvarez nodded, backing his partner up.

Captain inched closer. "And do you have a name for your suspect?"

"Markus Schneider."

Captain's face tightened in a moment of doubt. "Have you made contact?"

"Working on it."

"What's Markus's current location?"

"Unknown."

"You have nothing, Detective." A stony expression fell over Captain's face.

"We know Markus is the one bringing the pastor's secret to light."

"And how do you know this?"

"A very close and trustworthy CI." King couldn't mention his confidential informant was also *Times* reporter Samantha Bell without really getting his ass handed to him. "If Markus is the second shooter, he'll go after the pastor—"

"And LT," Alvarez interrupted.

I nodded. "We need to have the pastor protected."

The captain balled his hands into tight fists. "Have you thought how that might look? If we protect the pastor, don't you think it's possible the conspiracy already swirling around him would then appear to be true? Imagine the spin the media would put on it and the fallout of this department."

"I understand what you're saying," King argued. "But if he's murdered and we could have put a stop to it—"

Captain held up one hand again, getting King to snap his mouth shut. "Relax, King."

King's brows pinched.

"I sent a car to his church this morning." Captain grinned. "If the media asks, the patrol car is only there because of the risk the funerals being conducted there present. Understood?"

"You knew?" King sounded surprised.

"I only know the pastor isn't the most popular person right now."

"Maybe that is exactly what the perp wants," King heard Alvarez mutter beneath his breath.

A knock on the desk behind the men had them all turning to see who it was.

"Captain, we just received word from a suspect I'm assuming is the shooter." The uniformed officer skirted past the two detectives and slid a letter into Captain's hand. "The email came in five minutes ago."

King watched Captain read the printed email. His eyes lit up. Pulling his shoulders back, he shouted, "Call that patrol unit outside Michaels's church and send back-up right away."

King stepped forward, stole the printed sheet, and read the note.

*...more people will continue to be killed until Kenneth Wayne is exonerated of all charges. -Sincerely, Your Patriot of God.*

"King. Alvarez." Captain's eyes flashed with adrenaline. "I'll send word to LT. You two get over to Park Hill. Canvass the area and be on the lookout. Whoever is doing this knows how to shoot and if this is Markus, he'll want to make this personal."

He already has, King thought.

# CHAPTER SIXTY-TWO

Erin was staring at me bug-eyed and battle-ready when I was slow to peel my cellphone away from my ear. My body was cool with sweat when Erin started firing off her questions.

"Rick attacked Susan? Call the cops?" Her brow twisted. "What's going on, Sam?"

My throat felt like gritty sandpaper, my mouth parched. Dizziness engulfed me as I stood staring at the class list thinking about Chandler Turner. Erin reached out and violently shook my arm. I snapped out of my thoughts, blinked my eyes, and finally relayed Susan's phone call to Erin.

Erin's entire body was frozen stiff but her head kept shaking with the same disbelief I was struggling to process. "That's why no one was picking up when I called their house," she said. "No one was there."

"I don't understand Rick's end goal." A dull ache throbbed in my locked jaw. "What is it he's trying to achieve by ramping up his threats?"

"It's clearly about money."

"Is that all, though?"

"Notoriety? A compulsive need to not be seen as a victim for what his son did? The list could go on, Sam. Either way, he obviously thinks he has the power to rile up his community, does he not?"

I nodded and agreed, but it didn't make it right. We still didn't know who'd left the medallion for Pastor Michaels to find. I glanced down the hall in the direction of Croft's office. My head swam in the details of our investigation. It seemed like all three of our most likely suspects were choosing to make a move at the same time. "Who do we go after first?" I murmured.

Erin sighed. "We already talked to Croft. We could stay here and keep an eye on him, though I don't think it will be a good use of our time. And Rick gave Susan a deadline for tomorrow."

"So that leaves us either Chandler or Markus."

"It's your decision."

The room spun. I could hear the seconds ticking away as I was paralyzed with indecision. My cell vibrated in my pocket. I pulled it out and read the message. As if knowing my struggle, King had written, *You were right. It's Markus. We're going after him now.*

My heart jolted with an electrical shock. "King confirmed. It's Markus. Markus is the second shooter!"

Erin bounced on her feet around me. I started typing my response to King, wanting to know where he was when suddenly a call came through. Allison.

"Hey babe. Did you break into Tim's accounts?" I tried to remain as calm as possible, but with Erin nipping at my heels her anxiety kept me nervous.

"I'm afraid it's not as simple as that."

"What do you mean?"

"You need to see this in person."

"I'm kinda in the middle of something."

"Trust me. You'll want to see what I found. If I could tell you over the phone I would."

Erin paused and stared. She heard Allison through my ear piece. I was about to open my mouth and tell Allison it had to wait when Erin said, "King's got Markus, let's see what Allison has to show us."

"We'll be there in ten."

We were in Erin's car and racing across town, beginning to guess what in the world Allison had discovered. We had a dozen different theories going by the time we arrived. Erin parked out front and we bolted into Allison's beautiful office. Allison grabbed my hand and tugged me into her back office.

"Look here." Allison explained her technique on how she'd hacked her way into Tim's Facebook account, but it was mostly over my head. She hit play on a video.

My scalp prickled the moment Tim's voice came through the computer speakers. I held onto Allison's hand and I felt my fingers go cold. We watched him spouting off political banter that didn't make any sense. A lot of his words were racially insensitive but all I could hear were the cries from the parents as they stood outside North High that cold morning on the worst day of their lives. When I thought about Mason, I couldn't take any more.

"That's enough." I looked away, not wanting to see Tim ever again.

Allison hit pause. "Well, now you know he definitely considered himself a Patriot of God."

"What else did you find?" I asked.

"More hate speech. He kept repeating a couple of names that I had to look up." Allison released my hand and searched her desk for notes. "Douglas Davis and Kenneth—"

"Wayne," Erin said.

"You know them?"

"Davis and Wayne were the founders of the Patriots of God movement."

"I suspected as much." Allison sat behind her desk and curled her fingers over her keyboard. "So I worked backwards, hoping to find Tim had visited Wayne in prison."

Curiosity drew me closer, wanting to know what she had found. "And did he?"

"No." Allison clicked her mouse. Her screen populated with a list she printed out. She reached for the paper as soon as the printer spit it out and said, "Instead, I found this."

I took the paper and Erin tilted her head to have a closer look with me.

"Those are the names of people who *have* visited Wayne in prison sometime during the last ninety days." Allison paused to allow us time to catch up. "Recognize any names?"

"How did you get this?" Erin asked.

"The same method I get most things not easily accessible." Allison's eyes sparkled.

I touched my throat when I saw his name. "Markus Schneider."

"Visited Kenneth Wayne three times in the last three months." Allison nodded. "A coincidence?"

My gut flexed with worry for King.

"Now, what do you think they were talking about?" Allison asked no one in particular.

Erin was gripping my arm when she said, "King must have just learned this himself."

Allison tipped her body forward in her chair. We caught her up. Her dark cheeks lightened and I watched her eyes glaze over. We didn't have time to arrange a visit with Wayne, but we had to catch up with King—if only to be sure he knew what I was holding in my hand. But before I handed back the list to Allison, I caught sight of another familiar first name.

*Chandler.*

But the last name was different. *Davis.*

I pointed it out to Erin. She looked me in the eye and said, "You're not thinking that..."

"I don't know what I'm thinking."

"Did Douglas have a son?"

I shrugged. "Or any family, for that matter?"

"Do we know anything about Chandler Turner's family?"

"I don't really know anything about Chandler."

Allison's eyes bounced between Erin and me as we ping ponged our thoughts back and forth. The coincidence of us speaking with a Chandler and having another Chandler recently visit Wayne in prison was much too big for me to ignore. Sure, the last names were different, but I didn't know many Chandlers to begin with. It wasn't a common enough name for me to ignore. "We could be on to something," I said.

"Then we better acquaint ourselves with Chandler Davis before we mistakenly go accusing Chandler Turner of being someone he's not."

# CHAPTER SIXTY-THREE

ALVAREZ TOSSED ON THE EMERGENCY LIGHTS AND SLAMMED his foot down on the gas pedal. King lurched back in his seat and held on to the chicken handle. He kept glancing at the clock, worried they might be too late or that their suspicions were wrong. But King was certain of one thing. He could feel it in his gut; the shooter was planning his next attack. It was imminent. But who was his target? The pastor or Lieutenant?

King's muscles were tense as they raced east down Colfax.

With both hands gripping the steering wheel, Alvarez barely tapped the brakes as they blew through red lights. A minute later, the tires were squealing north on Colorado Blvd. Lucky for them traffic cooperated and as they entered the Park Hill neighborhood, they arrived to a still angry crowd.

Coke bottles exploded across their windshield.

Naturally, King flinched at the sudden impact. Alvarez hit the wipers and found refuge in the police barricade consisting mostly of marked patrol cars parked like a wagon caravan outside Dennis Hall's house, which was still an active crime scene.

Kicking the door open, King stood and stared into the

crowd. Mouths screamed, fists pumped into the air, and faces were mostly of color. Spotting Markus should have been as easy as seeing a cob of corn on a snowy field, but King didn't see anything that stuck out.

"I'm heading to the house." Alvarez took off to find Lieutenant.

King acknowledged his partner's move and kept his attention on the crowd.

Picket signs stabbed the air, hot blood thrashed between his ears, and King turned his focus to the rooftops.

It would be so easy to pop off a couple shots and disappear like a ghost, King thought. The shooter had done it once; King knew he could do it again. Except now there was security everywhere. They knew their suspect's skills and that he was a highly trained sniper. But Markus would be a fool to try to get to Lieutenant in the middle of all this.

"He's not going to take the shot here," King whispered to himself. He spun around and saw Lieutenant emerge from the house. He was dressed in full uniform, flanked by a half-dozen officers all keeping an eye on his personal safety. King thought he had the look of a lion. Even from where King stood, he could see the intense focus in his lieutenant's eyes.

"We are people, too!" The crowd shouted. "We will fight until the end! No justice! No peace!

King pushed his way through the throng of people, continuing his search for Markus. He was fooled with a sudden rush of excitement at a couple false sightings, so by the time he *did* see Markus's face he stopped and had to blink out the blur just to make sure.

Markus stood back, blending in with the crowd. He had a gray hoodie pulled over his head and his upper body was wrapped in a jet-black leather jacket. The crease between his brows was deep and it was clear he was staring directly at the lieutenant.

More shouts bellowed into King's ears.

A helicopter flew overhead and cracked the air.

The crowd swayed from this side to that and soon blocked King's vision.

Losing sight of Markus, King jumped and ran toward where Markus was just standing, determined this time not to let him get away.

# CHAPTER SIXTY-FOUR

THE SNIPER struggled to ease his racing heart. He hurried to the spot he'd mapped out earlier and quickly dropped into position. His blood pressure was through the roof. He knew that if he didn't get it done quick, he might miss his shot.

Taking his rifle into his grip, the small stones he lay on cut into his knees and elbows.

He inhaled, exhaled.

Closing his eyes for only a second, he placed himself firmly into one of his warmest memories. It was a sunny day and he was perched out on a granite rock high up in the alpine tundra deep in the San Juan Mountains. Cotton candy clouds drifted lazily across the bright blue summer day—a day he would never forget. Mule deer grazed in the grass below. His happy spot.

When his eyes opened, he readjusted his grip on the rifle handle and glassed the area through his scope.

Melting into the rooftop, he knew he had been made. His identity was no longer a secret. They knew who he was and they were coming for him. Time was no longer on his side.

Adrenaline replaced his anxiety. He had nothing left to lose. He swore to himself he would die with guns blazing before ever surrendering. *Martyrdom.*

Through his crosshairs, the Sniper paused on an officer's bored face.

A smirk tugged at the corners of his lips.

He checked wind speed and direction and fingered the trigger.

Closing one eye, he sighted in his target. His breaths eased and his heartrate dropped so low he might as well be dead. With his nerves relaxed and serenity closing his ears to the sounds of heavenly tunes, he whispered, "Time to meet your maker."

# CHAPTER SIXTY-FIVE

A PAINFUL BURN SLID DOWN THE BACK OF KING'S THROAT. He couldn't believe he'd lost Markus. There one second, gone the next.

Fighting his way through the wall of people, he slammed his shoulder into others, was blocked and tripped, and he stumbled as he grunted and kept moving. By the time he resurfaced in the exact spot he'd last seen Markus, he was spinning around without sight of his man.

Turning toward the house, Alvarez was at the lieutenant's side.

Lieutenant stared as Alvarez spoke passionately with his hands. King knew what was being said and, by the look on Lieutenant's face, it was clear he understood the danger. But he lacked the surprise King had expected to find.

"You already knew," King whispered to himself.

Recalling the conversation he'd had with Lieutenant the day King informed him of the shooter's connection to the Patriots of God, it all came back to him. He wondered if Lieutenant had been waiting for this day, expecting it to come in some form but never able to say because of the secrets he and the department had.

King's chest thumped as his heart kept drumming.

The hairs on the back of his neck stood, feeling that eyes were on him.

When King rolled his neck and glanced to his side, the world slowed to a colorful blur and time ceased to exist. A web of emotion spun around him as he suddenly found himself locked in a stare with Markus Schneider.

Markus dove his hand inside his jacket pocket—King thought he was reaching for a gun. A split second later, Markus ducked his head and took off sprinting toward the lieutenant.

King followed but kept hitting barriers of people no matter how hard he waved his arms through the air out in front of him.

"Alvarez!" King screamed but his words were drowned out by the crowd.

King kept fighting his way forward.

Markus had once again disappeared.

Waving his hands over his head, King kept screaming to gain attention. Nearing the police line, an officer caught sight of King. He jumped into a defensive stance and put his hand on his holstered gun just as King caught sight of Markus flanking the officer from the side.

King dove past the officer and wrapped his arms around Markus. They crashed to the pavement, tumbling hard.

"I know what you're up to, asshole." King wrestled with a shocked Markus and soon King had him on his stomach, his hands cuffed behind his back. Frisking his suspect, King's jaw dangled when he couldn't find a gun. "Where is your weapon?"

"Weapon?" Markus screeched. "I don't have a gun."

"King!" Alvarez ran toward King.

Jamming his knee between Markus's shoulder blades, King flicked his gaze to his partner. "He doesn't have a gun."

Alvarez calmed the uniformed officer who nearly pulled his handgun on King. Then Alvarez pulled Markus to his feet and tossed him up against a patrol car. Patting him down, Alvarez also found no signs of danger.

"This isn't any way to be treating an old friend." Markus sneered.

King fisted Markus's coat and violently shook him. "You think this is funny, scumbag?"

Markus grinned.

"King. Relax." Alvarez peeled King's hands off of Markus. "Not here. Not when cameras are around. You'll get your chance; trust me, buddy. Just don't do it now."

King stared into Markus's eyes and grinded his teeth before shoving him away. King moved to the side and glared at the officer who'd nearly pulled a gun on him. He moved further away, fire scurrying up his spine.

"What are you doing here, Markus?" Alvarez asked his suspect.

"I think you know why I'm here." King watched Markus flick his gaze in the lieutenant's direction. "I came to speak with Baker. To tell you boys that you're not safe here."

# CHAPTER SIXTY-SIX

ALLISON WAS LOCKED IN ON HER COMPUTER WHILE ERIN was on another, busy scrolling through Tim's accounts, and I still couldn't get it out of my head that maybe Chandler Turner was actually Douglas Davis's son.

"Here, I got something." Erin flicked her gaze to me.

I rolled my chair over the floor and tipped forward. Erin played it from the beginning. The video did a quick buffer and, as soon as it started up, I couldn't believe what it was I was seeing.

"Shit. That's him," I murmured as I listened to Timothy Morris and Chandler Turner speak into the camera.

"And they sound like Croft." Erin stared.

I held my hand over my mouth, unable to take my eyes off the boys. "He had us fooled. Made us believe he didn't get political."

"That's him, Sam." Erin nodded. "No question about it. That is Chandler Turner."

I knew it was but didn't want to believe it. He'd convinced me he was only in Croft's class for the credit—and maybe he was—but while he was there, he and Tim had obviously taken their politics to the extreme.

Allison rolled her chair to Erin's computer. "Which one is Chandler Turner?"

Erin pointed him out.

Allison was close to biting through her cheek when I said, "He was one of the first people we interviewed after the school shooting." Allison was awfully quiet and I wondered what she had dug up when working her magic this last half-hour of our day. "He's a student in Professor Dean Croft's Political Science class."

Allison rolled her eyes to me and I knew she had found something.

"You got sucked down one of your rabbit holes, didn't you?" Allison was still staring like a doe caught in headlights when she nodded. "What did you find?"

She swallowed like she was choking when she rolled her way back to her computer. "I was able to tap my way into the video surveillance of the prison," Allison was speaking a million miles per minute, "and am pretty sure that this is Chandler Davis."

Erin stopped working. We both sprang to our feet and leaned in as close as possible to stare at the face Allison had displayed on her computer screen. She zoomed in, enhanced the image, and did all her little tricks to make it as clear an image as possible. It didn't matter. I knew who I was looking at. Exactly what I was afraid of. Chandler Turner *was* Chandler Davis.

"But how is that possible?" Erin asked the room.

Allison's fingers tapped fast and hard. I didn't ask what she was doing—didn't want to interrupt her focus.

I went back to Erin's computer, scrolling through more old posts before stopping on a video made nearly six months ago. "Did you play this one?"

Erin stood over my shoulder, shaking her head no.

"Look here," I said, scrolling down, then back up. "They changed. Their outfits. The confidence in their face. Something happened where these boys were initiated into men."

"Play it." Erin jutted her chin.

Truth was, I was afraid to. My palms sweated as I rolled my neck and stared at the paused image of our little-known terrorists. Finally, I punched the mouse with a single tap from my index finger.

The boys were in complete camouflage and had an arsenal of weapons on display. "We are the Patriots of God," Chandler declared fiercely for the camera. "When Douglas Davis was murdered in cold blood, the system put his son into foster care in an attempt to scrub the boy's memory free. They tried to erase the family heritage, rid it from this green earth." Chandler laughed. "But what they failed to realize is that an ideology is something that you can't take away, not even in death. It lives. Grows. And just like water, will find its way into the roots of those ready and willing to accept the truth. We," Chandler flung his arm around the shoulders of Tim and pulled him closer to the camera, "are here to bring justice to those who did my daddy wrong."

When I gasped for air, a small whimper passed over my lips. Alarm bells were going off inside my head. It wasn't Markus. It was him—Chandler Davis. King had the wrong guy.

"I got something." Allison broke my trance. "Chandler Turner was born Chandler Davis. It's here on his birth certificate." She shared a quick glance and kept reading. "His mother died during his birth. After his father's death, his foster parents officially adopted him four years later and that's when he changed his name to Turner."

I reached in my pocket, gripped my cellphone, and called King.

The line rang.

My heart pounded so hard it felt like my ribs would bruise.

It went to his voicemail.

"Shit!" I swung my hand through the air and hit redial. I heard the line click over. "King?"

"Sam..." the line rustled.

"It's not Markus," I yelled. "You have the wrong guy. The shooter is Chandler Turner."

"Chandler who?"

"Chandler Turner. Markus isn't the shooter."

Suddenly King's voice got clearer. "I know."

I craned my neck like a giraffe. "You know?"

"We have Markus in custody. Who is Chandler Turner?"

"He's the guy we're looking for." I rolled my eyes, frustrated by the cell reception. Not wanting to waste another second, I spilled everything we'd just learned about Chandler Turner. "He's nineteen-years-old and was the one to radicalize Timothy Morris."

"How do you know all this?"

I glanced to Allison. "Best I don't say over the phone."

A loud uproar erupted through my earpiece. I pulled my phone away and felt my belly tie itself in a dozen different knots.

"Where is Lieutenant Baker?" I spit into the mic before my phone was back on my ear.

"He's fine. I'm looking at him now."

There was more screaming and it did little to settle the pit in my stomach. My mind spun around a debris-filled orbit and my eyes popped. "If the lieutenant is there, then who has eyes on the pastor?"

# CHAPTER SIXTY-SEVEN

"YOU SHOULD REALLY STAY INSIDE," ONE OF THE TWO uniformed officers said to Pastor Michaels.

"Yet you won't give me the specifics of why you're parked in front of my church." Pastor Michaels grinned and backed away from the open car window.

"Just following orders."

The pastor chuckled. "And so am I." He backpedaled and pointed to the heavens. "Enjoy the warm coffee. There is more inside waiting for you when you're finished with that."

The officer raised his cup and thanked the pastor once again.

Turning on a heel, the pastor smiled. He enjoyed the short conversation he'd had with the police, particularly adored seeing them accept his offer of coffee. He thought they could use something warm to drink on a cold blustery day like today. It made him feel good. After so much time inside devoting his attention to those who were suffering, he could use the fresh air, too.

His heart was at peace. He waved and greeted a couple

members of his congregation leaving his church when suddenly a hot searing pain cut through his heart.

The sound of air popping followed a second behind the initial surprise of being shot.

Hot blood splattered into his hands, pouring down his chest.

His lungs deflated and his knees gave as the pastor fell to the ground, lying on his back. Staring up into the heavens, the pastor stared into the bright sunlight feeling no pain at all, only peace as he whispered, "Forgive me Father for I have sinned, and now I'm coming home."

# CHAPTER SIXTY-EIGHT

Susan sat behind her work desk with her eyes closed. The taste of a completely chewed plastic pen cap filled her mouth and all she could hear was her employees' fingers tapping away on their computers with the occasional soft murmurs sparking up every few minutes. She tried to focus on the task at hand but couldn't. Her nerves were still raw and jittery and she was anxious for the attorney to arrive.

The doorbell chimed and crashed through the stagnant air.

Her eyelids flickered wide open.

The blood left her cheeks and her heart skipped a beat when all she could think of was how it better be the attorney and not another visit from Rick Morris.

Rolling her gaze to the front of the office, she curled her throbbing fingertips into the palm of her hand. They were still clammy from the events that had unfolded this morning. After her threatening visit with Rick and talking with Sam, she'd locked the front doors and given her staff specific instructions to not let any visitors into the building unless first approved by herself.

The doorbell chimed again.

Carly popped her head into Susan's office. "Want me to get that?"

Susan stood, moved to Carly, and ironed a friendly hand down her shoulder. "It's all right. Better if I answer it."

She sailed confidently toward the front, her heels making her appear taller than she was. One look through the glass and she could safely see the visitor wasn't Rick. She turned the lock and twisted the deadbolt free. Opening the door, a tall man with a full head of dark hair and wearing an expensive suit said, "Ms. Young?"

Susan angled her head sideways.

"Attorney Gregory Kilmartin." He extended his right hand, offering it to Susan. "Philip Price's recommendation."

Susan cast her gaze to his opened hand. "I'm sorry to have to ask, but do you have any identification?"

Mr. Kilmartin paused, stared, and flashed Susan a quick questioning look. "Certainly." He dove his hand into the inside of his cashmere topcoat and produced a business card.

Susan took it and scanned his credentials. "I do apologize," she said, handing the card back. "We have been victims of threats and you can never be too sure people are who they say they are."

"You keep it." Mr. Kilmartin nodded to his business card. "I've been following the events and I apologize, myself, for not arriving sooner."

Susan nodded. "Please, come inside."

As soon as Mr. Kilmartin entered the office, Susan closed the door behind him and once again locked it. "We have the conference room waiting."

"Perfect."

"I'll be completely honest with you, Mr. Kilmartin, my staff and I are in over our heads with this immense undertaking."

"My understanding is that you weren't given time to prepare."

Together they meandered their way into the conference room and Susan watched Mr. Kilmartin set his leather briefcase on top of the center table and remove his coat. "That's right. We were nominated without warning."

"I've handled dozens of situations like this before, Ms. Young, and I can assure you that we'll get through this one as well."

"It's good to have someone with experience finally able to assist us."

Carly entered the room, introduced herself to Mr. Kilmartin, and dropped a stack of folders in front of Susan. "So, where would you like to begin?" Susan asked Mr. Kilmartin.

"From the beginning."

Susan knew this would take a while when she turned her attention to Carly. "Carly, please make a fresh pot of coffee. If I need anything else, I'll give you a call."

As soon as it was just the two of them again, Mr. Kilmartin asked Susan, "Tell me what has been donated."

Over the next several minutes, Susan broke down the numbers and how her team created a list of the victims they believed should be compensated.

From behind his reading glasses Mr. Kilmartin studied the data. "Have you released a statement to the media?"

"Planning on doing it today." Susan twisted the ring around her finger.

"Let's hold off on that until we have a solid grasp on how this money will be distributed. Better to keep families in the dark for a day longer than overpromising something we can't deliver on."

Susan bit her cheek and felt a wave of heat bloom across his chest.

"Something wrong?" He stared.

"We received a call from a reporter at 9News this morning."

Mr. Kilmartin removed his glasses and cocked his head to the side. "I need to know everything you said, and don't hide anything because I'll find out about it if you did soon enough. Trust me. Transparency is the best method going forward. I can't help you if I don't have a clear picture of everything you've done up until the moment I arrived."

Susan shifted in her chair. Then she reached over the table, opened up a folder, and handed the attorney the check written for $10,000. "That's generous," Mr. Kilmartin said after looking at it.

"It came with specific instructions."

Mr. Kilmartin arched a single eyebrow.

"To be given to Timothy Morris's family."

"The school shooter?"

Susan nodded.

Mr. Kilmartin's eyes went back to the check he was still holding with both hands. "Well, this is certainly a point of tension."

"It was delivered in person."

The attorney leaned back in his chair. "Did you know them?"

Susan shook her head no. "It was given anonymously."

Mr. Kilmartin took a moment to stare at the bank check. "Any idea who might be behind this?"

"No." Susan furrowed her brow. "Does it matter?"

The attorney sighed. "No." He locked his gaze on Susan. "But it is an unusual request considering all that has transpired since the school shooting."

Carly knocked and said, "Susan, sorry to interrupt, but the afternoon news cycle is beginning."

"Thank you." Susan stood, reached for the remote, and

flicked on the flat screen on the conference room wall. "I just want to see if they're reporting on our call from this morning."

Mr. Kilmartin kept busy with the papers as Susan kept one ear on the television. Nothing was said about the victims' fund for a full fifteen minutes, then they both lifted their heads when they heard the news anchor mention Susan's business's debt and that some in the community worried that she would use the money for personal gain.

"This is insane." Susan pointed at the TV and shook her head. "It's not true."

Mr. Kilmartin rolled his eyes to the screen.

"I swear," Susan reiterated. "They're twisting my words."

"Call your accountant." Mr. Kilmartin's tone sharpened. "Let's just be sure that all your numbers are in order and a reporter hasn't uncovered something that you are unaware of."

Susan nodded and left the conference room for her office as she heard news breaking. Feeling lightheaded, she didn't bother to stop. Instead, she dropped into her chair and pinched the bridge of her nose, wondering how she'd found herself living this nightmare. She couldn't believe this was happening. No way was she committing anything close to fraud. They had it all wrong.

Suddenly, her cellphone rang. Susan snapped out of her depression and answered Benjamin's call. "Hey handsome." She tried her best to sound uplifting but it came out sounding flat.

"Hey beautiful."

His voice was the relief she needed. Without him prompting her, she told him how her day quickly unraveled soon after he dropped her off. Benjamin heard the fear in her voice when she spoke about Rick and could feel her pain at the accusation being thrown at her for supposedly stealing from the victims. Benjamin was sorry, sympathetic throughout it all, but added, "Did you hear?"

"What now?" Susan stopped breathing.

"Pastor Dwayne Michaels was shot and killed outside his church just a little while ago."

Susan's eyes watered with tears. "Oh my god."

"Susan," Benjamin's voice dropped to a whispery breath, "I'm worried about you."

# CHAPTER SIXTY-NINE

ALLISON LEARNED OF IT FIRST. WHEN ERIN FLICKED ON her police scanner app, we knew it was true. There was a murder at the pastor's church. Without hearing the details, I knew it was him.

"No. No. No," I cried.

We were too late. I had lost connection with King and couldn't get through to him again no matter how many times I tried. We'd known the pastor's life was in danger, yet we'd done nothing. Not even he'd known how to stop what was coming.

A sharp pain of guilt stabbed me in the side. I ran out of the room and barreled my way into the tiny bathroom in Allison's office. Falling on my knees, I heaved my stomach into the toilet. Pellets of sweat filled my face. When there was nothing left inside of me, I dropped my bottom to the floor and fell back against the wall.

Crying, I knew this was Chandler. No doubt about it.

We were so close, even had him pinned as the suspect we were after, yet we couldn't get to him fast enough.

I swiped my hand over my face, wiping the tears away

from my cheeks. Forcing myself to my feet, I stood at the sink swishing cold water in my mouth. When I swept my gaze up to the mirror, I stared into my own reflection and said, "Don't give up, Sam. Go get him and make him *pay*."

It was the pep talk I needed to hear. As difficult as it was to know the pastor had been killed, there was still at least one other person we knew for sure that Chandler wanted to take out.

I ran back into the office and found Erin already getting ready to hit the road. Allison had her head buried in one hand and, when I went to hug her, I said, "I love you, baby. This will all be over soon."

"My eyes are blurry." She flicked her gaze up to me and flashed a weak smile. "That's all."

I reminder her about Lieutenant being a target, and Allison told me to go.

Erin and I dashed to her car and raced to Pastor Michaels's church. I wasn't sure what we were going to find or why we'd chosen to come here instead of searching for Lieutenant Baker, but maybe I was hoping to find King already on scene. And maybe luck would have it that Lieutenant would be here, too.

The moment we arrived on the church's street, we were stopped and couldn't get past the police barricade. With my pulse throbbing, I was on high alert. Keeping an eye out for anything that might give me some kind of answer to what had happened, it didn't take me long to see several detectives canvassing for possible witnesses to the crime.

I hit redial on King's number.

He still didn't pick up his phone and panic knocked the air out of me.

Spinning in circles, I watched the lab team begin collecting evidence and witnessed people being interviewed by the cops. There were too many obstacles in my line of vision to know where the pastor had been shot—inside or outside, I didn't know. My guess was outside, given our shooter's history.

Holding one hand on top of my head, I didn't like the casual energy surrounding me. No one seemed to be in a rush. Even the paramedics had the back of the ambulance shut with lights off.

I palmed my cell and checked the display screen again.

The coroner arrived and I followed him to the body I knew to be that of the pastor.

A tremor rocked my core so hard it nearly knocked my feet out from under me. I swallowed down a deep breath and stared. A sheet already covered his body and suddenly a flash-flood of memories came swirling to the front of my mind.

The day Pastor Michaels officiated my marriage to Gavin. The compassion he always held for members of his community. The concern I saw in his eyes the other day when he asked about Mason. Even my conversation in the park last night.

Everything went quiet as I felt the stone harden in my throat.

"I'm going to go try to find out what happened," Erin said.

I nodded, unable to get a single word past my constricted throat. Then I felt my cellphone vibrate inside my hand. Excitement filled my lungs with a wistful breath.

"Irene, I'm at the church," I said, assuming she had already heard the news and that was the reason for her call.

She caught me off guard when she asked, "Is Mason with you?"

Bile gurgled up my esophagus as I felt my insides try to wring out what little there might still be in my stomach. "No, I thought he was with you."

Irene remained silent and I felt the tips of my toes go numb. I was too afraid to ask.

"Mason is gone."

I closed my eyes, willing myself to stay strong. "Did he tell you he was leaving?"

"He said he was going to the corner store. That he wouldn't be long. That was over an hour ago. I'm sorry, Sam. I know I shouldn't have allowed him to leave with all that is going on out there in the neighborhood, but he convinced me that he would be quick."

"It's not your fault, Irene."

"I didn't know what to do. I feel awful."

"I'll give him a call," I said, promising to keep her in the loop. "I think I might know where he ran off to."

# CHAPTER SEVENTY

I LEFT ERIN AT THE CHURCH TO CONTINUE PIECING together what happened to the pastor. She promised she'd call if King arrived or if she learned anything that might be useful in tracking down Chandler. She handed me the keys to her car and I was off to find Mason.

I chewed on a fingernail as I drove.

Even with unease keeping my body rigid, I tried to convince myself that Mason's disappearance was one big misunderstanding. He was a sixteen-year-old boy struggling to communicate not only his feelings but his plans. We had all been there. But his timing couldn't be worse.

Within minutes I was rolling into the convenience store Grandma Irene thought Mason said he was running off to. I parked and entered the small store, heading directly to the clerk hiding behind the front cash register.

"I'm looking for my son. He said he was coming here about an hour ago. Have you seen him?" I flipped my phone around and showed the older black man an image of Mason.

He studied it for a minute before shaking his head. "Nope. Haven't seen him."

"Are you sure? He would have been here alone."

His grey eyes moved back to the picture of Mason. "No one his age came here alone."

I lowered my head and felt my heart shrink. "If he comes in, please call me." I left my *Times* card with the clerk and stepped out of the building, putting a call in to Mason.

Nothing. Straight to voicemail.

I glanced up the block and back down the other way, convinced Mason had gone to visit Nolan. I just couldn't see him doing anything else. It was what he wanted to do, and something I promised him we could do together if I found a moment's break. Mason *had* to be there.

Once back inside Erin's car, I backed away and pointed the car west, driving to St. Joseph Hospital.

Mason had done this before and, in the end, it had been nothing, or at least not as big as I'd made it out to be at the time. I didn't want to overreact but I hated not knowing where he was or why he didn't tell anyone the truth of where he was going.

*Or, maybe he did tell the truth and something happened to him?*

I withdrew inside myself, shriveling up like a raisin, convincing my brain that the fears it was conjuring up were entirely irrational. But even I knew it was a lie. My fears were real. The school shooting proved that. Tim wanted Mason dead, and maybe Chandler did, too.

I slapped the flat part of my hand on the steering wheel and shrieked out a curse.

Pinching back the threat of tears pooling in the backs of my eyes, I tried calling him again.

It went straight to voicemail and I knew he had turned his phone off or the battery had died.

Fifteen minutes passed in mostly a blur. As soon as I reached the hospital, I dove the hood of my car into the dark belly of the parking garage, stopping at the gate and punching the button to retrieve my ticket.

My legs grew restless as it seemed to take forever in finding an open parking space but, finally, I did. It wasn't too far from the building's entrance, the doors unlocked.

Galloping through the hallways, I headed to the west wing and rode the elevator to the fifth floor. Nolan's door was open when I arrived and a flood of optimism perked up my eyes.

Time slowed as I approached and, when I noticed the silence inside the room, I knew that Mason wasn't here.

Natalie was sitting in the corner arm chair reading when I knocked. She lifted her head and I smiled and greeted Nolan. "Natalie, can I speak to you?"

Her brows pinched as she made her way across the room. She folded her arms across her chest when she stepped into the hallway. "Hey, Sam, about last night, I'm sorry I left like I did."

"Water under the bridge." I could tell by the look in her eye she hadn't seen the news unfolding. "Have you seen Mason?"

She shook her head. "No. Not since yesterday."

My phone beeped with an email notification and I glanced down to see that it was from Nancy Jordan. Without thinking, I opened it and read it in front of Natalie.

*As promised, here is the information I have. Professor Dean Croft was behind the $10K donation to the Morris family. Now maybe you could tell me why he would do that.*

"Sam..." Natalie brought me back to the present.

"I don't know where he is," I said, meeting her eye. My voice cracked when I told her how he'd just left and never come back from his grandparents' house. As I talked, I could see my own terror reflecting in Natalie's pupils.

"Maybe Nolan knows where he is?" Natalie stepped back

into the room and I heard her ask her son if he had heard from Mason when I received a call from an unknown number.

I stared at my phone, debating whether or not I should answer.

It could have been work, a source, someone tied to the pastor, or even...Mason.

I tapped the green call button with my thumb and answered. "Hello."

"I thought maybe you wouldn't answer." His voice sent a chill down my spine.

A sharp pain settled in my jaw as black spots filled my vision. I wobbled on my feet when I said, "What do you want, Chandler?"

"To meet."

Hot breath spewed from my nostrils as I reminded myself of the people he had killed. "I have nothing to say to you."

A psychotic shrill of laughter filled my ear. "Maybe not, but," his tone flatlined into something dangerous, "I have something I know you want."

My hand flew over my mouth to stifle the moan working its way up my chest. "You're making a big mistake."

He gave me the address and told me a time. Then he said, "Come alone and don't even think about involving the police. Trust me, you'll regret it if you do."

# CHAPTER SEVENTY-ONE

"HE CALLED YOU?" ERIN COULDN'T BELIEVE IT EITHER. "Chandler actually called *you?*"

I was lucky Erin answered at all. Not wanting to chance Chandler's intelligence, I played it safe and asked Natalie if I could make the call from her phone. She happily agreed without asking too many questions. With Mason gone, and Nolan not having heard from him either, Natalie understood everything I was feeling. But I couldn't tell her that maybe Mason had been kidnapped. I kept that piece of the puzzle a secret.

"Yeah, just now." I kept glancing over my shoulder, thinking I was being watched. It was that prickling feeling that wouldn't go away. I kept telling myself that maybe Chandler had seen me at the church and followed me here to the hospital.

"Sam, it's pretty tight-lipped over here but it was definitely him who killed the pastor. You shouldn't go. Especially not alone."

I bit my lip, wishing I had the guts to tell Erin that Chandler had Mason. "Just find King and tell him where I'll be."

"Sam," she protested.

Finally, I snapped. "I think he has Mason."

"Did he say that?"

"He said 'I have something I know you want.' Mason is missing and he's what I want."

"Shit."

Erin didn't have to say it. I knew Chandler wanted to finish what he started. Maybe he realized killing Lieutenant Baker would prove too difficult so he decided to take an easier target. One that would not only get my attention but that of the department he'd declared war against, too.

There was movement behind me and, when I turned, I found Natalie staring with trembling eyes. She'd overheard what I just said. I couldn't take it back, couldn't cover my tracks. The secret was out. Covering her mouth with her hand, tears began falling from her eyes.

"There is no other way," I said to Erin, making sure to lower my voice. "I have to go."

"Then let me come with you."

"I can't. Chandler said to come alone and to keep the police out of it. That's why I called you from this phone. In case he's somehow tracking me."

"I don't have a good feeling about this."

Neither did I, but I kept my fears to myself.

"Then keep your wits about you and stall him for as long as you can until help arrives."

As Erin's words became reality, the severity of my situation finally sank in and buried itself deep. My outlook was grim, but it was our only option.

"Just find King. I'll see you there." I killed the call before I started to cry.

Natalie wasn't too far and I moved to her, thanking her again for allowing me to borrow her phone. Staring into her watery gaze, I said, "Don't worry. This will all be over soon."

# CHAPTER SEVENTY-TWO

MY HEART HAMMERED INSIDE MY CHEST. SWEAT POURED down my sides, my nerves heating my core to an intolerable level. Even with the window cracked, there was nothing I could do to cool down.

I was afraid Chandler might take Mason away from me; scared that I might do something to get myself killed and leave Mason all alone. But, mostly, I was terrified of what might happen if I didn't confront Chandler. There was no telling what he might do next, how far he might take this battle of his or if it would even end with the killing of Lieutenant Baker.

With one eye on the lookout for traffic cops, I kept my foot heavy on the accelerator as I sped my way from St. Joseph's toward Denver International Airport.

I checked my phone.

I wanted so badly to get in touch with Mason or King but decided against it.

I hadn't heard back from anyone and all I could hope was that Erin would find King before time ran out.

It didn't take me long before I was exiting off Pena Boulevard and heading north on Tower Road. Making my way to the very open and exposed USAirport Parking area, all I could think about was how foolish it was for me to agree to meet an expert sniper, here of all places.

The tires slowly rolled over cold pavement and I listened to the pebbles crack and grind as they crumbled beneath the car's weight. I took my ticket at the gate and worked to find an empty spot when my phone chimed with a message from Chandler.

*Drive to the far eastern end of the parking lot. I'll meet you there.*

I did as I was told despite feeling like this was a setup to put me in the crosshairs as he'd done to the pastor. But I needed to get Mason back.

I chose a spot between a black Toyota Sequoia and a bright red Ford F250. I figured they could shield me from a bullet if that was what Chandler had planned for me. Better to play it safe than risking it all.

*You better have what I want,* I messaged back, then stepped out of the car and began looking around.

The gusts of wind were relentless and the cold air nipped at my nose. Tumbleweeds scurried across the windswept grass and I caught sight of a jack rabbit darting his way through the field. Back on the other side, I watched an airport shuttle scoot along picking up and dropping off passengers. Other than that, I was out here alone—giving Chandler exactly what he wanted.

As I stood there waiting, my mind kept playing tricks on me. I kept hearing my phone ring when it didn't, and there was a very real feeling that Chandler was watching me from afar through his rifle scope. But I stood between the big vehicles with my hands buried in my pockets and continued to wait.

I just wanted Mason back.

To get him home safely.

We weren't part of Chandler's fight. Somehow, Chandler had made it our concern the moment Tim decided to make Mason a target.

Staring at the parking lot entrance, I watched a black Honda Civic stop at the gate.

I kept an eye on it from behind the Toyota. It slowly rolled east, getting closer. My stomach tensed and anticipated this to be the arrival of my guest. Its window tint was so dark it was impossible to see inside. Squinting through the sun's glare, I couldn't know for sure if it was Chandler or not. I watched it weave through the rows before finally coming down the lane where I was parked.

It had to be Chandler.

Stepping out just far enough for the driver to see me, there was a brief burst of engine before stopping not more than five feet away from where I stood.

The passenger window rolled down and I held my breath. Chandler's piercing green eyes stared as he said, "Get inside."

"Where are we going?" I asked, remembering Erin's advice to stall for as long as I could.

Chandler grinned, glanced forward, and shook his head. Then he lifted his arm and pointed a gun, aiming it between my eyes. "Don't make me tell you again."

I swallowed a difficult breath and inched my way to the passenger door. Reaching for the handle, it was cold to my touch as I pulled it open and asked, "Where is Mason?"

"Sit."

I sat, keeping a close eye on his trigger finger. "Do you have him or not?"

"Now shut it." Chandler waved the muzzle of the gun through the air, pointing at the car door.

The door clicked shut and he brought the gun into his lap but still pointed at me. "Toss your phone out the window."

I did as he said. Satisfied with my response, he began

driving. The mood was tense, the drive quiet, and I was overly suspicious of his intention. He exited the parking lot and headed north on Tower Road where he took me to the nearby landfill.

"Is Mason here?"

Chandler parked the car in a dirt pull-off and told me to get out.

"Where are we going?"

He leaned over and I caught a quick sour scent of his body odor. Pointing his gun to the top of the landfill he said, "There."

"Mason is there?"

"Get out." He pushed the muzzle deep into my side.

I did as he said, knowing he wouldn't hesitate to pull the trigger if only out of pure frustration and a burning desire to prove he was in control.

I was on foot being led up the steep incline by a madman. We trudged our way up the grassy knoll before rounding the ridgetop and coming within sight of his sniper rifle already set up and waiting near the southwestern edge.

I glanced behind me and found him smirking. "Mason isn't here."

"Where is he?"

"Wish I knew. Timothy would have liked to know I'd finished the job he couldn't complete."

Balling my fists at my side, I clenched my teeth and asked, "Then what do you have for me?"

His brows raised in delight. "A request."

Staring at him from beneath my brow, I said, "And what would that be?"

"Don't worry, Samantha, you're already halfway to completing it." He jutted his chin to his rifle. "Look through the scope and tell me what you see."

A stiff breeze blew my hair over my eyes. I stared at

Chandler through the curtain of hair, already knowing he had his rifle pointing at Erin's car. My insides quivered with the realization that he had used me as bait to draw in and kill King, knowing I would have never come alone without first telling him my plan. I was too caught up with getting Mason back to realize my mistake before it was too late.

# CHAPTER SEVENTY-THREE

AFTER HIS CONVERSATION WITH SAM, KING LEFT MARKUS with Lieutenant Baker and he and Alvarez raced across the neighborhood toward the church.

A sharp pain of regret kept his side stitched in agony.

"Here we go," Alvarez said, reading from the police's online database. "Chandler Davis. Son of Douglas Davis. Put into foster care after his father was killed. Chandler was one-year-old at the time." Alvarez picked up his head from his smartphone.

King readjusted his grip on the steering wheel. "He doesn't have any recollection of it ever even happening."

"Doesn't mean he doesn't know what happened." Alvarez cast his gaze back to his phone's screen. "At age five he was adopted by his foster parents and his name was changed from Davis to Turner."

King scrubbed a hand over his face. "That's what Sam was telling me. How did we miss this?"

Alvarez shrugged.

"Not because we have to jump through bureaucratic

tape." King flicked his gaze to his partner. "Maybe we're just not as good as Samantha."

Alvarez rolled his neck, too filled with pride to admit they needed Samantha as much as she needed them.

"She's good." King nodded. "Maybe now you'll understand why I trust her as an informant."

Alvarez didn't respond by the time King reached for his phone. Pinching his brows, the screen was dark and blank. He tapped it. There was no sign of life. The thing was dead. He breathed out a whispery curse and tossed it onto the dash. It must have busted during his scuffle with Markus.

The CB radio crackled and King turned it up.

He and Alvarez listened intently. When news of the pastor's murder broke, King stomped on the gas pedal and the car lurched forward.

"Dammit." Alvarez punched the dash with a closed fist.

King clenched his jaw and felt a ball of fire scurry up his spine. He wanted to do something. Anything. But there was nothing he could do. It was too late. They didn't act fast enough and now the pastor was dead because of a decision he'd made.

"We should have never left him with only a patrol car," King muttered.

"It doesn't matter." Alvarez stared out his window and shook his head. "Not if it's the sniper who shot him."

King knew his partner was right but it didn't ease the guilt he was feeling. He blamed Markus, he blamed the pastor's secret, he blamed Captain's lack of urgency on the matter. Mostly, he blamed himself.

Nearing the church, he hit the brakes. The tires squealed and as soon as the car was parked, the two detectives kicked their doors open and ran to the crime scene tape. The patrol officers were on scene, doing nothing.

"Why aren't you doing anything?" King screamed as he approached the body, flashing his badge.

"It's too late. He's gone," Alvarez said.

"It came out of nowhere," an officer said as he glanced at King's badge.

King kneeled and pulled back the sheet covering the pastor's body. "Son of a bitch."

He clamped his hand on the nape of his neck as he stood and stared at the pastor. His feet shuffled in an endless dance and he thought he might vomit. He glanced to his partner. Alvarez's dull and distant eyes were a clear reminder that they had both seen too much over the years.

"We'll get this asshole," Alvarez said. "He'll get what's coming for him."

Feeling the rage build inside of him, King swung his closed fist through the air and made contact with his opened palm. He swiped Alvarez's hand off his shoulder and marched his way back to their car. Taking the radio receiver into his hand, he called dispatch and put word out about the possible suspect. "Name, Chandler Davis, 19 years old." He gave the specifics of what he knew and then heard his name being called from somewhere behind him.

Twisting his spine, he looked over his shoulder and saw Erin waving her arms above her head from behind the police tape. King ran over to her and, as he did, he couldn't help but notice how she seemed frantic, anxious like time was about to expire.

"Erin, don't look," he said. "It's not worth it."

"I know. I can't help myself."

King looked around for what was missing. "Where's Sam?"

"That's just it." Erin's eyes locked with King's. "She left."

"What do you mean?" King's heartrate suddenly blasted through the rooftop. "Where did she go?"

"Alex," Erin inhaled a deep breath of air, "Sam believes Chandler took Mason."

King's chest caved in as Erin unleashed the details of everything she knew. When Erin was finished telling him how Mason went missing and how Chandler called Sam, King asked, "Why the airport?"

Erin shrugged.

"It doesn't matter. We have to go. Now." King called to Alvarez and waved him along. He grabbed Erin's hand and led her to his car. The three of them piled inside and King sped off.

"Where is the lieutenant?" Erin asked from the backseat.

Without taking his eyes off the road, King responded, "He's safe. We're not taking any chances until we can be sure we know who is behind these shootings."

Alvarez was on the radio putting out an APB for Mason while they sped with sirens wailing, weaving their way northeast to I-70, then east to Denver International Airport.

"Why does he want to meet Sam way out here?" King asked again. "They couldn't be hopping on a plane; they would never get through security without tipping somebody off." When no one responded, he flicked his gaze to the rearview mirror and locked eyes with Erin. "Any ideas?"

Erin shook her head no.

"You and Sam must have come across something," King pressed further.

Erin's expression pinched as she thought back to what it could all mean. "Just that the pastor lied about his testimony in the Kenneth Wayne trial and that Chandler Turner was born Chandler Davis."

With frustration building, King yanked on the wheel and sped past a couple of slow commuters who remained oblivious to the lights and siren wailing. "It makes no sense to take his fight here," King lashed out at Erin.

The car fell quiet for a moment as they took their race onto Pena Boulevard. Then, just before the exit to Tower Road, Alvarez said, "You ever hear of the conspiracy theories that surround the airport?"

"For Christ sake," King growled.

"Just hear me out. I think it might be why Chandler came way out here." Alvarez told everyone briefly about the theories of how some think the airport was built by a Nazi group of the New World Order. "Apparently, the airport's runways are shaped like a swastika when viewed from above."

"Maybe. But it doesn't explain what he's doing here with Sam."

"The symbolism must resonate with the Patriots of God."

The airport was now within view and they exited off Pena Boulevard and headed north on Tower Road when suddenly King slammed his foot down on the brakes and cut the wheel sharp enough to make the tires squeal. The car he cut off behind him honked and King ignored him as he pulled into the Conoco gas station within clear view of USAirport Parking.

"King, what the hell are you doing?" Alvarez was breathing hard. "You nearly got us hit back there."

King stared ahead. His mind churned. Shaking his head, he said, "How did we not think of this sooner."

"What are you talking about? Think of what?" Alvarez snapped like a Doberman.

King turned his head and stared at his partner. "This is a setup. They're not there."

"And you can tell that from way over here? I can see the parking lot but I couldn't tell you if they're there or not."

With her nose pressed up against the glass, Erin said, "You're right. It's what he does."

King scanned the horizon. "He wants us to step into his crosshairs. Just like he did to everyone else he's killed."

"So, what do we do?" Alvarez huffed. "The clock is ticking."

King reached for the radio receiver and said, "I have an idea."

# CHAPTER SEVENTY-FOUR

I COULDN'T BELIEVE WHAT I WAS SEEING. MY LEGS WERE numb as I lay in the prone position, squinting through the rifle scope with my right eye. The ground was cold and hard but I didn't notice anything other than Erin's car caught between the crosshairs.

Chandler had fooled me into believing he had Mason. Now that I understood his plan, the question became, what would he do with me once he took out the cavalry I knew was coming to save me?

My left eye opened as I pulled away from the scope. With my palms pressing into the dirt, I pushed myself up and dusted off my thighs. The rifle's metal glint reflected in the glaring sunshine. I knew I needed to act quickly.

"If you're hoping Lieutenant Baker will be coming for me, you're wrong."

"Now why would you pour water on my dreams like that?" Chandler's eyes were wild. "Baker killed my father."

"Your father was a criminal."

"He was a patriot." Chandler lunged forward and stomped

his boot down hard into the ground. He stared at me with dark eyes hiding under his brow. A fire burned within.

My heart raced knowing just how unpredictable he was.

"My father was a man who fought and died for his country."

I kept a close eye on his movements as I dug deep into my memory. I couldn't recall reading anything about Douglas Davis's record of service in the United States military. Then again, maybe Chandler was referring to the Patriots of God movement his father started. It didn't matter.

"It doesn't have to end like this," I said, pointing to the rifle on the ground behind me.

"Revenge is the only way this ends." Chandler waved his handgun around in the air between us.

"Is that what Kenneth Wayne told you? I know you've been visiting him."

"You don't know what it's like." His laugh was filled with pain. "No one does. The only reason Kenneth is imprisoned is because the pastor lied under oath."

"Is that why you killed him?" I paused, hoping to get Chandler to confess. When he didn't respond I continued, "Because you think he committed perjury."

"I don't think, I *know* he did." The boy released a guttural roar. "And I know you know it, too."

"Tell me. Maybe there is something that I don't know. Maybe I have the facts wrong."

Chandler flicked his fiery gaze over my left shoulder before saying, "The police department has gotten away with hiding the truth for long enough."

He reached for my arm and clamped a tight hand around my elbow. Dragging me away from his rifle, he spun me around and pushed me to the ground. "Put your hands behind your head."

Everything was moving so fast it was hard to keep up. My

vision blurred and my blood thrashed in my ears, making me dizzy with thoughts that this was it. "If Kenneth Wayne didn't kill those two black men, then who did?"

Chandler closed a pair of handcuffs around one wrist before yanking my hands off my head and tying them behind my back. My head was light as I struggled to suck enough air into my lungs. With death on my doorstep, I refused to give up hope.

"See, you don't even know." I looked over my shoulder and kept talking. "You were too young to remember. But I can tell you, it was an ugly time and you might not have been told the complete story of what happened."

"Don't tell me what I don't know."

Chandler put his foot between my shoulders and kicked me face-first into the dirt. My skull cracked against the stone and I winced as the sharp pain traveled through my spine.

"I know what it was like." Chandler marched around me. "How do you think I've been able to fracture the city in just the last forty-eight hours? My life was ruined because of what the cops did. They took my family away from me. Do you know what that feels like?"

I lay on my stomach, my legs splayed, my hands cuffed behind my back with blood dribbling down my face like hot tears as I thought about Gavin. "I do know what it's like. I lost my husband."

Chandler stopped pacing. "But you still have half a heart left. Me, I have nothing."

"You have a foster family who I'm sure loves you. You have school and a whole life to look forward to. Don't make it worse for yourself. You can still get out of this alive."

"It's too late to turn back." Chandler moved closer to the ridge, keeping his eye on the parking lot in the distance.

My thoughts drifted to Mason. "Why did you target North High?"

"That was Tim's idea. He hated it there. Wanted to kill everyone. Once I knew of his anger and how impressionable he was, I saw my chance. It was a perfect opportunity for me to begin my war against the police. Tim got what he wanted, but he also gave me enough time to complete my own mission."

I peeled my head off the ground and raised it high enough to see Chandler. He was still standing with his back to me, watching for King to arrive. I wondered what was taking him so long and wished there was a way for me to warn him to not come at all, to spare himself.

"And my son? Why did Tim want to kill Mason?"

"That was Tim's decision. He hates Blacks as much as I do."

Every fiber in my body flexed as I thrashed in an attempt to wiggle myself free. I had never wanted to hit somebody as much as I wanted to smack him now. He disgusted me. I wished I would have caught on to him sooner.

Chandler heard my feet kicking in the dirt and turned around. He walked over to me, laughing at how pathetic I looked. "You know, the day I saw you and your hot little blonde sidekick walk into Croft's class I thought I was done for." The toe of his boot tapped my outer thigh, firm but not hard enough to bruise. "But you came there to talk to him." He laughed into the thin air. "Wayne told me everything, including how the system tried to erase my heritage. But, you know what? Despite the entire world's attempt to cleanse me of my family's past, I found out."

Chandler crouched down low next to my head and brushed my hair out of my eyes. I flinched and spat in his direction.

He flicked my saliva off his hand and said, "You know how I learned of my history?"

I stared into his face and clenched my jaw.

"Professor Croft." He smirked. "Irony is a bitch, ain't it? If it weren't for his stupid assignment, I might have lived my whole life not knowing who I truly was."

Chandler kept his eyes on me, smiling, as he stroked my rosy cheek.

"You have beautiful skin," he said. "Shame that you had to taint yourself by marrying a black man."

Suddenly, Chandler stood. He seemed to have a sixth sense for knowing when his target arrived. I strained my neck and watched him gaze through a pair of binoculars. I could feel it, too, see it in his stance. Either King had arrived with Erin, or it was another officer who'd come looking for me. Either way, no matter who it was, I knew they weren't safe.

"What is it?" I asked, hoping he would reveal what I couldn't see.

"It's about time they came looking for you," Chandler said as he positioned himself behind his rifle. "I knew you would tell someone our little secret."

# CHAPTER SEVENTY-FIVE

ERIN HAD NEVER BEEN SO NERVOUS IN HER ENTIRE LIFE. Her knees wobbled and she could hear her breath shake each time she exhaled. She knew this was what they had to do to save Sam and get Mason back from the monster they were with.

Everything was riding on King's theory. It was the best conclusion they could come up with. The clock was ticking down and no one knew what Chandler would do once he learned that the entire police force was coming after him. He could kill Sam, Mason too, or take them hostage. Anything was possible, but only one thing was certain. The department was out for blood—frothing at the mouth for an opportunity to take down the cop killer who'd murdered their brothers in blue.

Erin closed her eyes and said a quick prayer. Her heart told her Samantha was still alive, but until she reunited with her friend, there was always a chance she could be wrong.

King slid a bulletproof vest over her head, the Velcro ripping as he adjusted the straps. "Are you sure you're up for this?" he asked her.

Erin peeled her heavy eyelids open and licked her dry lips as she nodded.

"At any point you feel uncomfortable, just lay down on the ground behind a car and wait for help to arrive. Got it?"

Erin swallowed a difficult breath and muttered, "Got it."

King gave her shoulder a firm squeeze and stepped back, opening the trunk. Erin watched King arm himself with extra cartridges of ammunition, holster his handgun, and load up his tactical rifle. King slammed the trunk shut and said, "Let's roll."

Alvarez was already waiting in the driver's seat when Erin took the front seat with King piling into the back.

"Just got word that Chandler has a black Honda Civic registered in his name."

"All right. Keep your eyes peeled," King said as they all began the search.

The wheels rolled at a fast clip as they exited the Conoco gas station and headed north on Tower Road. It wasn't long before Erin spotted Chandler's car.

"That's it, all right," Alvarez said as he slowed the car down to read the plate.

Erin tipped her head back and scanned the landfill horizon. It was the only significant elevated land in the area and she knew Chandler was up there with her friend.

Alvarez drove to the backside of the landfill and dropped King off in a place he could confidently jump the fence.

"Don't play hero," Alvarez reminded his partner.

"Just show yourself long enough for him to want to take a shot. Hopefully, by then, I'll have him in sight and can stop him before he pulls the trigger."

Alvarez nodded and King slammed the back door shut. Alvarez spun the wheel and sped back to the parking lot in search of Erin's car with King sprinting toward the wired fence.

"This is crazy, right?" Erin asked Alvarez.

Alvarez flicked a quick knowing glance in her direction but said nothing. Once at the parking lot entrance, Alvarez punched the button, took the ticket, and immediately turned the car east.

Erin pushed herself up in her seat. She looked for her car among the hundreds of others. Like searching for a needle in a haystack, they had to put themselves in Chandler's shoes.

"This side of the parking lot gives him the clearest shot."

"If he's on top of the landfill." Erin's nerves fluttered her stomach. They could have this all wrong.

"He's up there. We saw his car."

"There." Erin pointed at her car. It was parked between a black SUV and a red pickup truck.

Her heart hammered in her chest. She felt like she was being watched—was certain Chandler had them in his crosshairs and at any time could take them out. They knew he was a great shot. They also knew he was out for blood.

"Stay down," Alvarez said. It was the first time she could hear the uncertainty quaking his voice. It wasn't much, just enough to make her second guess what the hell she was doing. "If I get shot," he said as he slowly approached and parked behind her car, "hide, and stay hidden until backup arrives. No sense in getting you killed, too."

# CHAPTER SEVENTY-SIX

KING LANDED SOUNDLY ON BOTH FEET AFTER CLIMBING THE fence and he hit the ground running. He kept one hand firmly gripped around the handle of his rifle while the other pumped and was used for balance as he scurried up the slippery grass slope.

Keeping his head down, nothing was on his mind except bringing Mason and Samantha home safely. That was all that mattered. Chandler would receive his day of judgement one way or the other. Whether it be today, or a year from now, justice would find him. King would make sure of it.

He slipped again on loose rock but kept scrambling up the hillside.

King's lungs burned and his heart drummed but nothing could slow him down. Not today, not with Samantha's and Mason's lives on the line. King would do whatever it took to make sure this ended well. The very real fear of losing everything he loved kept him focused on making sure that didn't happen.

Keeping his head down, King searched the fields he could

see. He looked to the ground for tracks or any signs they might be near.

Nothing.

He kept climbing.

The earth crumbled beneath his feet and it didn't take him long to reach the ridge. There, he stopped and crouched down low. Hiding behind the grass, he could hear soft murmurs of voices nearby. Adrenaline opened his veins. They were here. Not far. It was definitely Samantha's voice.

*She was alive.*

Slowly, he stood with both hands on his rifle. His eyes popped when he caught sight of them less than one hundred yards away—the wind was to their backs and they were looking in the opposite direction. Picking the soles of his shoes off the ground, King approached from behind and quickly noticed there were only two of them.

He paused, held his breath, and swiftly assessed who was who.

Samantha was on the ground—her hands tied or cuffed behind her back.

Chandler lay prone behind his sniper rifle only five feet away from her.

Mason. *Where was Mason?*

Fear wrapped its lasso around his heart. He snapped his jaw shut, lifted his rifle, and aimed it on Chandler's head. He wanted to make sure he didn't miss *if* he had to use deadly force.

# CHAPTER SEVENTY-SEVEN

I SLITHERED OVER THE LUMPY GROUND LIKE A RATTLESNAKE intent on striking.

"Come any further and I'll put this bullet in your head," Chandler said without looking.

Not willing to risk my own life on a theory based off assumption, I stopped. Chandler didn't move. He kept peering through his rifle scope's glass. I wanted to know what he was glassing, who had come, if it was only Erin, or Erin and King.

Arching my back, I lifted my chin and squinted into the low angle light hoping to see what Chandler was seeing. It was too far. There was too much tall grass that stood in my way.

"What are you going to do after you take your shot?" I asked.

Chandler kept quiet.

"You might have escaped capture after you murdered the others, but that was before you had me."

"Who says I'm planning to take you with me?" Chandler's words were muffled by the breeze.

"I am."

"And why would I do that?"

I had Chandler talking and that was a good thing. Either he didn't have a shot, or no one had come yet. "To have a bargaining chip," I continued, distracting his focus. "Use me as collateral. You want to keep me because I know things you don't."

"Shut up!" he snapped.

I gasped and felt my heart surge into my throat. My eyes went back to fighting through the grass, trying to see what he was looking at. The grass kept moving back and forth like wipers on a windshield and, through the blur, I somehow managed to find Erin's car. Two people were spinning in circles nearby. It had to be Erin and King.

"Your blonde friend looks afraid."

I regretted ever calling her. "She didn't do anything to you," I argued.

"No. She didn't." Chandler's words were too calm for me to feel comfortable. "And it would be such a waste to see her go, but..." Chandler checked the wind, adjusted a few dials on his scope and I held my breath just as I heard someone scream for Chandler to put his hands in the air.

Hope inflated my lungs.

Panic filled my chest.

All hell broke loose when Chandler dropped his left shoulder, rolled on his side, and pointed his handgun at the man marching directly toward us.

A shot popped off and I screamed.

A deep tremor quaked in my bones as I watched Chandler's head explode.

He lay limp on his shooter's mound with his brain splattered in a thick fan on the grass in front of me. I blinked and hyperventilated as I looked around. The air had been knocked out of me. I was completely vulnerable having my hands cuffed behind my back.

Rolling around, I kicked and flailed in the dirt, ignoring the pain. When I turned, I saw a dark silhouette running directly for me. He had broad shoulders and was carrying a rifle. Through my muffled ears, I heard my name being called.

*King.*

Tears filled my eyes. "You came. Oh, thank God you came."

"Are you okay?" he asked, still pointing the muzzle of his rifle at Chandler's lifeless body.

My neck released and my head fell back into the dirt. I nodded and started to cry.

King confirmed Chandler's death before turning his attention to me. "Sam, where is Mason?"

I squeezed my eyes shut and shook my head. "I don't know."

"Did Chandler have him?"

"I don't know. I don't think so, but I can't be sure."

King gently pulled me up into the sitting position. He brushed the dirt off my face and dabbed at the blood drying from the cut above my eyebrow. "We have to get you out of here. Did Chandler put these cuffs on you?"

Nodding, I told King where I saw Chandler hide the handcuff keys.

King dug them out of Chandler's pants pocket and released me. As soon as my hands were free, I flung my arms around his neck. My body trembled as he held me. All my emotions poured out of me. I wished he hadn't shot Chandler. He might have known where Mason was. But, if King hadn't taken the shot, Chandler would have killed him.

King pulled me to my feet, wrapped his arm around my waist, and walked me down the steep slope. I wouldn't have been able to walk without his support. My legs barely kept me upright.

He put a call in to Alvarez to come pick us up—told him that it was over, Chandler was dead. We left Chandler on top of the landfill for the investigators and coroner to come clean up the body and, by the time we were at the road, Alvarez was pulling the car to the side with Erin jumping out and running directly toward me.

She slammed into my chest and wrapped her arms around my neck, nearly knocking me over. My face dug into the hard protective vest she was wearing as she told me how happy she was that I'd made it out alive.

"Mason is still missing," I said, shock still sending shivers through my body.

Erin pulled back, her eyes shining. "They found him, Sam. Mason is alive and well."

"What? Where?" My mind spiraled out of control. I was relieved, excited, and totally confused. How did this happen?

"A patrol unit picked him up in the neighborhood where the Morris family lives." Erin cupped my face inside her palms and smiled. "I can't wait to hear what he was doing over there."

"I'm going to ground that boy."

Erin laughed. "He's on his way here now. Oh, and we found this in the parking lot." She handed me my phone. "I knew you shouldn't have gone alone."

Sirens wailed in the air and soon the road was blocked with a dozen squad cars. Teams of investigators climbed the landfill and got statements from both King and me. By the time I was finished, I stepped back to Erin and said, "Nancy Jordan finally responded."

"A little too late." Erin rolled her eyes.

"Maybe not."

Erin looked to me and raised both her eyebrows.

"The ten grand donation given to the victim's fund, guess who wrote the check?" Erin's lips rounded. "Croft."

"No way."

I nodded. "Would explain why he wanted to keep it anonymous."

"Except Croft still didn't do anything to ease the tension."

I shrugged, folded my arms across my chest, and rested my tailbone on the hood of King's unmarked cruiser next to Erin. "There are just some people I will never understand."

A black SUV arrived and was surrounded by two other unmarked police cruisers. We watched it with great curiosity, hoping Mason was inside. Lieutenant Baker was the first to step out. We made eye contact as he moved to the front of the vehicle and then the opposite back door opened and my son emerged.

I ran over to him. Sweeping him up into my arms, I squeezed him tight. "What were you doing in the Morris's neighborhood?"

"I don't know, Mom. I just thought maybe I could comfort Tim's parents."

"Jesus." I stroked the back of his head with my hand. "You need to start letting someone know your plans."

"My phone died."

I pulled back and locked my eyes with his. They were young and worried and I didn't have it in me to stay angry at him. He was alive, and so was I. That was all that mattered.

Lieutenant Baker made his way to me. When I saw him coming, I told Mason to go talk with Erin. "I didn't mean for it to work out like this," I said.

"The outcome is favorable. You did good work, Samantha."

"Thanks, Lieutenant."

"Though I would prefer if you didn't write up your story until after our investigation is complete." He winked.

"I might be able to hold off for a little while." I smirked.

"I spoke with Markus Schneider." Lieutenant narrowed his eyes and stared. "You know what he asked me?"

I shook my head no. It could have been anything. Markus seemed to know everyone's secrets.

"To forgive him." Lieutenant flicked his gaze and I watched him sweep his eyes up the hillside behind me.

"He knew Pastor Michaels lied under oath," I said.

"And now the pastor is having that conversation with God."

I swallowed the lump that had lodged its way into my throat and felt a cold shiver send shock waves throughout my body.

"I'd prefer it if you kept that part out of your story as well."

"You can't hide from the truth."

"No. We can't." He paused. "Markus told us everything, Samantha." Lieutenant held my eyes inside of his. "Including his visit with Kenneth Wayne."

"Did he tell you why he went to visit him? Chandler Davis also visited him," I said, pointing to where I'd last seen Chandler.

"Markus wanted to make peace with all the people involved during that time."

"And you believe him?"

"Is there reason I shouldn't?"

I licked my lips, unable to find one.

"Yes." His words were firm and authoritative. "I believe that Markus came back with good intention. It's our theory that Kenneth Wayne saw Chandler as his opportunity to finally seek revenge and Markus gave us enough evidence to support that theory as well. It will all be written in the report and I'll make sure that you're one of the first to see it outside the department."

I glanced toward Mason talking to Erin and watched King make his approach. I turned back to the Lieutenant and asked, "Are there any other known links to the Patriots of God still out there, waiting to pick up arms and continue the fight?"

The corners of his eyes crinkled. "Funny, I was going to ask you the same thing."

"I guess it's over then."

"For the record, Gavin was one of the best cops I have ever known."

"Thank you," I whispered as I watched Lieutenant step away, promising to be in touch soon. King and Mason walked over to me and I hooked each of my hands onto them, saying, "Let's go home."

# CHAPTER SEVENTY-EIGHT

*FIVE MONTHS LATER...*

I was tucked away in the back dank smelling corner of our pathetic newsroom, hoping to find inspiration for my next story when slowly my thoughts drifted to the morning of the school shooting.

A cold shiver reminded me of the sick feeling I had when rushing to the school. A warm bloom spread across my chest when I remembered how I felt the moment I knew both Mason and King had made it out alive. I would never forget the terror or relief.

There was nothing more satisfying than knowing I had helped the police solve the Chandler Davis sniper case but, with every high, there was a deep and lingering low.

Unfortunately, that low for me happened to come today.

My eyes flicked up to my computer screen. The curser on my blank Word document continuously flashed, challenging me to question and doubt everything I had accomplished as a journalist up until this point.

After Chandler's arrest, the police department granted me first access to their internal report as promised. I kept my word with Lieutenant Baker and told Pastor Dwayne Michaels's story and possible reason for being targeted by Chandler without ever mentioning his false testimony against Kenneth Wayne. I thought long and hard about that and, in the end, I liked how the Lieutenant had phrased it; Pastor Michaels could have that conversation with God. His life was over. It was better to keep his legacy intact as a way to heal the deeply divided community.

And deeply divided the community had remained. The damage that Chandler had inflicted was deep, reigniting old wounds that would take time to heal. Many months and an independent investigation later, the department was cleared of any wrongdoing in Dennis Hall's cold-blooded murder.

But that didn't reverse the damaged relationship and lack of trust the public felt toward the police. It was clear that that was exactly Chandler's plan all along, and there was still plenty that needed to be done to undo his work.

I turned my head away and nibbled on my fingernail. Sitting here was useless. I had nothing. No story that inspired me, and certainly nothing as exciting as the sniper case. Deep inside, I held a secret of my own. After solving two big cases back to back, I suddenly found myself addicted to the danger and excitement those stories brought me. Not only did I find King to be a friend and a partner, but I was rediscovering myself. These stories made me feel alive. They filled me with a sense of purpose beyond measure, and I was due for another big one.

My knee bounced beneath the desk as I struggled to push my thoughts of inadequacy out of my mind. I could feel the electric buzz crackling deep in my bones. Dawson had me working the crime beat—DUIs, assault, gang related crimes —but the stories were small and boring. Though he never came out and said it himself, I knew Dawson was hoping for me to get my next big break sometime soon, too.

Finally, I closed up shop and headed out the door. Susan had the girls getting together for margaritas at the Rio and that sounded better than just sitting here while not getting anything done.

Slinging my purse over my shoulder, I exited the building and headed for my car when I caught sight of movement out of the corner of my eye.

Glancing to my side, I put on the brakes as I noticed a familiar face lock eyes with me. It had been months since we'd last spoken and I thought we might never see each other again.

"Ginny," I said with a smile.

"I'm sorry for not calling to schedule a meeting."

Ginny Morris was wearing jeans and a winter coat. Her eyes were still as sad as I remembered them the last time we spoke. She had aged considerably, and I attributed it to the stress and grief of dealing with the fallout of knowing her son was a cold-hearted killer.

"No, it's not a problem. It's good to see you."

"You too." She sighed. "Look, I just wanted to say thank you for keeping your word."

The air grew silent between us and together we shared a solemn look of mutual understanding. Ginny Morris was referring to my story that followed the school shooting. Most of the story was told and published in the paper but the part Dawson had cut, I'd added to my website feeling like it wasn't complete without being shared. Inside the editorial, I told the harsh truth of the Patriots of God movement Tim got caught up in and how it could have all been prevented if decisions in the past had been made differently. It wasn't to make any excuses or justification for what he'd done, but to act more as a warning to remain vigilant in the world in which we lived.

"I heard Tim's funeral went well," I said.

"It was a peaceful and respectful ceremony."

"He deserved as much," I murmured, thinking how Rick went quiet after Susan and her attorney Gregory Kilmartin silently gave them the money donated by Croft without incident.

Ginny's eyes watered as she turned and looked away. "It gave both Rick and me the proper closure we needed in order to move on ourselves."

My limbs grew heavy as I stood there in the cold feeling sorry for all she'd been through and what she had lost. I could only imagine the difficulties these last few months must have brought her. It must have been the hardest months of her life, always hearing whispers behind her back, having people glare and think she was the monster her son was.

"Rick didn't want me to come speak with you, but I know he's too proud to apologize for the way he acted."

"I'm glad you did. I've been thinking a lot about you two."

Ginny flashed a weak grin. "Anyway, I better get going."

I spread my arms, stepped forward. Ginny fell into my chest and wrapped her arms around me tight. Tears popped out of her eyes as she cried. I held her until she was finished. When she stepped away, she wiped at her eyes and gave me one last look before turning on a heel and disappearing around the corner of the big concrete building.

I drove to the center of the city, choking back my own tears. I prayed for the Morrises, hoped that they could find peace within themselves. They had a difficult road ahead and I certainly didn't envy them.

I was the first to arrive at the Rio and was quickly seated. I ordered my margarita and, by the time I was taking my first sip, both Erin and Susan were stepping through the front door. Shedding their winter coats, they both fell into the booth just as more drinks were served.

"Has anyone talked to Allison?" Susan wrapped her lips around her straw.

Erin rolled her eyes to me. We both shook our heads and shrugged. "I thought you talked to her," I said.

Susan pinched her brow. "I did. She said she was leaving the office early."

"Maybe she had other stops before coming here?"

We shrugged it off as no big deal with the expectation that Allison would arrive any minute. As soon as our first plate of appetizers arrived, I was telling Erin how I still didn't have a story to get excited about.

"It will come," she assured me.

"What are you looking for?" Susan asked.

I couldn't admit to them what I really wanted. It was too embarrassing and would only elicit unwanted lectures I wasn't in the mood to hear. "I don't know. Something deeper than what I'm currently working."

"Well, Benjamin has me going to a business conference with him in Boulder."

I perked up, happy to shift the conversation away from my life. "Are you organizing the event?"

Susan shook her head and laughed. "Not quite. Apparently, he's reserved a swanky hotel room tucked up against the Flatirons."

"Romantic," Erin and I teased.

"I couldn't resist the offer even if I'll be subjected to a day of conferences I'm not interested in."

"Do you have to go?"

"I promised him I would."

"Geeze, is it really worth it then?" Erin gave Susan a skeptical look.

Susan looked back, wiggling her eyebrows. "Totally worth it."

We all giggled until our glasses were empty and we were

ordering a second. As soon as we were starting on the next round, a woman of about my age with cascading dark hair hesitantly approached our table.

"Excuse me, you're Samantha Bell, right?"

I peeled my shoulders off the back of the booth and scooted forward. "That's me."

"I've been following your website." The woman shifted her gaze to Erin. "And listening to your podcast. I'm a huge fan."

Erin's spine straightened. "Thank you."

Suddenly, Susan's cellphone started ringing. She excused herself from the table and left us alone with our fan.

"I've been reading and listening to your podcast since the Chandler Davis case." She tilted her head and paused, shifting her feet over the floor as if there was something she had to say but didn't know how to say it. "Anyway, a friend saw you two here tonight and called to tell me."

"Is there something we can do for you?"

Her half-mast eyes raised. "I need your help."

I shared a quick glance to Erin.

"My daughter," the woman swallowed hard, "vanished after having dinner at my place and no one knows where she is."

"Have you gone to the police?"

She nodded, clutching her purse like a cat kneading its claws.

"When did this happen?"

"Two nights ago." The bags beneath her eyes puffed up and swelled like balloons. "I know I should wait for the police to conduct their investigation, but it isn't like my daughter to just disappear without letting me know where she was."

"And you would like us to assist?" Erin asked.

"At least look into it." Her eyes filled with hope. "I know

how thorough you two are and thought maybe by speaking to you directly I could win over your sympathy."

My mind was scrambling to decide whether or not I could help this woman with her interesting request. There wasn't any harm in at least looking into it. Maybe something was there that I could use to pick me up out of my own personal funk. Before I could respond, Susan was hurrying back to the table with a glimmer of fear shining in her eyes.

"That was Patty O'Neil who just called." Susan was breathless as she spoke. Her cheeks flushed in sudden panic as she lunged across the booth, reaching for her purse. "Allison collapsed at the office and was rushed to the hospital."

Erin and I scrambled when gathering our own possessions.

"This is awful," Susan kept saying. "We have to go now."

I slid out from the booth, stood, and turned to the desperate mother still looking to me for help. Handing her my card, I said, "Send me the details. I'll see what I can do to help find your daughter."

*Continue the series by reading Bloody Bell. Click here and start reading today!*

# AUTHOR NOTE:

*Thank you for reading BELL HATH NO FURY. If you enjoyed the book and would like to see more Samantha Bell crime thrillers, **please consider leaving a review on Amazon**. Even a few words would be appreciated and will help persuade what book I will write for you next.*

One of the things I love best about writing these mystery thrillers is the opportunity to connect with my readers. It means the world to me that you read my book, but hearing from you is second to none. Your words inspire me to keep creating memorable stories you can't wait to tell your friends about. No matter how you choose to reach out - whether through email, on Facebook, or through an Amazon review - I thank you for taking the time to help spread the word about my books. I couldn't do this without YOU. So, please, keep sending me notes of encouragement and words of wisdom and, in return, I'll continue giving you the best stories I can tell.

# ABOUT THE AUTHOR

Waldron lives in Vermont with his wife and two children.

Receive updates, exclusive content, and **new book release announcements** by signing up to his newsletter at: www.JeremyWaldron.com

Follow him @jeremywaldronauthor

facebook.com/jeremywaldronauthor

instagram.com/jeremywaldronauthor

bookbub.com/profile/83284054